MW01172145

PAY BACK

A DETECTIVE MARCY KENDRICK THRILLER

THEO BAXTER

INKUBATOR
BOOKS

Published by Inkubator Books
www.inkubatorbooks.com

ISBN (eBook): 978-1-83756-454-5
ISBN (Paperback): 978-1-83756-455-2
ISBN (Hardback): 978-1-83756-456-9

1

IT'S JUST BUSINESS
THE ENTREPRENEUR

Monday

"It'll be fine. She's not goin' to do anythin'; she's nothin' but a wannabe princess livin' in her fancy house, lordin' it over all of us, treatin' us like peasants." I sat in my car, a used, silver Toyota Corolla that had too many years and way too many miles on it, and listened to my friend give me every reason under the sun why I shouldn't do what I was about to do.

The trouble was, the advice was wrong. I had *every* reason under the sun to do this.

She was expectin' me to show up today, since I was supposed to be deliverin' the merch we'd acquired in our recent heist. Our original arrangement was me and my crew boosted the product she wanted, I delivered it, and she paid me for our efforts. The product we were lifting was worth thousands of dollars, but she only paid me a couple of hundred bucks, which I had to share with the crew.

Why should some rich Karen get all the profit? Why shouldn't we, the ones doin' all the dirty work, make more of a cut? What made her so special? Nothin'. She sat high and mighty in her luxury mini-mansion, and we were out here barely scraping by, tryin' to feed ourselves on the bread-crumbs she gave us.

That was gonna end today.

I had a plan. Nothin' could go wrong; it was foolproof. No cap.

"You there?"

I blinked and realized I was still on the phone. "Yeah, but I gotta go. She's expectin' me. I'll meet up with ya later." I ended the call and turned the phone off, slidin' it into my back pocket. I'd pulled over to take the call about a block from my destination. This wasn't exactly the best neighborhood to do that in because I was callin' more attention to myself than I probably should be, given my car was held together with rust and spit, and the house I was parked in front of was probably worth millions. That couldn't be helped.

Turnin' the car back on, I finished the drive to her house. As far as I could tell, she lived alone in her mini-mansion with the manicured lawn. I'd never seen anyone hangin' around her place anytime I'd been by. Of course that could be because of the nature of our acquaintance. What we were doing wasn't exactly somethin' she'd want to advertise to her church group or fancy friends and nosy neighbors.

I pulled into her driveway, which was fairly long, drove up to the house, and parked behind her black Mercedes, next to the path that led to the front door.

"You can do this," I muttered to myself. "She's not better than you."

My heart started to race as I reached into the glovebox and pulled out the 9mm Glock I'd picked up from a guy who knew a guy who sold this kind of thing. I knew how to shoot it, thanks to a former gangbanger friend who was too stupid not to get out of that life and had ended up dead. If he'd lived, maybe he'd have been here with me as part of my crew, and I wouldn't have to be the one doin' this. I could have sent him to take care of it.

That was the problem though, if I had sent him, he'd have fucked it up, just like he fucked up everything else and ended up dead, I thought. No, it was better I take care of this. What was the sayin'? If you want shit done right, do it yourself? Yeah. That was where I was at. No cap.

I slid the Glock into my waistband and tugged my shirt over it before climbin' out of the car. I almost felt like a gangster as I walked up the path, a little swagger in my steps. I was a badass. I was about to take a step toward entrepreneurship.

I walked up the steps to the door, steelin' my nerves for what was about to go down. A moment later, I pressed the doorbell and waited. A nervous energy filled me, made me hyperaware of everythin' around me.

The door swung open, and my bottle-blonde, mid-forties trying to look like mid-twenties, bitchy client stared at me, her arms crossed over her fake boobs. "You're late."

I didn't bother to wait for her to invite me in. I just stepped through the doorway and shut the door behind me, then pulled the gun. "I'm right on time."

"What the hell is this? What are you doing?"

"What the fuck does it look like I'm doin', bitch? I'm robbin' you."

"Huh? What? Why're you doing this? I don't understand!"

I laughed. "Because I can. We're done being your slaves for less than minimum wage. We're goin' into business for ourselves, and I'm takin' back the merch we got you. Where the fuck is it?"

"No, I'm paying you fair and square. You can't even turn it; that's why you work for me in the first place! Now put that stupid gun away, bring me the stuff I ordered right now, or I'm calling the cops." She picked up her phone from the table next to the front door.

I shook my head and slapped the phone from her hand. "Try me, bitch! Where the fuck is the rest of the merchandise? Where do you keep it?"

She glared at me; her green eyes glittered with hatred. "I'm not telling you shit; get out of my house, you low-life scum-sucker," she spat at me, her face turnin' pink in anger.

I pulled the slide back on the Glock, chamberin' a round. I wasn't goin' to shoot her, but I wanted her to feel the threat. "Watch your mouth! Show me where it is!"

Instead of doin' what I asked, she lunged at me, grabbin' the muzzle of the Glock, tryin' to take it from me. I held tight, my finger on the trigger. "Let go!" I screamed as I struck her cheek with my left fist.

Her head shifted to the side at the force, and she gasped, but didn't let go of my gun. "You let go! What the hell do you think you're playing at? You think this is some game?"

She twisted my arm, and I struggled to keep hold of the weapon. She was usin' both hands now, one grippin' the muzzle of the gun, the other on my wrist, tryin' to wrench the gun free. My finger began to pull out of the trigger guard, and I reflexively squeezed.

The gun went off, and she gasped, her hands droppin' from the gun, from my wrist, as she stumbled backwards. She looked down at her boobs, her hands pressin' against the gaping bloody mess of her chest, and fell backwards to the floor as she struggled to breathe.

"Stupid Karen! Why did you have to do that?" I screamed at her.

I had no time. I didn't know if anyone had heard the shot. I needed to get the shit I was after and get out. I put the gun back in my waistband and started runnin' through the house, openin' doors, scannin' rooms.

As I looked for the merchandise, I also checked for signs of a home security system. I didn't see any, thankfully, but I did find the products in her office. She had shelves of high-end makeup and perfume, all stuff that me and my crew had boosted for her. A table was set up with boxes where she must package it all to send out, and a desk where her computer sat. I grabbed a couple of the shoppin' bags she had folded next to the shelves and started clearin' the products, dumpin' them into the bags, but I was panicked.

What if she died?

Fuck.

What if she didn't?

My stomach twisted in knots. I looked over at her laptop on the desk and grabbed it too. I wondered if she had a safe and if I could get into it. Probably better not to try lookin' for one. It would take too much time, and I wouldn't know the combination anyway.

I made my way back to the kitchen and noticed her purse

on the counter. Openin' it, I dumped everythin' out, then took her cash and cards out of her wallet.

I was just about to leave when I realized my prints were everywhere. "Fuck!" I shouted, lookin' around.

What had I touched?

Grabbin' a kitchen towel from the counter, I set the bags of cosmetics and perfume down next to the fridge and ran back through the house, wipin' doorknobs as I went. When I reached her office, I ran the towel over everythin' I'd walked past, then returned to the kitchen.

I picked up the bags and headed for the front door. I saw her lyin' on the floor, her green eyes glassy and dead, starin' off into nothin'. She was gone. She wouldn't be tellin' a living soul who killed her.

Bile rose up from my stomach. I needed to get away. Pressing my lips together, I used the towel to open the door, leaving it open so I wouldn't get my prints on it, then ran for my car. I tossed the bags and towel in the back, hopped in the driver's seat, and sped away.

I couldn't think. All I could see was her dead eyes starin' at me, accusin' me. The blood on her blouse, on her hands, had been bright red. It had pooled under her, around her as she lay on the wooden floor of the front entryway. I glanced at my hands on the steering wheel. Flecks of red covered the backs of them. I looked down at my shirt; there was blood on it as well.

I felt sick.

Pulling over, I barely made it out of the car before I lost my lunch. Twice. I'd shot her. I'd killed her. I'd never done anything this bad in the past. Never thought I was capable. But here we were.

"She's dead," I muttered as I wiped my mouth.

There was nothin' I could do about it. I didn't have a time machine to go back and change things. Wasn't sure I wanted to do that even if it was possible. She'd been a bitch. If she'd done what I'd asked, she'd still be alive, no cap. But no. She just couldn't be a decent human for once in her fuckin' life. She had to have things her way. Well, where did that get her? She fucked around and found out; that's where that got her.

I grabbed my keys from the ignition and went around to the trunk. I had some extra clothes in a backpack in there. I took off the T-shirt I was wearin' and tossed it into the trunk before pullin' a clean one from the bag and puttin' it on. The blood on my hands was dry now, but I wanted it off me. Noticin' a half-drank bottle of water in the back of the trunk, I grabbed it and poured water over my hands, then used my dirty T-shirt to rub off the blood.

Feeling better, I tossed the empty bottle and wet T-shirt back into the trunk, then slammed it shut. I needed to get out of here before someone stopped and started askin' questions. Taking several deep breaths, I got back into the car, put on my seatbelt, and then started the car.

"You've got this; nobody knows you did this." Except someone did. I worried for half a second, but then smiled. She'd never say anythin'. "Nobody who would rat on you knows you did this," I assured myself.

I only had a slight niggle of doubt that I could be wrong as I drove to meet up with my crew.

2

LIFE OR SOMETHING LIKE THAT

MARCY

Monday

"It's not like I want to do this, Frank. I'm under orders," I said as I ran the brush through my hair. I'd had Callie, Angel's girlfriend, cut and style it into a stacked bob, so it was easy to care for and didn't get in my way.

"Why isn't the press secretary dealing with this? Or your captain?" Frank asked from where he was sat on the edge of the bed, watching me. "Hell, why isn't the police chief handling the press? You'd think they'd want to take all the glory for themselves, anyway. Why do they keep roping you into dealing with them?"

"We've been over this." I tossed him a look over my shoulder as I picked up my mascara. I leaned toward the mirror and applied the lengthening black goop to my lashes. I didn't wear much makeup normally, but being on camera made me a little more self-conscious. "With all of the bad press we've had lately, the mayor and the police chief decided it would be a good idea to have me and Angel in front of the camera as the faces of the LAPD."

"I know you two kick ass. I'm not questioning that. My concern is about you drawing unwanted attention from the wrong people. Namely El Gato's men."

I put the wand back in the bottle and closed it, then grabbed some clear lip gloss and applied it before turning around to look at Frank. He seemed genuinely concerned, and I sighed. "I get that, but you know I can handle myself. There's nothing to worry about except me losing my cool on camera and throttling the journalist for asking stupid questions."

Frank's lips twitched. "You would never."

I laughed. "You're right, I wouldn't, but I'd be thinking about it and would probably cut them down to size with my tongue once the cameras were off." I stepped into his outstretched arms and sat on his lap. "Look, I'll talk to the captain and see if this can be our last interview. I don't want to be doing them any more than you want me to be doing them."

"Okay." He wrapped his arms around me and pressed his lips to mine. "I just worry about you. The more your face is out there, the more likely some jackass with bad intentions will come after you to make a point. You've worked on several high-profile cases. I just don't want some Zodiac Killer type deciding to play cat and mouse with you."

"And that's a good point. The more I'm in the press, the higher the chance some psycho will decide to do that. I'll bring it up with the Brass. But you know I can't guarantee they'll listen to me."

"I know." He nodded. "Maybe we should run off to Vegas again, but stay longer than a weekend this time."

I laughed and shook my head. "Vegas was fun, but I don't think that's the answer. Besides, neither of us really want to give up our jobs to become full-time gamblers. At least I don't."

"Not sure why, Mrs. Gotrocks. You made a killing at the craps tables."

I rolled my eyes. "I wouldn't call seven hundred and fifty-two dollars a killing. Nor would we survive on that, especially considering you lost four hundred on blackjack."

Frank sighed. "True. Back to work it is, then." He stood up and set me on my feet. "How about some breakfast before you go?"

Glancing at the clock, I saw I had half an hour before I needed to leave. "Okay, something quick. I'm supposed to pick Angel up in forty-five minutes. The new lieutenant is starting today."

"Can't believe they didn't offer the job to you. After everything, it should have been yours." Frank's back was to me as we walked into the kitchen, so he didn't see my smile.

"I don't even care. I don't want the job, not now."

He turned and looked at me as he opened the fridge to pull out some eggs and bacon. "Why not? I thought you went after it before, but lost out to Jordan?"

"Oh, I did, but after seeing what Jordan went through, the kind of stress he was under, how he didn't really get to go out on cases anymore and was basically stuck behind a desk and in meetings all the time...I've changed my mind. That's not the kind of job I want. I'm a detective, and I want to keep doing what I'm doing."

Frank nodded slowly. "I get what you're saying, but

wouldn't you like to slow down? Not put yourself in peril all the time?"

I put my hands on my hips and grimaced. "Honestly?"

He set the carton of eggs and package of bacon on the counter, then turned to look at me. "Yes. Honestly."

"I like the rush. Not being part of the action would kill me."

He turned back to the counter and started cracking eggs into the pan, then lined the bacon in another. Once the bacon and eggs were on the stove and cooking, he faced me. "I've thought about it. Going for lieutenant."

I reached for the coffee pot and switched it on. "You'd make a good LT." I looked back at him. "Not in my department," I added, my lips twitching.

He chuckled. "No, I think that might cause us some issues. You've already stated your boundaries on working together, and I respect that."

"The bump in pay would be nice. That's the only reason I'd consider it. But I don't think it's worth it, not for me." I poured a cup of coffee for each of us as he flipped the eggs. The smell of the bacon sizzling in the pan had my mouth watering. I was hungrier than I thought.

"So where's this new LT coming from? Do you know who it is?" Frank asked as he turned the bacon.

I got out a couple of plates and some silverware. "Somebody out of San Diego. I don't remember his name. Captain said he was divorced and looking to get away from his ex."

"Hopefully that doesn't become an issue later."

I knew he was thinking about my ex, who also happened to be my previous lieutenant, Jordan, who had turned into a stalker. He was currently residing in a psych facility for the next several months. I wished it were longer. If I never saw Jordan Brasswell again, I'd be happy.

Frank put the eggs and bacon on the plates, and I carried them to the table. We worked well together in the kitchen. Hell, we worked well together in nearly everything, but I didn't want him as a partner or co-worker. That only caused problems. I'd learned that lesson well with Jordan.

"What time do you have to be in?" I asked, taking a bite of the eggs.

"Nine. I'm on till nine tonight. You?"

"Barring a new case, I'm off at five. I'll come to yours tonight if nothing kicks off."

He smiled. "Here's hoping it's a quiet day for the LAPD."

I finished my plate and swallowed down my coffee, then rushed to the bathroom to brush my teeth. I didn't need food in my teeth for this interview. I reapplied my lip gloss, put on my holster and checked my service weapon. I was wearing black slacks, a pink blouse, a black blazer, and low heels. I'd change into my tennis shoes after the interview.

"You look smart. Stylish," Frank offered, coming up behind me and kissing my neck.

I turned in his arms. "Thanks. I'd better go. See you tonight." I kissed him.

"Be safe." He walked me to the door. "I'll lock up on my way out."

"Thanks. You be safe too." I picked my purse up from the table by the door and pulled out my car keys.

"Tell Angel I said hey."

"I will," I replied as I walked outside. I waved and gave him a nod as I climbed into my car. Setting my purse on the floorboard of the passenger seat, I put on my seatbelt and pulled out of the driveway.

The closer I got to Angel's house, the more my nerves picked up. I hated doing these interviews. They made me jumpy, and that wasn't me. I could chase down bad guys all day long, but put me in front of a journalist with a camera, and I was ready to jump out of my skin.

I thought about my conversation with Frank. I really did hate doing these interviews, and he had a point about putting myself in the limelight. I knew he was concerned about something happening to me. He'd become slightly overprotective since the El Vibora incident at my house. I snorted. *Slightly* was an understatement. If Frank had his way, I'd be wrapped in bubble wrap and protected by him twenty-four seven. That was another reason I was glad we worked for different precincts.

Honestly though, I didn't mind him being overprotective as long as he didn't keep me from doing my job. And so far, he hadn't interfered. I knew he was struggling though, considering everything that had taken place over the past year in both our lives on and off the job. I was glad he'd been going to therapy; it had been a big help in getting him to deal with his issues.

I'd never been big on therapy with what happened when I was a kid, after my mom was murdered in front of me. However, after dealing with the copycat killer who had targeted me, I'd changed my tune. I'd started with one-on-one therapy with Dr. Fellows and online group sessions several times a week, but now I was down to just my group therapy once a week. It was cathartic to share with others the things that were going on in my life that caused me stress. Of course I couldn't share details about specific cases, but they all knew I was a detective with the LAPD Homicide Special Section Unit, so they understood.

Katrina was one of my friends from the therapy group. I recalled I was supposed to have lunch with her later in the week. I'd need to give her a call later to confirm.

Angel was waiting for me as I pulled into his driveway. I waved as he came toward the car and opened the passenger door. "Frank said to tell you hey," I said.

He sat down and pulled the door closed. "How's he doing?"

"He's good. How's Callie?"

"Sleeping," he replied with a grin, his eyes flashing back toward his house.

"I thought that was her car in the drive."

"She stayed over last night," Angel said as he buckled in.

"She's been staying over a lot lately." I smiled as I backed out and headed for the news studio where we were supposed to be interviewed.

Angel smirked. "Things are going really well," he replied.

"I'm glad. You ready for this?" I asked, referring to the interview.

His expression changed to one of distaste. "Not really, but let's get it over with."

"You took the words right out of my mouth."

3

INTERVIEW WITH THE VULTURES
ANGEL

Monday

"You're enjoying these interviews about as much as I am, I take it," I said, glancing over at Marcy.

She looked great today. I had to admit, the cut Callie had given her suited her and showed off her heart-shaped face to perfection. Her lips were shiny, she'd added some kind of gloss to them, and it drew my attention, but I did my best to look away. She was with Frank. She wasn't mine, never would be, and I was okay with that. Didn't mean I didn't struggle occasionally with the desire I had for her. She was my best friend. We had a connection that was strong. A bond that went beyond us being partners on the job and just regular friends.

Were things different, I knew we'd be great together as a couple, but it wasn't meant to be. Not in this lifetime anyway. I swallowed the sigh that wanted to slip out, and buried those feelings for her. Besides, I had Callie, and I really did like her a lot. We'd had a rocky start, but we were good together. I'd met her when I was trying to get over my feelings for Marcy. At first, she'd been a great distraction, but she'd become more than that. I could see myself with her for the long haul.

I was planning to take her down to Mexico to meet some of my family this fall. After that, we'd see where we were. I hoped we'd be in a good place. *So far, so good*, I thought.

"I hate them," Marcy said.

Startled, I shifted my gaze back to her and then recalled I'd commented about not liking these interviews. "Yeah."

"After this one, I'm talking to Robinson about not doing any more. Frank's not happy about me doing them either."

I arched a brow. Since when did she care what anyone else thought about what she did? "Why?"

"He's worried about me being in the spotlight because it might draw attention from El Gato's men or from some new serial killer who might target me."

I supposed Frank had a point. The more we were on camera talking about the case, the more attention we got from the public. "I doubt Robinson will have a say about it since this is coming from the police chief and the mayor."

Marcy sighed. "I know, but I'm hoping he'll talk to them, and we can stop."

"It's a big case, Marce, and we were front and center for it. It's good PR for the LAPD." I didn't know why I was arguing with her about it. I didn't want to be doing these interviews either. Every one of them was a rehashing of how we caught El Gato when Vice hadn't been able to for the past ten years.

"You think I'm not aware of that?" She frowned at me,

her rosy lips squished into a mewl, her eyes narrowed before she turned back to watch the road.

"I know you are. I'm just stating the obvious. Brass isn't going to give up good press, which is what they think this is."

"It may be, but they could hire a press secretary to do this crap. Yeah, the reporters might not get firsthand details, not that they're getting that anyway, but they would still get the good press."

"I think it's more the chance that one of them *might* get us to give those details that keeps us in this PR campaign."

"Yeah," she muttered as she pulled into the parking lot of the news studio.

"Come on, put on your professional smile, and let's go beard the vultures in their den." I knew I was mixing metaphors, but it made her smile. I gave her a wink as I climbed out of the car.

THE INTERVIEW HAD BEEN STRESSFUL, but we'd gotten through it. The hosts of the *LA Morning Show* had tried to get me and Marcy to share details of the bust, but we'd deflected like professionals.

"I'm glad that's over," I said as we got back in the car.

"Me too. I need coffee. Something with a lot of sugar," she murmured, starting the car.

"Sounds good." *I could use some coffee myself,* I thought as my phone rang. "Hey, sweetheart, is everything okay?" I answered.

"Everything's fine," Callie replied. "I just wanted to tell you that you looked handsome on TV."

I chuckled. "Thanks. I didn't know you'd be watching."

"Of course. I wouldn't miss it. Tell Marcy her hair looked perfect."

Smiling, I glanced over at Marcy. "Callie says your hair looked perfect."

"Tell her thanks. She's coming with you Saturday, right?"

"Marcy wants to know if you're coming with me to her barbeque on Saturday. You are, right?"

"I wouldn't miss it. Does she need me to bring anything? I can make potato salad."

Marcy must have overheard her because before I could relay the question, she said, "No need, I've got everything. Just need you there."

"Okay, great. See you Saturday, then, Marcy," Callie replied, raising her voice.

"You coming over after work?" I asked, hoping she would.

"I planned to. Let me know if you're going to be late, okay? I'm going to pick up dinner."

"I'll let you know. Better go now. I'll text you later."

"Okay, bye."

I hung up as we pulled into the coffee shop drive-thru. "Get me an Americano."

Marcy nodded and placed our orders. Five minutes later we were back on the road and headed to the precinct. It was much less stressful being in the office since Jordan had been fired, and I really hoped the new lieutenant wasn't a control freak like Jordan. I could do without the animosity toward Marcy as well. Working under him had been like working in hell.

As soon as we walked through the door, the captain waved us over. "Kendrick, Reyes, come here for a minute."

Next to Robinson stood a well-dressed, dark-haired man.

He reminded me of a rugged movie star from back in the eighties.

Marcy and I made our way over. "Morning, sir. We just finished that interview, and I was hoping to talk to you—" Marcy started.

"I saw it, Kendrick, good job, both of you. Mayor Taylor was thrilled with the interview." Robinson smiled. "I wanted to introduce you to Lieutenant Lukas Chenevert. You're the last two to meet him. Chenevert, meet Detectives Marcy Kendrick and Angel Reyes."

"Pleasure," Lieutenant Chenevert replied, holding a hand out for me and Marcy to shake. "I look forward to working with you both," he added, with an accent I couldn't place.

"You too," I offered.

"You're not from California," Marcy said, studying him.

The man smiled, showing off perfectly straight white teeth. "Not originally, no. I'm from New Orleans. Did most of my detective work down there, moved to San Diego about five years ago, made lieutenant two years ago, and well, here we are."

"It's good to have new blood in the LAPD." Marcy smiled. There was a slight pink tint to her cheeks.

"Thanks, I'll let y'all get to work."

"We're having a briefing after lunch, barring any new cases coming in," Robinson said before turning toward his office with Lieutenant Chenevert at his side.

"Yes, sir," I said as Marcy and I headed for our desks.

I sank down in my chair. The lieutenant seemed nice, but I'd reserve judgment until we saw him in action. Though anyone had to be better than Jordan.

"Damn, the mayor should put the new lieutenant on

these interviews. The press would eat him up," Marcy murmured, her eyes focused on Robinson's now closed office door.

I followed her gaze and then frowned. "Better cool it, or I'll tell Frank you've got a thing for the new lieutenant," I teased.

Marcy looked over at me and rolled her eyes. "He's not my type, but he is easy on the eyes." She paused for a minute and then added, "He reminds me of a young Sean Connery, if he had a Southern accent instead of a British one."

"Yeah, I can see that," I agreed.

"Kendrick, Reyes, can you go out on a call?" Jason called from his desk.

Marcy glanced over at him; her brow furrowed. "What have we got?"

"Store clerk at the Bodega on East Temple and Center Street called in an armed robbery just happened, two customers have been shot, and he was injured but didn't say how. We've got a bus on the way; perp is in the wind."

"Yeah, we'll head over," Marcy answered for the both of us.

We spent the next two hours working the scene. We didn't typically go on these kinds of calls, but with the recent trouble the LAPD had been in, and the fact we'd lost a lot of officers for various reasons, it was all hands on deck so to speak.

"I'll be happy when we're back at full staff," I muttered as we drove back to the precinct. There was no time for lunch now, not if we wanted to make it to Robinson's meeting.

"Me too. Why don't we grab something from one of the trucks before we head in. We might not be able to eat it immediately, but at least we'll have it later."

"Yeah, that's a good idea. Hopefully, it'll be something that will keep."

Marcy pulled into the parking lot and parked. We looked over at the two food trucks parked near the building: Rolling Burger Barn and Lobsta. I glanced at her, and we both said, "Burgers," before heading over there. As much as we both loved the Lobsta truck, it was better eaten as soon as it was purchased. A burger would keep for a bit.

We made it inside just as Robinson was calling everyone to the conference room. It wasn't just HSS, but also Vice and the regular LAPD homicide and robbery divisions, which were also under his command. The only people who were not attending the meeting were those still out on calls. They'd be caught up on what they'd missed as soon as they returned.

Marcy and I stood against the back wall, as all the seating was already taken by the time we got in there. I noticed Hummel and Vance had seats up near the front. Probably hoping to get in good with the new lieutenant.

Robinson was quietly talking to the new lieutenant as we waited for everyone to find a spot. Chenevert seemed focused on what Robinson was saying and actively listening to him. I wondered what kind of guy Chenevert really was.

"Maybe we should invite Chenevert for drinks after work," I said quietly to Marcy.

She turned her head slightly and arched a brow at me, but didn't say anything.

"You know, welcome him to the division? See what he's actually like before Hummel and Vance get in good with him and start turning him to the dark side?"

Her lips quirked. "I don't think he'd fall for it. They don't have cookies."

I chuckled. "What do you think? Should we?"

"Sure, why not?" She shrugged and turned her gaze back toward Robinson and the lieutenant. "Should we invite Robinson too?"

"Think he'd come? He hasn't been out for a drink with us since the divorce."

"Wouldn't hurt to ask."

"Sounds like a plan," I offered as Robinson started waving for everyone's attention. "After this meeting, then."

4

AN UPRISE IN CRIME
MARCY

Monday

I wasn't sure it was a great idea to invite the new lieutenant for drinks after our shift, but it would tell us more about the guy. Right now all I knew was Chenevert was a good-looking man with dark brown hair and brownish-green eyes. He was tall, probably about the same height as Frank, give or take an inch. He was lean but muscular and filled out his suit to perfection. It looked like an expensive suit too. Not one typically worn on the job.

None of that told me what kind of cop he was or if he'd be good for the department, which was really all I cared about. I wasn't looking to date the man. I just hoped he wasn't as controlling as Jordan.

"Settle down," Robinson said, waving his hands at everyone. "As you are all aware, today is Lieutenant Chenevert's first day with HSS. He's just getting acclimated to how we do things in that department, and while we are still short-staffed in various other departments, we'll be spreading out cases and utilizing every available detective when needed. HSS will still take the high-priority, high-profile cases, but will assist robbery/homicide as well as Vice when needed."

There was a murmur among the officers about us being so understaffed.

"I am aware how overworked and stressed you're all feeling, especially with the way the media has been trying to paint us in such a poor light—"

"Except for Kendrick and Reyes," someone called out.

"Yeah, the media darlings," someone else added.

I felt my hackles rise. "Not by choice," I said, unable to stop myself.

Lieutenant Chenevert's gaze landed on me, and I felt my cheeks flush. His expression didn't change from the stoic look, but the scrutiny made me want to squirm. Still, I held myself in a relaxed position, not wanting to be intimidated or show any kind of bother. His gaze moved on, and I slowly let out the breath I'd been holding.

"As I was saying"—Robinson drew everyone's attention back to him—"I know how stressful things have been; however, it doesn't look as though things will be slowing down any time soon. It seems there's been a bit of chaos on the streets, with El Gato having been captured. A power vacuum has caused various criminal elements to vie for control, and we've had more dead gangbangers than normal over the last few weeks. And it's not just the normal gangs doing the killing. Several new crews have popped up, trying to get a piece of the action.

"And we've had a recent wave of gang activity from mobs of teenagers targeting high-end shops. They're also boosting cars and breaking in to a lot of homes in the wealthier neighborhoods. Reports have skyrocketed over the last few weeks all across the board."

I knew from experience that when the economy took a dive, crime increased, and we were definitely feeling the economic pinch right now, so I wasn't completely surprised by the uptick in theft. Though if you coupled the flailing economy with the animosity toward police and a few of the new laws on the books, it made for a perfect storm of crime.

There was more murmuring from the corner where Vice, or what was left of Vice anyway, was sitting. Then a hand went up.

"You have something, Martin?" Robinson asked.

Devon Martin, who'd been with Vice for at least fifteen years, cleared his throat. "They aren't exactly old-school gangbangers. These are more organized mobs of teens who raid various businesses, steal as much merchandise as they can carry, and then run out during the chaos. The new laws about shoplifting haven't helped, and the stores are no longer stopping the thieves; they've told employees to stay out of it and not to confront the shoplifters."

"Right," Robinson acknowledged. "Though many of these teens have been armed, most of them are just taking advantage of the chaos to steal the merchandise. There have been a few shootings, mostly when someone does try to stop them. We've lost three off-duty officers in these mob scenes."

"So what's the solution, sir?" a detective from robbery/homicide asked.

I thought it was Jill Rice, but I couldn't be sure since she had her back to me. We'd never worked together. I'd just seen her around the precinct occasionally.

"Police Chief Warren, Mayor Taylor, Deputy Mayor

Freeling, Lieutenant Chenevert, Lieutenant Hernández, Lieutenant Daniels, and I will be working on various solutions going forward."

As Robinson said the names, I realized the lieutenants from the various divisions were all standing close to Chenevert. I wondered if that was planned or if they just naturally gravitated toward being front and center with the captain. I supposed that Robinson had asked them to be up there, as they were the leads of each division. Normally he briefed them separately, but maybe he didn't want to hold two briefings this week. Who knew?

Robinson continued, "For now I wanted to brief you all on what we're facing. Violence seems to be scaling up between the various new gangs—yes, I know they don't call themselves gangs but crews, but that is beside the point. The point is they aren't just starting to get violent with the people they're robbing, they're getting violent between themselves, resulting in several deaths already this week."

Jill raised her hand again and then timidly stood as Robinson nodded to her. "Yesterday I had to answer a call to a Wellness Pharmacy. The store manager and pharmacist were able to get the pharmaceutical medication area locked up and hid back there, but they left two young employees to fend for themselves. They were both shot dead." Her voice shook. "From the surveillance videos, it looked like there were at least thirty teens who hit that store."

I raised my hand. "Sir, how would you like us to proceed given what's going on?"

Robinson looked beyond stressed, more so than he'd been while in the middle of his divorce, and that was saying something. Had it only been a few months ago that he'd taken a leave of absence? It seemed like a million years had passed between then and now.

"Cautiously, Kendrick. I don't want anyone engaging with these crews and getting into an OK Corral situation. We want to take them down safely without a lot of bloodshed." Robinson looked out over the room, then added, "Ideally, we'd like to take each of these crews down the way you, Reyes, and all our great uniformed officers took down El Gato. It was clean and organized, precise."

I arched a brow. He was wrong about it being precise, it had been just this side of chaotic, but we'd gotten the job done without any LAPD fatalities, which was a win. I wasn't about to argue with him about it in front of everyone here though.

"The first step will be identifying those in charge of these crews," the captain continued. "I'll have more information after my meeting with the Brass and I'll start assigning people to the task force at that time."

I nodded, but secretly I hoped I would be left out of it. I didn't want to spend hours of my day going through video evidence looking for whoever these leaders were. Give me a serial killer to chase and I was good, but this? It seemed like a headache waiting to happen. I could already feel the pressure behind my eyes building at just the thought of having to dissect body language and listen to hours of video to find the person calling the plays behind each of these mob shoplifting scenes.

"You look stressed," Angel muttered close to my ear. "You okay?"

"I *am* stressed about possibly being tasked with watching all those videos," I whispered.

He snorted. "Can't say I blame you. Doubt it will be us

though. Not to toot our own horn, but they've got us on the press circuit right now. Don't think they're going to take us off that to sit at a desk and do something a monkey like Hummel can do."

My lips twitched. "Who knew there'd be a silver lining to doing the press junkets?" I said, keeping my voice low enough so I wouldn't be overheard by anyone around us. Maybe I wouldn't ask Robinson to get us off the interview circuit quite yet.

5

HOME INVASION HOMICIDE
MARCY

Monday

"Unless there's any more questions, then that's all I have for now." Robinson looked around the room and then added, "You're dismissed."

Angel and I lingered as others filed out of the room. We were waiting for Robinson and the lieutenant to head in our direction so we could invite them to join us for drinks after shift. We still had several hours before that, but we wanted to make the offer.

"Kendrick, Reyes, was there something else?" Robinson asked, seeing us waiting.

"Not about the crime spree, sir. Reyes and I were talking before the briefing about heading to the Short Stop tonight after shift and wondered if you and the lieutenant wanted to join us. Sort of a welcome to HSS for the lieutenant here." I nodded toward Chenevert.

Robinson paused, and his face lightened briefly before returning to his normal serious look. "Good idea, Kendrick. You up for that, Chenevert?"

The lieutenant looked from the captain to me and then to Angel as if trying to assess the situation.

"We'll make sure the whole department is invited if you're able to come," I added, not wanting him to think this was us trying to sway him to treat me and Angel differently than anyone else.

A smile twitched on the man's lips for a moment before he gave me a nod. "Sure. That would be nice. I'm afraid I don't know where the Short Stop is, though."

"Right. We'll get you the address for your GPS. Or you're welcome to follow one of us to the bar," Angel offered.

"Perfect. I'll look forward to that."

"Anything else?" Robinson asked, looking at us.

"No, sir, that was all."

"Then get back to work. You've got reports to write up on this morning's shootings, right?"

"Yes, sir," I said with a nod. I looked at Angel, and the two of us headed back to our desks.

As I reached my desk, I noticed that my burger was half eaten, and all my fries were gone. I looked around the room and saw Vance wiping his mouth. "Vance!" I glared at him.

He shrugged and smirked at me. "Shouldn't leave food around like that, Kendrick."

I rolled my eyes, picked up my burger and tossed it on his desk. "Asshole." I wasn't going to eat it now that he'd had his mouth on it. "We're all meeting at the Short Stop tonight after shift to welcome Chenevert to the team. You get to pay for our drinks." I stared at him, my brow arched.

"Yeah, okay," Vance agreed, almost looking happy about that.

I stared at him suspiciously, wondering why that had him nearly gleeful.

"Kendrick, Reyes," Robinson called, sounding urgent as he stood next to Jason's desk.

I hadn't even gotten to sit down. "Yes, sir?"

"Just got a call. Homicide in lower Hollywood Hills. Looks like a home invasion or robbery homicide. You two take it. Jason'll send you the address."

"Yes, sir." I grabbed my purse from my desk drawer as Angel gathered up his food.

"Get the car. I'll grab you another burger—" Angel started to say as we were walking out the door.

"Naw, leave it. I'm not that hungry anyway. I'll just get something later."

It took us twenty-five minutes to get to the address Jason texted to me. I parked in the long driveway behind two patrol cars. There were more parked on the street. As I got out, I noticed the CSI team and the coroner, Damien Black, pulling up. We headed for the front door, which was being guarded by Officers Braun and Garcia.

"What do we know?" I asked as we reached them.

"Homeowner dead in the front hall, GSW to the chest. No gun in sight. Part of the house looks ransacked."

"So are we thinking she walked in on the robbery or...?" I left the last bit open-ended because there were too many possibilities to suggest.

"Couldn't say. The daughter, Lauren Richards, found the front door wide open and her mother dead just inside," Garcia answered.

"Where is the daughter?"

"With Jenkins. Allen is inside. They were the first team on the scene."

"Okay, thanks," I said as Lindsey Stone and her CSI team, as well as Damien, came up behind us, their equipment in hand.

We headed in and saw a blonde woman dead on the stone tiled floor. "Allen, I forgot to ask Garcia, do we have a name on the victim?"

"Yes, ma'am, Helena Richards, she's a divorcée. Lived here alone, ran a home business."

"And we're thinking a home invasion or robbery type of event took place?"

"That is our initial assessment, ma'am. Lauren Richards came by when she couldn't reach her mother on her cell. She found the front door open, and her mother lying there." Liz Allen nodded at the victim.

"Did the daughter go any further into the house?"

"No, ma'am, Ms. Richards said she immediately went back outside and called us. She was afraid the killer might still be in the house, so she ran to her car and locked the doors, then called."

"Good to know. You cleared the house?" Angel asked.

"Yes, Jenkins stayed with Ms. Richards, and when Garcia and Braun arrived, the three of us cleared the house. That's when we discovered the theft."

"Okay, can you show us while Dr. Black goes over the body?"

"Of course," Allen replied. "It looks like there are two areas the perp focused on." She led us through the hall to the kitchen and gestured toward the counter, where the contents of a purse were scattered. "It looks as though the perp got the homeowner's credit cards and any cash she had. The wallet was empty."

"I'll have it bagged," Lindsey said, pulling out an evidence bag and handing it to one of her team.

"Where else?" Angel asked.

"Through this door and down the main hall. It looks like it was a home office." She stopped at the door.

I glanced into the large room. The walls were lined with shelves that were mostly empty. There was a table with boxes and packing peanuts, as well as rolls of bubble wrap. In one of the boxes that looked almost ready to ship sat a couple of boxes of the new Kardashian facial cream that was supposed to make your skin supple and youthful. I only recognized it because I'd seen it advertised online.

"You can only get this stuff at really high-end cosmetic shops," I said, nodding toward the box.

Next to the table with the boxes was a trash can from where Lindsey pulled a wrapper out. "This is a Luxe wrapper. See the gold lettering?" she pointed out.

"Bag it. Bag anything in that trash. We'll want to trace it." I studied the room and then moved toward the desk. "If this was a home business and this was her office, I'd assume she had a computer in here...where is it?"

Liz shook her head. "I didn't see one. Maybe it was taken along with whatever merchandise was on the shelves?"

"You could be right. Where's Jenkins with the daughter?"

"They went around to the back patio so Ms. Richards could sit down. Figured that would be okay and would keep Ms. Richards off camera if the news studios sent reporters to investigate the scene."

"Good. You checked it first, right? No sign the perp was out there?"

"Yes, ma'am. The back of the house was locked, and the gate to the backyard was closed as well."

"Okay, thanks. Lindsey, we'll leave you here to do your thing. Let me know if you find anything I need to know about."

"Will do." She nodded without looking at me.

Angel, Liz, and I headed back toward the kitchen and out the glass door to the deck, where Officer Sarah Jenkins was sitting with a well-dressed, dark-haired woman. She had teary green eyes and was sniffling as she wiped the tears away with a tissue.

"Ms. Richards?" I asked.

"Lauren, please."

I gave a small nod. "I'm sorry for your loss, Lauren, and I'm sorry you were the one to discover your mother."

My words made her sob, which wasn't my intention. I sank down on the outdoor sofa next to her. Sarah sat on her other side, her hand on Lauren's forearm, rubbing up and down in comfort. I glanced at Angel.

He nodded, understanding that I wanted to give Lauren a moment with just me and Sarah. "I'm going to check in with Damien. See what I can learn."

I mouthed, "Thank you," to him as he turned back toward the house. I looked back at Lauren and rubbed her back as she continued to cry. We hadn't exactly ruled her out as the perp, but given how upset she was, my gut told me she was just a grieving daughter, not the one who'd murdered her mom.

After Lauren calmed again, I said, "I know how hard this is, but I need to ask you a few questions. Do you think you're up to answering them?"

She nodded, but stayed quiet.

"What can you tell me about your mom's home business?"

She blinked and wiped her eyes again. "I...I wasn't involved in what Mom did. I don't know a lot about it. Just after Dad left, Mom needed to get a job to maintain the life she was accustomed to. She used the money she got in the divorce to start the online business."

"Okay, it was an online business, so she has a computer?"

"Yes. It should be in her office. It's in the house. Um." She scratched her head and tucked some hair behind her ear. "Down the hall off the kitchen, third door on the right."

"There wasn't a computer in there. Could she have moved it?"

"No, I don't think so. She has a different computer for other things. The one in her office was strictly for work."

"Alright, we'll keep looking for it." I didn't want to tell her that I was pretty sure the work computer had been stolen along with her mother's inventory. "What kind of things did your mother sell in her online business?"

Lauren sniffled and wiped her nose. "Just...stuff. Cosmetics, perfume. That kind of thing. Here, I can show you her website." She pulled her phone from her pocket and searched for the site, then handed me her phone.

I glanced through it and saw everything on there was name-brand, high-end products for drastically low prices. Well, low for the products, anyway. I wondered how Helena was able to afford to give such discounts on things she had to be paying a crap load of money to acquire. I made a note of the name of the business—Belle Elite Boutique—so I could have the Tech team go over the site.

"Thank you." I handed her phone back. "Lauren, can you

tell me a little about your mom? How was her relationship with your dad? Did she have any enemies?"

Lauren frowned. "My dad? He didn't do this. We haven't even seen him since I was five."

"I'm sorry, I was under the impression that her divorce was more recent than that."

Lauren nodded. "It was, but not from my dad. She never married him. Richards is my mom's maiden name. I don't have my dad's last name. She was married to Roger Wrexler. The carpet king?"

I recalled the commercials. "I see. Was their divorce amicable?"

She shrugged. "As far as I know, it was. Mom wasn't exactly happy with the settlement, but she got the money to buy this house when they sold theirs, Roger gave her the car and the club membership, as well as seven hundred and fifty thousand dollars, and she retained his life insurance policy. I tried to get her to buy a smaller house, maybe somewhere cheaper, but she wouldn't."

"Why wasn't she happy with all that?"

Lauren rolled her eyes, and a small smile ghosted her lips. "She wanted a stake in his business as well so she could have an income coming in. He refused. That's when Mom decided she'd run her own business. She had a degree in business, you know."

"I didn't. Was it doing well?"

"Yes, I think so. She said she was often selling out of product and had to order more."

"Thank you. I was told you didn't go any further into the house than the hallway, but did you happen to notice if anything valuable was missing?"

Lauren shook her head. "I didn't really look." She closed

her eyes for a moment. "Everything in the front room looked untouched though, from where I stood."

"Okay, thanks, it'll just help us to zero in on your mother's killer if we know what all was taken. If you think of anything else, anyone who might have wanted to hurt your mother, please call me. Here's my card."

Lauren took the card I offered. "Thank you. I will."

"Officer Jenkins will drive you home." I didn't want her driving in the state she was in.

"Oh, I have my car—"

I smiled gently. "We want to make sure you get home safe, so we'll have someone bring your car to you."

"Okay, thank you."

I left them and went back into the house to find Angel. He and Damien were hovering over Helena's body. "So what can you tell me?" I said as I approached them.

"Just what it looks like," Damien replied. "GSW to the chest, looks like a 9mm, but I'll know more once I find the bullet. Judging by liver temperature and the fact rigor has just basically set in, I'd say it happened between eight a.m. and noon. I'll have a better idea once I get her back to the lab."

"Okay, thanks." I turned to Angel. "You check in with Lindsey?"

"I did. She found more of those wrappers and bagged them. No sign of a computer in the office, but one of her team found one in the bedroom. They're sending it over to Tech."

"The daughter said she has two, one for personal and one for work. Said her mother always kept the work one in the office."

"So it was probably stolen along with the merchandise."

I nodded. "Lauren gave me the name of her mother's website, so we can have Tech look at that as well."

"Great. Anything else we need to do here?" Angel asked.

"I think we're good. Let's turn the scene over to Lindsey and Damien and head back to the precinct."

Five minutes later we were back in the car. "Mind if I head to the Jack-in-the-Box's drive-thru?" I asked, seeing it up ahead.

"Sure, get me a soda," Angel replied. "Figured you'd stop somewhere."

My partner knew me well. "You figured right," I said with a smile.

"Can't believe Vance had the nerve to eat your food. You'd think he had a death wish."

I smirked. "Right? But he'll be paying for it tonight though."

"Did something about his acceptance of that seem off to you?"

Now that he mentioned it, I had noticed, but hadn't had time to talk to him before now about it. "Yeah, what was he so happy about?"

Angel shook his head. "Not sure, guess we'll find out tonight."

I placed our order, getting the large fries, knowing Angel would want some even though he said he only wanted a soda; then we continued on to the precinct.

6

THE SHORT STOP

MARCY

Monday

"I've been thinking about this case..." I said as I pulled into the station.

"Yeah?" Angel asked. "What are you thinking?"

Something was bugging me about those wrappers and the merchandise Helena was selling. "I'm just wondering how she was able to sell the products at those prices. Is she some kind of, I don't know, subsidiary for those brick-and-mortar retailers?"

"That's a good question. We'll have to check that out."

We headed in, and I paused on the way to our desks. "Should we brief the lieutenant on the case? I know we normally go to Robinson these days, but with the new lieutenant...what do you think?"

Angel shrugged. "Wouldn't hurt to let him know we're back."

Changing direction, we headed toward Jordan's old office and knocked on the door.

"Enter," Chenevert called out.

"Sir? We just wanted to let you know we're back."

"Good. What's the case? Robinson said possible home invasion homicide?"

"It does look that way, though most of the house was left alone. The owner's home business seems to have been the target."

"Do we know if the victim is the owner?"

"Yes, Helena Richards. She owned the house and the online business. She ran a website called Belle Elite Boutique, selling high-end cosmetics and perfume."

"Okay, do we have any leads?"

"Not yet, sir, but Lindsey Stone, head of CSI, is checking for prints, and there is quite a bit of evidence to go through, so we're hopeful we'll have some leads soon. Dr. Black, the coroner, will get back to us when he's got more on the body. Right now the best he could give us was she was killed between 8 a.m. and noon."

"Okay, y'all keep me informed. I'll share what you've told me with the captain."

"Yes, sir." I turned to leave, then hesitated.

"What is it, Kendrick?"

"Do you want us to stay past shift change to see if Dr. Black or Lindsey come up with anything?"

He paused and thought about it for a moment. "No. I don't think this is going to be a time-sensitive case. It's not a serial yet, this could be a one-off, and we don't have any perspective perps in our sights, so let's wait and see. Tomorrow will be soon enough."

"Yes, sir. Still up for drinks, then, after shift?"

"Sure. Just send me that address."

"Right, sorry, meant to do that earlier," Angel replied as he pulled out his phone. "Is there a number I can text it to?"

Chenevert rattled off his number, and Angel typed it into his phone, then sent the text with the address to the Short Stop. "See you there," he said.

Angel and I left and returned to our desks. It was nearly time to leave, but I figured I could at least get the report on this morning's shooting written up.

At five, the evening shift appeared, and Angel and I got ready to go. I had gotten Lieutenant Chenevert's email address from Jason and emailed my report to both Chenevert and Robinson, then switched off my computer.

"Want to ride together?" Angel asked.

"I would, but I'm headed over to Santa Monica after this. Frank's on until nine."

"Sure that's a good idea? I mean, it gives you a long drive in the morning."

"Yeah, I know, but I can't let Frank make that drive every day; it's not fair to him."

Angel smiled. "I guess. Anyway, I'll see you there."

Nodding, I headed out. As I closed my car door, I pulled out my phone and sent Frank a text.

> Hey, going for a drink with the HSS team to welcome the new LT. Be at your place around 8. Anything special you want for dinner?

I didn't wait for him to reply, just set my phone aside and turned the car on. I heard my phone ding as I made the drive over to the Short Stop, but didn't look at it. I found a spot to park, grabbed my phone and my purse, then headed in. Half of the team was already there, and they waved as I entered. Angel joined me at the bar a minute later, and we ordered drinks.

"That'll be twelve fifty-seven," the bartender said.

"It's on Vance's tab," I replied, pointing him out to the bartender.

The bartender looked at the group, and then he nodded. "Okay, I've got his card. I'll add it."

"Thanks," Angel said.

Angel and I took our drinks and started toward the team when Robinson and Chenevert came in together.

I paused and turned toward them. "Sir, drinks are on Vance; the bartender has his card."

Robinson arched his brow, giving me a questioning look.

I shrugged and smiled; then we continued on to the table. "Hey, Vance, thanks for the drinks; you should steal my lunch more often."

Angel laughed. "No, don't; she gets cranky when she doesn't eat."

"I do not."

"You know that Snickers commercial? You get hangry."

Rolling my eyes, I sat down.

"I don't mind paying for the drinks to welcome in the new lieutenant; it's an honor," Vance said with a smirk. "So drink up, everyone."

I stared at him. *Of course he's happy to brown-nose; should have known,* I thought. "I can't stay too long. I've gotta go home before I head out to Frank's."

"How's that going?" Detective Bailey asked.

Regina Bailey had made detective while Angel and I were working the El Gato case, and had been assigned to the HSS division recently. She was partnered with Ashton Clark, a transfer in from robbery/homicide. I didn't know either of them well, but she at least seemed nice.

I smiled at her, not sure why she was asking. "Um, sorry, I'm just wondering—"

"How I know who Frank is?" She smiled for a moment, then she looked down, and her expression changed. "I knew his brother."

I sucked in a breath and stared at her, waiting for more information.

"I was a patrol officer with the SMPD when I first started," she said, keeping her voice low. "I transferred to LA about three years ago, figured I'd have a better shot at making detective here, which I did."

Sighing, I nodded. "I see. Well, we're glad to have you. And yeah, Frank and I are doing pretty good."

"I'm glad to hear it." Regina smiled, and her whole face lit up. She leaned in closer to me and said, "So what do you know about the new lieutenant?" Her gaze flitted over the man and back to me. "Is he single?" she added, running her fingers over the braids she wore, which were pulled back into a bun at the base of her neck.

I grinned. "He is pretty handsome, right?"

She nodded. "The man is damn fine."

"I know he was born in New Orleans and made detective there, then moved to San Diego. And I'm pretty sure he's divorced," I said, keeping my voice low enough that the chatter around us drowned me out to anyone else but her.

"How did you find that out?"

I glanced around the table to make sure no one was giving us any attention. "Captain said he wanted away from his ex. Plus, if you look at his left hand, you'll see a faded tan line where he used to wear a ring."

"Girl, I missed that. Sure he's not just playing away?"

"That's always a possibility, but I doubt it. Not with what Robinson said."

"Good to know." Regina looked speculatively at the new lieutenant.

"Can I offer a piece of advice?"

"Sure."

"You weren't around when we had my ex as our lieutenant, so you wouldn't know, and I'm not saying Chenevert would be the same way, but be careful. It can turn the workplace toxic if things don't go well."

"Food for thought, definitely, thanks. And yeah, I've heard about that. Not sure how you survived that toxicity."

"Hey, Kendrick," Hummel called across the tables, "you buying the next round?"

"Hell no, all the drinks tonight are on Vance. Besides, as soon as I finish this, I'm out." I lifted my highball glass and swallowed the rest of the alcohol, feeling it burn my throat. "Sir, welcome to HSS," I added, looking at Lieutenant Chenevert.

"Thanks for the welcome." He lifted his glass.

I stood and said, "I'll see you all tomorrow."

As I gathered my purse and waved, they jokingly said I was breaking up the party early, but I just laughed. "Bye," I called as I headed for the door.

I stopped at the taco truck outside the bar and grabbed a taco before getting in my car and heading home. It wasn't dinner, more of a snack.

At home, I recalled that Frank had texted me back, and pulled my phone out to look at it.

> Hey, TT, sounds good. Order pizza? That way you won't have to get out?

I smiled at his endearment for me. TT stood for tiny tornado, and it always made me smile. His idea was a good one. If I ordered pizza, I could plan for it to arrive right before he got home, and it would still be hot. He had a couple of favorites, so I asked which he wanted.

> Abbots or North Italia?

He texted me back while I was in the shower.

> North Italia. Order the Funghi pizza and the spicy rigatoni vodka and anything else you think sounds good. You've got my card, right?

I smiled. He always offered to pay, and I did have his card number, but I would get it this time, I told him.

> Babe. No. Use the card. I'll see you around nine fifteen. Love your body, Larry.

I laughed out loud at the line from the '80s movie *Fletch* with Chevy Chase.

> You aren't Mr. Underhill. I'm not sticking you with the bill.

I tossed my clothes for tomorrow in a bag as I waited for the inevitable reply.

> I would hope not. I'm not that much of a prick! Still, though, use the card.

Grabbing my stuff, I headed back out of my house to the car. Before I pulled out, I sent him another text.

> We'll see. I'm leaving now. See you when I see you.

I added a kiss emoji to the end and hit send, then tossed my phone on the passenger seat.

"BABE?" Frank called as he walked through the front door.

"In the kitchen," I replied, raising my voice so he'd hear me.

He joined me a couple of seconds later, wrapped his arms around my middle and leaned over my shoulder, then kissed me. I sank back into him, loving the way he enveloped me in his arms.

"How was your day?" he asked. "I caught the interview; you looked good."

"Thanks, hopefully I can stop doing them soon. My day was messed up after that though. Had to deal with the aftermath of a teen mob robbery that turned deadly, and then a woman was murdered in her home in what we think was a home invasion."

Frank shook his head and pulled a couple of plates from the cabinet. "Things are getting wild out there in LA lately. You'd think we have a lawless society."

I grabbed the silverware from the drawer and a serving spoon for the rigatoni and handed it to him. "Pretty much do with these new shoplifting laws where they can steal a ton and only get a slap on the wrist. Kids are out of control."

"Tell me about this home invasion," he said as he

scooped some of the pasta onto each of our plates, then added slices of the pizza.

I grabbed a couple of beers from the fridge, and then we carried everything into the living room to eat on the sofa before I told him about the case. Well, what I could tell him at any rate. "The woman ran a home business, and aside from her purse being ransacked, it was basically only the stuff for her business that was taken."

"So the perp didn't take anything else that was valuable in the house?"

"Not that we found or that the daughter of the victim noticed." I took a bite of my food and chewed it slowly as I thought about the case. "The weird thing—well, I don't know if it's weird, but it seemed off to me—there were all these cellophane wrappers in the garbage from Luxe, you know, that high-end cosmetic shop? Anyway, there was no product to go with the wrappers. No partially used products, nothing opened. We found a few boxes of product already in some boxes ready to ship, but they had a cellophane wrapper that matched the victim's business name."

Frank paused with the slice of pizza halfway to his mouth, then set it back down. "Wasn't Luxe hit in one of the teen mob theft sprees just last week?" He pulled his phone out from his pocket and started typing. "Yeah, they were." He handed me the phone.

I looked at the article and then back to him. "Okay...so what are you thinking?"

He took a couple of bites of his pizza and chewed thoughtfully, then wiped his mouth on a napkin. "What if the wrappers in the garbage were from the stolen goods, and your victim was rewrapping them in her own cellophane and selling them?"

I stared at him, my plate of food going cold in my hands as I thought about his suggestion. "You could be onto something...I just don't know how to go about proving that."

"Maybe talk to the detectives over in robbery/homicide? They probably have someone working the shoplifting mob cases, right?" he suggested. "I bet they'll be able to give you some insight into how this all works. Robbery isn't exactly your specialty."

"You're right, it's not, and that's a good idea."

He grinned. "You know what else is a good idea?" he asked, wiggling his eyebrows at me.

I swallowed the giggle that wanted to burst from my lips and arched a brow at him. "What's that?"

"You and me making it an early night, if you know what I mean?" he said huskily.

I ran my tongue over my teeth and then grinned. "I like the way you think, Detective. Let's finish this up and move things to the bedroom."

7

EVIDENCE ABOUNDS
MARCY

Tuesday

"What's your day look like?" I asked Frank as we drank our coffee at the kitchen table the next morning.

"Eleven to nine today; want me to come to yours?"

"Would you mind? I'm not sure what time I'll be off shift tonight, depends on if we get a break in the case or not, but I'm also having dinner with Stephen."

"Okay, tell your brother hi from me. Talking to R and H will help, I bet. Do you know the name of the vic's business? I'm assuming since you said there was product in boxes ready to be shipped that it was online. She didn't have customers coming to her house, right?"

"Yeah, we're pretty sure it was all online. And we do have the name of the business. The daughter gave me the link to the website."

"Might want to have Tech dig into her business, see what they can find."

I smiled. He wasn't suggesting anything I hadn't already thought of as far as the online business went. "I planned to."

"Sorry, I started thinking about your case again this morning, and well...you get it."

Laughing, I nodded. He was a detective, so we thought of things in a similar way. Granted, he had more experience than I did with various kinds of cases. While I generally specialized in the harsher, darker world of murder, his were more diverse, and that gave him different insights sometimes. If he weren't with SMPD, he'd make a great LAPD detective, but then if he were LAPD, we probably wouldn't be seeing each other. I wouldn't say we absolutely wouldn't, because there was a reason people often said *never say never,* but it was as close as possible to never. I didn't date where I worked. I'd learned my lesson with Jordan, and I wasn't going down that road again.

I stood and took my travel mug to the coffee pot and poured another cup, then turned back to him. "I should probably head out," I said, glancing at the clock. It was nearly six a.m., and I was due in at seven.

"Okay, babe." Frank stood up and hugged me, then kissed me. "I'll see you tonight after my shift; it may be late. Have a good day and be safe."

"I will," I said, then gave him one last kiss before tossing my purse on my shoulder and picking up my overnight bag.

Frank opened the door for me and then took my bag, carrying it to the car for me. He put it in the backseat, then kissed me again. "I mean it, be careful."

"You too," I murmured before climbing into the car.

. . .

FORTY MINUTES LATER, I pulled into the precinct parking lot. I headed inside and was seated at my desk, finishing off my coffee, when Angel walked in. "Good morning, sunshine," I said, seeing how bedraggled he looked. "Rough night?"

"Need more coffee," he said grumpily.

I laughed. "How many drinks did you have last night?"

He shook his head and then groaned. "Ugh. Don't ask."

"I thought you were only going to have one and then head over to see Callie; did you not do that?"

"Callie had a last-minute client disaster she had to take care of, so I stayed at the bar and had way more than I should have."

I narrowed my eyes at him. "You were trying to keep up with Hummel, weren't you?"

"The man is a fish."

"Yeah, he is, dummy." I rolled my eyes. "Want me to go grab you a coffee? I saw the beignet truck out there this morning."

"You're an angel."

I laughed. "No, that's your name, not mine. I'm Marcy, remember?"

He didn't look amused, but I was having a great time teasing him. Without another word, he folded his arms on his desk and laid his head down.

I grabbed my purse and went back outside to the food truck and ordered the chocolate beignets and two coffees, because let's face it, you could never have too much coffee on this job, and then returned to the detective pool.

"Extra hot and strong. Had them add a shot of espresso to it," I said as I handed him the cup, then dug in my purse and pulled out a bottle of Aleve. "Take these for your head and then eat," I said, setting the box of beignets on his desk.

"Thank you," he murmured, opening the bottle, and dumping two into his hand. He tossed them in his mouth and took a swallow of coffee.

I pitched the bottle back in my purse and put it away in my desk drawer. "I'm going to go talk to MacHenry since we didn't get to do that yesterday before our shift ended, and then I want to head over to robbery/homicide and talk to someone about a theory Frank had about our case." MacHenry had become our go-to guy in Tech. He was the Tech commander's right-hand man.

"You talked to Frank about our case?" His bleary gaze focused on me as he took a bite of the chocolatey goodness.

"Just generally, nothing about the victim, more about the theft itself."

He nodded. "Sure, sure."

"Anyway, I'm headed over to Tech." I left Angel to his food, hoping he'd feel better by the time I made it back to my desk. In the meantime, I walked down the hall to the Tech department. I nodded at a couple of the cyber detectives and headed for MacHenry.

"Detective Kendrick, what can I do for you?" he asked, looking up from his computer.

"Hey, MacHenry, I was hoping you could do some of your tech voodoo magic on a website for me?"

He laughed. "Depends on the site and what kind of voodoo magic you want. Is it something I'm going to need a subpoena for?"

"Not sure, maybe? But we really do need the info. Our latest murder victim, Helena Richards, owned and operated the website Belle Elite Boutique. She sold high-end cosmetics and perfumes. I need to know if there's any record of where her inventory came from, what her financials for the company look like, how long she's been in operation... pretty much any kind of information you can get linked to that website would be great."

MacHenry pursed his lips. "Yeah, okay, I'll see what I can do. May have to wait to get her financial info with a subpoena. Is there a partner or a next of kin who can expedite permission for us to have access to it?"

"There isn't a partner, Helena owned and operated the business herself, but maybe her daughter will be able to give permission," I offered. "I'll give Lauren a call and let you know."

"Okay, great. Anything else?"

"Nope." I popped the *p* and smiled. "Thanks, see you later."

He was already focused on the hunt and didn't say anything more, so I headed over to robbery/homicide to talk to one of the detectives. As I passed through the door, I walked into a chaotic mess; at least that was what it seemed like to me. There were detectives moving quickly through the room, bringing people in cuffs from one spot to another, taking statements, and answering ringing phones. I had to pause and wonder if it was always like this.

I spotted Jill Rice hanging up her phone and made a beeline toward her before she could take another call or grab a perp to get a statement from.

"Jill, hi, do you have a minute?"

The blonde woman looked up at me, her blue eyes serious. "Barely. You're Marcy Kendrick," she said, surprise laced through her voice.

"Guilty." I nodded and then gestured toward the chair by

her desk. "May I?"

"Sure, yeah," she said.

I sat down. "Thanks. Sorry, I know you all are busy over here with all the mob stuff going on, but we just caught this case, and I had some questions I was hoping you could answer for me."

"What have you got?"

"So we're investigating a home invasion where the home-owner was killed, but it was her home business that was targeted. She sold cosmetics and perfume online. That's not really my question. We found a lot of packaging from Luxe in the garbage. I was speaking with another detective from SMPD, and he thought maybe our victim might have been selling stolen goods."

"Frank Maldon, you're seeing him, right?"

Her question startled me. "Um, yeah, actually. Do you know Frank?"

"Just in passing. I was down in Santa Monica a few years ago working a case. Well, he's right. Your victim could very well be selling stolen goods. These teen mobs rush the stores and take loads of things and then sell them to—well, we don't know who exactly. And they're not all street kids. Many of them come from good, decent homes. It's just a mess."

I frowned as I thought about that. "So some of them are just doing it for kicks? How much are they getting paid?"

She shrugged. "Probably. Most of the ones we've caught admit they make about a hundred dollars a job, but can't tell us who is paying them, or where the merchandise is going."

"They don't know who's paying them?"

"No names, that's what they all say. Nobody uses a real name. They think it's all a game."

"What, like *GTA*? What's next? Boosting cars and

running over prostitutes?"

"God, I hope not," Jill said, looking disgusted at the idea.

"Okay, well, thanks for the insight. I might have more questions later. Is it okay if I come back to you with them?"

"Not a problem. If I'm not here, you can text me." Jill grabbed a business card from her desk and handed it to me. "Oh, and you can always talk to Detective Jackson." She handed me another card. "Keith is my partner, but he's dealing with one of the kids who were picked up in this morning's hit. He'll know more about how these crews are run. He used to be part of the gang and narcotic division."

"Thanks. I appreciate it, Jill." I rose from my seat. "I'll let you jump back into the fray."

She rolled her eyes and gave a wry laugh. "Thanks."

I gave her a half wave as I left the department and headed back to the HSS detective pool with a sense of relief that we weren't so overwhelmed in our department. Not that we didn't deal with a lot of things in our division, but it wasn't nearly at the level as robbery/homicide. That was over-the-top busy; no wonder we were catching more cases than normal down here. Well, that and we hadn't had a serial killer to deal with since El Gato and his minion.

"Good, you're back. Lindsey called, she wants us down in her lab, and then Damien asked if we could head over to see him." Angel handed me a file as he stood up.

I opened the manila folder and flipped through it. It looked as though the CSI team had discovered a lot more at the victim's house. "You feeling better?" I asked.

"Yep, nearly back to normal, thanks for the breakfast and the painkillers. They helped."

We headed for the elevator and clicked the button for the CSI lab. It wasn't too far from Damien's morgue, so we'd go there after we finished up with Lindsey.

"HEY, Linds, what have you got for us?" I called as we entered the CSI lab.

"Oh good, you're here. Come on over." Lindsey directed us to join her at one of the counters. "So, we recovered all of this from the garage. Shopping bags, security tags, a removal system, and more wrappings from a few other storefronts."

"Wow, okay, so we're thinking Helena was selling stolen goods, then," Angel said, picking up one of the bagged security tags.

"It's looking that way, for sure," Lindsey replied.

"What about fingerprints?" I asked. I hadn't seen anything in the file suggesting they'd discovered any random prints in the house, but maybe it just hadn't made it into the report yet.

Lindsey shook her head. "That's a problem. There were prints of course, but they all belonged to Helena, her daughter Lauren, and the cleaning women she hired. However, what I can tell you is that the office, part of the kitchen, the front hall and door as well as all the doorknobs down the hall were wiped clean of prints."

"So our killer was smart enough to realize they'd left prints and wiped down everything they touched before leaving?"

"It looks that way. I've sent the team back over there to do a more thorough dusting for prints, check the walls, every surface, just in case the killer missed one. We'll know more soon, hopefully."

"Okay, sounds good. You got anything else for us?" Angel asked.

"We recovered a phone, and I've sent it over to Tech to get it unlocked."

"Perfect. Do they have an ETA on that?" I asked.

"Nope, and that's all I've got for now."

"Then we're going to head over to see Damien."

Lindsey nodded and started to turn toward her desk. "Lunch soon, yeah?" she said, turning back to me.

"Yeah, we should catch up," I agreed. "Let me know when."

"Will do."

Angel and I left the lab and headed down the hall to the morgue. "So what did MacHenry say?"

"He's going to look into the website. I need to call Lauren and see if we can get her permission to dig into the financials, but we may have to get a subpoena." I glanced at him. "I also talked to Jill Rice over in R and H; they have their hands full with all these shoplifting mobs. You would not believe the number of teens they've arrested. But so far, none of them know much about who's running the mobs. At least not that they're admitting."

"So we're still at square one, waiting for a break in the case?"

I nodded as we entered the morgue. "Hey, Damien, you have something for us?"

"Yeah, hi. One sec," he said, typing something on his computer. A moment later he stood up and gestured for us to join him at one of the slabs. "Afraid I don't have a whole lot to tell you about the victim."

"Well, give us what you've got," I said with a sigh. This seemed par for the course with this case.

"There are no defensive wounds on the victim, no skin or fibrous tissues under her nails. The GSW was at fairly close range, a 9mm Glock, which is a pretty common weapon. I've sent the recovered bullet over to the lab, but unless the gun was used in a previous murder or crime, not sure we can trace it. Best bet would be to catch this perp and recover the weapon for comparison."

"Great. We'll get on that."

"Anything else you can tell us about Helena?"

"She had eggs benedict for breakfast, along with an espresso. She wasn't a heavy drinker, judging by her fairly healthy liver. She didn't smoke and more than likely didn't spend much time around anyone who smoked; her lungs were in great shape. She'd had work done, breast implants, at least two facelifts, and there are signs of recent liposuction. I'd say she cared about her appearance and worked hard to maintain her looks."

"That's great, but not helpful." I rolled my eyes at him.

"Well, judging by the contents of her stomach and how digested it was, I can tell you she'd eaten about an hour before she was murdered. Considering the amount of rigor she was in by the time we got her here, I'd say with quite a bit of confidence that she was killed between nine and eleven in the morning."

"That's a smaller window than you had before, so that's good. Maybe Lindsey or the Tech team can make that window even smaller," I said, thinking about the phone Lindsey mentioned.

"Thanks, Damien," Angel offered as we left the morgue and headed for the bank of elevators. "So what do you think? Should we go canvass the neighborhood? See if any of the neighbors knew what Helena was up to?"

I nodded slowly. "We should definitely do that, but first I think we need to go through Helena's social media accounts, and I still need to put in that call to Lauren. Not sure how I want to bring up the stolen-goods aspect of her mother's business. If she knew about it and didn't report it..."

"She'd be an accessory after the fact."

"Right, but when we spoke to her before, she didn't seem to know much about her mom's business, so I don't want to flat out accuse her."

"Maybe don't mention it?"

"Maybe, we'll see," I said as we reached our floor and headed toward our desks.

I picked up the phone and dialed the number Lauren Richards had given me and waited, but it went straight to voicemail. I left her a message and then turned to Angel. "No answer."

"Okay." He looked thoughtful for a moment. "Tell MacHenry to push for the subpoena just in case, we'll look at the social media stuff, and if she doesn't call back by lunch, try again?"

"Sounds like a plan. We can go canvass the neighborhood after we eat."

Angel nodded. "I'll take Insta and TikTok."

"Fine, I'll take Facebook and Twitter, or rather X." I called MacHenry to give him a heads-up, then got to work.

An hour and a half later, we had built a pretty good picture of Helena's lifestyle based on the things she had posted over the course of her life. It also seemed she had posted pictures to a Facebook group at 9:27 a.m., so that helped narrow our timeline a little more if they weren't made from a third-party posting group. MacHenry or one of the other Tech gurus would have to look at it to be positive it came from her directly. I made a note of it and then closed down my computer. "I'm starved; let's grab lunch."

"No call from Lauren?" Angel asked as he shut down things on his end.

"Nope. I'll try her again when we head over to her mother's neighborhood." I grabbed my purse, and we left the precinct. "You don't think she was lying about how involved she was, do you?"

Angel shrugged. "It's always a possibility. Guess we'll have to wait and see, won't we?"

8

NOT SO NOSY NEIGHBORS
MARCY

Tuesday Afternoon

After stopping at the King Buffet just off the 101 on N. Western Ave. for lunch, we were back heading toward Helena's neighborhood. The Pan Asian seafood had really hit the spot, and I was stuffed. "So how do you want to do this?" I asked, glancing at Angel as I drove.

"I'll take the houses to the right of Helena's, and you take the left?" he suggested.

"Okay. What are we thinking, five or ten houses down, plus the same across the street?"

"Or to the end of the block? The yards are on the large side; too far down and the neighbors probably don't pay a lot of attention, you know?"

"So play it by ear." I parked in Helena's driveway, and we split up, Angel heading to the house to the right of Helena's, and I turned and walked over to the one of the left. Knocking on the door, I waited.

A Hispanic woman opened the door. "*Si?* I help you?" she asked in broken English.

"Good afternoon, my name is Detective Marcy Kendrick. I wanted to ask you a few questions about your neighbor Ms. Richards."

The woman tapped her chest. "No neighbor, I no live here. I get Mrs. Bartholomew for you."

I started to tell her to wait, but she had already closed the door in my face. I waited a moment, and then an elderly woman came to the door. "Good afternoon, ma'am, I'm Detective—"

"Rosia told me the police were here; what's this about? Is there a sex offender in the neighborhood? Another murder? What's going on?"

"As I was saying, ma'am, my name is Detective Kendrick, and I'm here to speak to you about your neighbor Ms. Richards."

"Oh. Her. I heard she was killed in a home invasion, shot, from what I was told. Horrible, and in this neighborhood. I put in a security system last year, with all the crime that's been going on, and now it's practically on my doorstep, and what are you people doing about it? Nothing."

I swallowed back the retort that lingered on the tip of my tongue. "It's good that you have a security system, ma'am. I am sorry that this crime was brought so close to your home and making you feel unsafe; however, we believe Ms. Richards was targeted specifically because she ran a business out of her home. Were you aware she was doing that?"

"No. Of course not. How could I be aware? What kind of business? Not...not prostitution, was it?"

"What?" I was taken aback. "Was Ms. Richards promiscuous? Was there a lot of traffic coming and going from her house?"

"You tell me. You're the one who said she was running a business out of her home. Was it drugs?"

"Wait...I'm sorry, I think you may have misunderstood. Ms. Richards ran an online business selling cosmetics and perfume. Are you saying you suspected her of selling drugs and herself? Were there a lot of people coming and going from her house?"

"I couldn't say. I don't pay attention to what my neighbors do. That was why I was asking. Are you saying she wasn't doing those heinous things?"

"No, ma'am. Not as far as we're aware." I felt as though I'd somehow walked into an alternate universe. "How well did you know Ms. Richards?" I asked, trying to get back to my list of questions.

"I didn't know her at all. Of course I knew what she looked like, but I didn't associate with her." Her tone said she didn't think very highly of Helena. "She was one of those women who chased after her youth; you know the type, I'm sure. Always having work done?"

"Yes, I am aware. Can you tell me how long you and Ms. Richards have been neighbors?"

"Oh, a few years now, I suppose. I did try to be neighborly when she first moved in; however, she made it quite clear that she wanted nothing to do with any of us here in the neighborhood. She never came to the events or parties any of us planned, nor did she participate in any of the neighborhood activities we arranged."

"I see. Well, thank you for your time, Ms. Bartholomew. Before I go," I said, holding up one finger. "Did you happen to notice anything strange in the neighborhood yesterday morning?"

"I did not, as I wasn't home after seven a.m. I didn't return until about four in the afternoon. I met my sister for breakfast, and we spent the day shopping."

"Okay, well, thank you again for your time." I gave her a tight smile and walked back down the path to her driveway.

I moved on to the next house, but that neighbor—Mr. Greene—didn't know much more than Mrs. Bartholomew did. It went downhill from there. Not one of these neighbors had noticed anything out of the ordinary, nor did any of them know anything beyond the fact Helena Richards was a divorcée who was always having work done to adjust her appearance. They were quite shocked to learn that she ran a business out of her home.

The general feeling I got was that living in that particular neighborhood, you should either be independently wealthy, or have a spouse who was a high-powered executive making eight or nine figures, or *be* the executive who made the eight or nine figures. Helena didn't seem to fit in.

I made it back to the car and waited for Angel. While he was gone, I tried Lauren again, and this time she answered.

"Lauren, it's Detective Kendrick. I was calling with a few more questions about your mother's business."

"Oh," she sniffled. "I don't really know much about her business, but I'll try to answer whatever questions I can."

"I appreciate that. First, I wondered if we could get your permission to go through the business' financials?"

"Um, sure? I mean, I don't know if I can give that kind of permission, but it doesn't bother me if it will help find who did this to Mom."

"That's fine, and as her next of kin, you can. I'll need you to call her bank and let them know, if you don't mind?"

"Sure, I can do that."

"Thanks. I also wanted to ask if you knew where your mom sourced her products from?"

Lauren paused and didn't say anything for a full minute, but I could hear her breathing and still sniffling in the background. "I don't think she ever told me. I was trying to recall if she'd ever said anything, but I don't think she did. Not even in passing. I mean, I never really took a big interest in what she was doing. It was really so beneath her, you know? She didn't want to work, but she felt she had to keep up her standard of living, as she called it. I thought it was ridiculous. She could have bought a smaller place or come to live with me, she didn't have to buy that place and keep up appearances, but that was Mom. She didn't want her friends to think less of her."

The car door opened, and Angel sat down in the passenger seat. Seeing I was on the phone, he didn't say anything.

"Do you have a list of her friends? Maybe someone she confided in?"

"Her best friend, Jessica Mannarino, maybe? Though, I doubt Mom told her she was running a business. Jessica is... well, she's very judgmental."

"Do you have her number? Her address?" I asked.

Lauren rattled off the woman's phone number and address for me. "Was there anything else? I have to go meet with the funeral home."

"Just one thing, was there anyone else your mom was close to she may have confided in?"

"Not that I can think of. Mom didn't really have other

friends, more rivals than anything else, and none that she would have told her darkest secrets to."

"Okay, thank you, I think that's all for now. If you would contact the bank, though, that would be great."

"I will. Goodbye, Detective." She hung up.

I pocketed my phone. "Any luck with the neighbors?" I asked, looking at Angel.

"Not really. Not one nosy neighbor among them. How about you?"

"Same." I turned the car over and put on my seatbelt. "I miss nosy neighbors in this kind of case. If just one of them had been paying attention, it would make things so much easier."

"What did Lauren have to say?" he asked as I backed out of the driveway. "Did you ask her about the stolen goods?"

"No. She said she didn't know where her mom sourced her products, and I didn't push it. She seemed sincere. She gave me her mom's best friend's name, number, and address. Maybe Helena confided in her, but according to Lauren, she may not have because Jessica Mannarino is very judgmental."

"Worth a shot though, right?"

"Definitely." I started thinking about where we were with the case, and I kept coming back to those stolen goods. If we could figure out where they came from, maybe we would get closer to who might have known that Helena would have all of that at her home. "I want to talk to R and H again, well, to Detective Jackson specifically."

"Why him?"

"Jill mentioned that he might have more insight into how these mobs of teens are being organized and how they work. He used to be part of gang and narco, but moved over to robbery/homicide. I'm hoping he'll be able to give us some avenues to pursue."

"Okay, let's see if he's in."

Back at the precinct, we went to R and H. I saw Jill and headed for her first. She'd given me Keith's card, but I'd never met him, so I was hoping she'd introduce us. "Hey, Jill, you know my partner, Detective Reyes?"

"Yes, of course, Detective, I've seen you around." She smiled and shook his hand, her eyes brightening a bit as she looked at him. "Did you have more questions?" she asked, looking back at me.

"Well, yes and no. You mentioned your partner might have some more insight into these teen mob groups. I was hoping you could introduce us."

"Oh, sure." She turned and waved to a tall, black man in a nice navy blue suit. "Keith, can you come here a minute?"

He said something to the person he was with, then walked over to join us. "What's up, Rice?"

"Keith, meet Detectives Kendrick and Reyes, from HSS."

"Sure, I know who you are. Seen you around the station; was there something I can help you with?" he asked as he held a hand out for us to shake. His voice was deep and had a smooth tenor to it.

"Actually yes. I hope so. Is there somewhere we can talk that's not so public?"

He directed us to an incident room. "Will this do?"

"Perfect."

When the four of us were seated, Jill told her partner, "Kendrick and Reyes are working that home invasion homicide from yesterday."

"Oh yeah? Heard about that."

I explained about Helena's business and how we were

fairly certain she was selling stolen goods. "Jill said you might have some insight into how she might have acquired the goods."

Keith unbuttoned his suit jacket and leaned back in his chair, looking comfortable as he propped a foot on his knee. "Sounds like she was buying the goods off some of these mobs that are hitting the shops. See, these kids answer ads on sites that advertise for flash mobs. Most of them think it's some sort of game. There are a few higher up in the ranks who are aware, but they're more careful about what they do."

"So how does it work?" Angel asked. "How do they set all this up? Is it people like our victim who set it up?"

"That's unlikely, at least from what I've been able to gather. It's more like they put the word out on what products they want, and then these crews are sent out by their bosses to gather the products. It's a pretty lucrative business, and the business owners stay relatively safe, as they only deal with the boss of the crew."

"So is there one boss sending out a bunch of different crews, or are there multiple bosses sending out their own gangs?" I asked.

"We're not sure because most of the kids we've caught don't know who their boss is," Jill replied. "They get paid in cash from someone lower on the totem pole, at least that's what they're told. Names aren't given. At least not real ones."

Angel frowned. "So walk me through it. If I were one of these teens, what does this look like for me?"

"Right. So say you were a teenager looking to make a couple of bucks doing something to 'stick it to the man'; that's generally what they think they're doing. You answer one of these ads and then go through some sort of test where you have to know a certain name or event, which is never the same. From there you're told to meet up with a group at a particular location and to wear a hoodie or something similar, a face mask that covers your nose and mouth, so no one can recognize you. That's where you're told what store you're hitting and what product is to be taken."

"Have you all tried to infiltrate these mobs by answering the ads?" I interjected.

A half smile curved Keith's lips. "Of course we have. That's how we know a lot of this, but so far, we haven't made it past the initial interview phase. We're trying to get one of these kids we've caught to turn informant for us, but so far, they couldn't give a fu—er...sorry, but you hang around with these kids long enough and it sticks. Anyway, they don't care about the law."

"Okay, so once they know where they're going, what happens next?"

"After they make the hit, they're told to bring the product to a random location that changes for each hit. At that point they're given their payment and told to watch for another ad if they want to make more. That's it as far as they're concerned."

"So the person or persons picking up the product, are they the bosses?"

Keith shook his head. "We don't know. Maybe. These kids don't think so; they're just other kids. Now whether those kids are the masterminds behind it all, and I'm not saying it isn't possible, remains to be seen. We haven't been able to get our hands on any of them so far."

"Which is why you're looking for a kid you can turn informant."

"Exactly."

"So let's look at the other end. Where is this product

ending up?" I asked. "Take our victim, for instance. Helena Richards has no criminal background, and she runs a business out of her home."

"From what you've said, it sounds like your victim was one of the fences," Keith explained. "We've tracked some of the product, shut down websites that sell the stolen goods, but as soon as you shut one down, three more pop up. Most of the sites are run by people who've never had a run-in with the law. They aren't criminal masterminds, but have business degrees and are tech savvy. They hide behind web domain names and fake names, setting up their profits to pass through various pay sites linked to email addresses that lead nowhere."

"So they keep their hands clean," Angel said. "The kids are the ones taking all the risk."

"Pretty much, yeah." Keith nodded. "We've had multiple kids shot, a few killed, in these mob events. Not to mention the fact that many of them are carrying now and hurting the employees of the stores they're robbing. We just had two young people killed the other day at a pharmacy."

"I heard about that," I offered. "Do you have any leads?"

"One, we're working on facial recognition, trying to get a name, but we have the perp on camera."

"Good. I hope you catch them."

"You and me both." Keith sighed. "I don't see them having any remorse, and I expect things will just get deadlier as this continues."

9

SHE WAS A BIT OF A KAREN
ANGEL

Tuesday Afternoon

M arcy and I left robbery/homicide with some new insights into how these crews worked, but I wasn't sure they were going to be very helpful in identifying who killed Helena. It was all well and good to know how she managed to get her hands on the products she was selling, but it didn't really tell us who could have killed her.

"Okay, so we have a couple of different theories on who might have done this to Helena," I said as we waited for the elevator.

"It had to be someone who knew her, right?" Marcy began. "Someone who knew she ran that business from her home. The neighbors were all oblivious, so that would rule them out."

"Right. So that leaves the daughter," I offered.

Marcy hit the button to close the elevator doors and said, "No, I don't think it was Lauren. My gut says she's a bystander, only in this because she discovered her mom's body."

"Well, we can't rule her out quite yet. Do we have an alibi for her?"

"Not sure we asked, but I can. I still don't think it was her."

"Okay, we'll set her aside for the moment. So then we've got a friend of Helena's who may have been jealous of her success. What was the name Lauren gave you? Jessica something?"

"Mannarino, and I suppose that's possible. This could also be a rival? Maybe someone who wanted to move in on her business? Someone who wanted to take over her product source?"

"Yeah, that's a good possibility." I stepped off the elevator, and we headed toward our desks.

"And then there's the mob crew. Maybe they did this thinking they could get paid a second time for stealing the product that they sold her?"

"But according to Keith Jackson, the mob crew didn't know where the product actually ended up. They dropped it off with the next level in the chain. So maybe not the crew, but a higher member up the chain?"

"Or the crew boss?"

"Right." I glanced at the clock. It was a quarter till five, and I was exhausted. The pain relievers I'd taken that morning had long ago worn off, and I needed a break. "So, let's set up a plan for tomorrow. What do you think?"

Marcy spun back and forth in her chair, twisting from one side to the other as she contemplated what she wanted to do. "I'd say, first thing, we check with Tech, see if they've got anything for us on the personal laptop, the phone or anything on the website."

"Okay, we'll do that and see where that takes us. You got plans with Frank tonight?"

"Later after he gets off shift. I'm having dinner with Stephen. You?"

"I'm gonna pick up dinner for me and Callie. Maybe make it an early night. I feel like a worn leather shoe right now." I gave her a half grin.

"Don't try to drink Hummel under the table anymore and you won't feel like this," she said with a laugh.

"Good advice, I'll keep it in mind."

"We should go brief Chenevert on where we are on the case," Marcy suggested, her eye on the clock too.

Thankfully, doing that didn't take very long. Chenevert asked a couple of questions, but didn't try to sharpshoot us or undermine our investigation, which was rather refreshing, and just told us to keep him in the loop. He really seemed like a decent guy, and I hoped he'd work out for us.

I waved goodbye to Marcy in the parking lot and pulled my phone out to text Callie.

> Hey, sweetheart, how is your day going? I was going to pick up dinner. Anything you're craving?

I sat behind the steering wheel and closed my eyes, trying to unwind as I waited. If she didn't answer, I'd tell her I'd just pick something and see her when she finished with her client, but I'd give her a couple of minutes. I knew with her job, she couldn't always stop what she was doing to answer me. Sometimes she was elbows deep in a dye job and couldn't pick up her phone.

I was just about to send that second text when she messaged back.

> Hey yourself, handsome. My day's been going pretty good, how about yours? How are you feeling after last night? Still hungover?

It dawned on me that I hadn't spoken to her all day except for this morning when I'd told her I was hungover.

> I'm tired, but the hangover is mostly gone. Do you have thoughts on dinner?

> I'm glad to hear that. I'm good with anything. Maybe just grab something easy? I've got thirty more minutes, then I'll head to your place.

> Okay, sounds good. See you then.

I tossed my phone on the passenger seat and pulled out of the precinct parking lot. She'd said something easy, so I headed downtown to Prince Street Pizza. I probably should have called it in, but seeing as she was still at work, I didn't worry too much about it. I ordered the Fancy Prince pizza and risotto balls, as well as Italian rainbow cake for dessert.

By the time I got to my house, Callie was already there. I'd given her a key to my place after our trip to Vegas with Marcy and Frank, wanting to make things with her more official. "Sweetheart?" I called, carrying the pizza, appetizer, and dessert into the house.

"In the bedroom," Callie called and then appeared a moment later. "Something smells divine."

"You said easy, so I got pizza."

"Perfect." She smiled and moved in for a kiss, then took the boxes from me. "Go shower, and I'll get everything set up."

I gave her another quick kiss and did just that.

Ten minutes later, I was dressed in a pair of low-slung sweatpants and seated on the couch, a cold beer in one hand, a slice of pizza in the other. "How was your day? Anything interesting happen at the salon?" I asked, taking a bite.

"You could say that. One of my clients was killed in a home invasion yesterday. It was all my stylists could talk about. Can you imagine being killed like that? Randomly in your home?"

I stopped chewing and stared at her.

"What?" She looked concerned. "Is that your case?"

I nodded, finished chewing and swallowed, then wiped my mouth. "You knew Helena Richards?" I dropped my pizza slice on my plate and turned to give her my full attention.

"I mean, we weren't friends or anything. I didn't even do her hair very often; she was a regular of one of my other stylists. Her and her best friend, Jessica Mannarino."

"Normally, I wouldn't ask, I wouldn't involve you, but... we're struggling a bit with this one, so anything you know about Helena might be helpful."

"Well, I don't really know much about her. Just what she shared in the salon." Callie tilted her head and looked thoughtful. "I know all about her divorce, her daughter, who apparently is very smart and successful and can do no wrong. I never met Lauren, so I couldn't say if that was true or not." She grinned. "Helena was a bit of a Karen. You know, always had something to complain about? Except when it came to her daughter. She would not hear one word against Lauren, ever, not even from Jessica."

"Oh?"

"Yeah. I remember this one time a couple of years ago, around the time Helena got divorced, Jessica said something about Lauren dating an intern from her office, and Helena lost it. Apparently, dating of staff at the law office was reason for dismissal; anyway, Helena took great offense at Jessica's suggestion that Lauren would date 'beneath' her." Callie used finger quotes on beneath.

"Funnily enough, I found out later from another client that it had all been true. Lauren had been dating her intern, or at least sleeping with him. It caused a big ruckus, and she lost her position at the firm."

I frowned. "So Lauren is a lawyer? She seemed a little young for that when I met her."

"Oh, no, sorry, she was a paralegal and still in college at the time. She was training as an intern, and well...you get the picture. Anyway, she was fired. I don't know if she actually got her degree after that."

"Hmmm," I murmured, thinking we might need to look a little closer at Lauren. What exactly did she do for a living? Could she have been lying about being part of her mom's business?

"I know that look. You're thinking about the case."

I chuckled. "Sorry. Just realized that we don't actually know what Lauren does for a job either."

"Oh. Does it have something to do with your case? I mean, does it matter what kind of job Lauren has?"

Shrugging, I said, "I don't know. It might if she lied to us about her mom's business."

"What do you mean her mom's business? Helena didn't work, at least not as far as I knew."

"She ran an online business selling cosmetics and perfumes."

"She did?" Callie shook her head and took a bite of her pizza. "So good," she murmured after swallowing. "Helena never spoke about having a business or a job of any kind. I guess I assumed she was just wealthy."

"That does seem odd. Tell me about this Jessica Mannarino."

"She's a regular drama queen. Very high-maintenance, you know? She comes in every six weeks for a root touch-up or full color. She's got a flair about her, she's outspoken, and she likes to poke the bear. She's always stirring up trouble with someone and then laughing about it."

"Would you say she's the jealous type? Jealous of Helena is what I'm wondering."

"No, I can't see that being the case. If it were the other way around, definitely. Helena could be petty, and she always seemed envious of Jessica's natural beauty. You know she had a lot of work done, right?"

"We're aware."

"Well, Jessica is all natural. Well, except for her hair color, her natural shade is dark blonde to light brown, and she gets it lightened and highlighted. Plus, Jessica is married to a Hollywood agent, and she's always getting bit parts in commercials and sometimes walk-on roles or the like. Helena was super jealous of that."

"So Jessica is an actress?"

"No, not really. She says she just does it for fun, not as a career, and the little bit of money she makes from the bit parts are only enough to fund a cruise once a year. She takes her mom, apparently."

"That seems like a nice thing to do," I replied.

"It is, but now that I think about it, I wonder if she knew Helena ran a business and Jessica mentioning that stuff was a dig at her?"

"Maybe so."

"Do you want me to ask her next time she's in?" Callie offered.

"No, no, better not. I wouldn't want it to affect your business."

Callie smiled and snuggled into my side. "I don't mind. She's not the greatest tipper."

I kissed her temple and picked up our empty plates. "Dessert?"

"Oh yeah, I've been dying for a piece of that rainbow cake."

I went to the kitchen, sent Marcy a quick text about what Callie said, and then grabbed the desserts and returned to the couch. Handing her one of the containers, I sat down next to her. We spent the rest of the evening watching a TV show I couldn't begin to tell you about because I was half asleep for most of it, and then headed to bed.

As I drifted to sleep, I couldn't help but think back over our conversation and wonder if maybe Jessica and Helena had had a falling-out, and in the heat of the moment, maybe Jessica had killed her and then fixed the scene to look as though it was a home invasion. It was something to consider, wasn't it?

10

UNCONDITIONAL LOVE
MARCY

Tuesday Evening

After waving to Angel in the parking lot, I headed over to Stephen's apartment. I'd promised him I'd come over and we could hang out and play video games like old times. We hadn't gotten much time together lately because he was often with Yazmine, and I was nearly always with Frank or working. It was the perfect night for it, since Frank was working late again.

I knocked on the door, and a moment later, he let me in. "Hey, big brother." I smiled and gave him a hug.

"Come in; pizza's getting cold."

"Smells good, whose did you get?" I asked, setting my purse down.

"Ricco's. Got the Ricco Special and an order of buffalo wild wings. Soda?" he asked, opening the fridge.

"Sure, I'll take an RC."

He tossed me a can and then grabbed a couple of paper plates and handed me one. "I've already got everything set up for us to play back in the living room. Pizza and wings are on the table. Help yourself."

We went back to his living room and sat down on the couch.

I fixed my plate and asked, "So what's up? You've been a bit...distant, I guess, for a few weeks. You okay?"

I tried to sound calm, but I was actually a little worried about him. Stephen had been struggling for years, but it had all cumulated in a serious mental breakdown nearly a year ago now. I hadn't known it, but it turned out our mom had abused him in the worst possible way, and he had struggled with dealing with the trauma from it. Not that I blamed him; that kind of trauma would break anyone.

I hadn't been abused by Mom, but hearing about his trauma broke me in a way, too, and on top of witnessing her murder, well, I'd ended up in therapy as well. Who knew talking things out would help me deal with all of the built-up anger and vengeance I had laying on my heart. I felt like I was in a good place now, mostly, and only occasionally did the group online therapy sessions with Dr. Fellows. I wanted Stephen to get to a good place, but he'd had another episode not too long ago and ended up in Shine View, a mental health facility. I really didn't want it to happen again, so I always worried about him and his mental health.

Stephen set his pizza down on his plate and put the plate on the table. "No. I'm not. Not really." He turned and looked at me, his gaze troubled.

My heart sank, and I put my plate down too. "What's going on? Talk to me."

"I just keep—" He broke off and looked down at his hands in his lap. They were squeezed together and turning red.

I reached over and took his hand. "Stephen, you can talk to me. I'm not going to judge you. I'm not going to yell and tell you that you're crazy. I love you. You're my brother. My only family. I need you. Please talk to me."

He nodded and looked away for a moment, I assumed trying to tamp down the emotions I could see were antagonizing him. "I keep wondering what it was I did to make Mom think that it was okay." His words were barely a whisper.

I squeezed his hand and murmured, "Stephen, look at me."

It took him a moment, but then he raised his gaze and met my eyes.

"You were a child. You did absolutely nothing wrong. Everything wrong that happened was on Mom. Not you. Never you."

"But I—" His voice broke, and his lips quivered. "I liked some of it..." His voice was so broken and almost angry. "She...she made it a treat...like a reward...and she would buy me stuff and let me stay up late because I would do what she wanted."

I gripped his hand harder. "She manipulated and groomed you; she used you. It was abuse, Stephen. You weren't old enough to consent to any of that. You didn't know what you were doing."

"She told me to keep it a secret. I couldn't tell anyone. I should have known. I should have realized—"

"Stop. No. That's not how it works. She was our mother. She was supposed to protect you, care for you, care *about* you. I don't know what happened in her life that made her that way, and of course, there's really nobody left to ask who would actually know. I doubt even Rick would know. Mom didn't share anything about her past with anyone. We both know that. But look at her life choices. Neither of us know who our fathers are.

"I used to think she was doing her best by us, making sure CPS didn't come and take us, but now I wonder what our lives would have looked like if we had alerted them. Told a teacher or another adult what was going on. I know I didn't because I was sheltered from most of what was going on by you. You protected me, not only from the johns Mom brought home, but also from Mom herself. You made sure I was safe always."

"But—"

I stopped him. "But nothing. So what if you enjoyed the times she rewarded you for doing what she wanted? You were a child, Stephen. Stop feeling guilty because Mom bought you a game system when you kept your mouth shut and didn't tell on her. Stop feeling guilty because she let you stay up late when I had to go to bed at eight. Stop feeling guilty because she would buy you McDonald's. It was all her manipulating you. Don't let her win. None of that is on you."

Stephen took a deep breath and then gave me a small smile. "Sorry."

"Don't you dare apologize for feeling the way you feel. And if those thoughts start bogging you down, you need to check in with Dr. Faulkner. Maybe have an extra therapy session. What you went through was so traumatic it's going to take a good long time to deal with it, but you *are* dealing with it, and you aren't burying it again with booze and women."

"Thanks, sis. I'll call Dr. Faulkner tomorrow and make an appointment. You're right. Talking about it with you helps. Talking to her does too." He picked up his plate again and took a bite, chewing slowly. "I think it's all coming up again because I've been considering telling Yazmine. She knows what happened to Mom, and that we ended up at a group home, but I haven't told her about what Mom did to me. About the abuse."

I nodded and pulled him into an awkward hug. "I'm glad you're considering it, but maybe this is your mind, your heart protecting you? Telling you that you aren't ready to share that yet? I'm not saying don't tell her; I'm just saying maybe not yet. Dr. Faulkner would be better at making sure you're ready for that conversation, but judging by how upset you are right now, I think it might be best to wait."

"Maybe you're right. I just don't know how Yazmine's going to react to it. What if she doesn't want to see me anymore?"

"That is a real possibility. She may not be able to handle it, and she may decide to walk away. Are you prepared for that risk? Again, I'm not saying she will do that. She may take it in stride and understanding and see how strong you are to have broken the cycle of abuse. You are getting help. You have a support system."

"I'm not sure I'm ready to take that risk yet. I'll talk to Dr. Faulkner, and maybe we can work on getting me prepared for that." His voice was lighter now, like a sliver of hope had pierced his mind.

"That sounds like a great idea," I said as my phone buzzed in my pocket. Frowning, I pulled it out and looked at the incoming text from Angel.

Hey, Callie just told me Helena was a client at her salon. She's been giving me some insight into her character. She also has Jessica Mannarino as a client, and I've learned about her too. Thinking we need to go see her soon. She may know more?

"What's up? Do you have to leave?" Stephen asked, looking worried.

"No, it's just Angel. He found out some information about our victim from his girlfriend of all people." I sent Angel a text back telling him that I agreed, and we'd talk in the morning.

"Oh, yeah, you've got a new case?"

I shoved my phone back in my pocket and picked up my pizza again. It was a little cool, but I didn't mind eating cold pizza. Sometimes it was almost better that way. I took a bite and swallowed before answering, "Yeah, home invasion, but the woman ran an online business. Thinking it may tie in with some of these shoplifting mobs. She was selling stolen goods." I stopped talking as I realized I might have been giving out more information than I technically should be. "Keep that to yourself, okay? It hasn't been shared with the press or anywhere else."

"Of course. But you're probably right; if she was selling stolen goods, she probably bought them off one of those shoplifting crews. There are a lot of online platforms that allow people to set up random online stores. And it's really hard to get them taken down. Those sites don't care if what they're selling is legit."

"Oh? So she might be selling on different platforms than just her website?"

"More than likely she has set up accounts on sites like E-shop and Zipcart. She pays them a fee, and they basically put whatever she's selling in front of their users, and they can click and buy."

"So we need to look at those as well, thanks for that. I wouldn't have known. I'll get Tech on it tomorrow first thing." I finished off my pizza and ate two of the wings. "Okay, you ready to get your butt kicked in *Super Smash Brothers*?" I grinned at him.

"Never going to happen, sis," Stephen said with a laugh, picking up his controller. "It's on like *Donkey Kong* now."

"Bring it," I taunted, happy to see him in a better mood.

"SURE YOU GOTTA GO? If we play another round, you might beat me," Stephen said as I finished cleaning up our dinner mess.

I laughed. "No, you are clearly the king of the *Smash Brothers*. Next time, we're playing *Mario Cart*."

"You've got it." Stephen pulled me into a hug. "Be safe driving home."

"I will. I'll see you Saturday, okay?"

"Yazmine and I will be there. Need me to bring anything?"

"Just your smiling face." I kissed his cheek. "Bye."

"See you." He waved from the balcony as I walked down the stairs and over to my car.

I waved to him before getting in and heading home. It was almost ten, and I knew Frank would be arriving at my place at any time now. It was nice knowing he'd be there.

The drive home was uneventful, thankfully, but as I

pulled into my driveway, I could see Frank on my front step, arguing with someone in the dim moonlight.

I wasn't worried about Frank, but the guy looked a little unhinged, and I was concerned that they were at my house. Was I about to walk into some sort of danger here?

11

IT'S A MOOT POINT
MARCY

Tuesday Night

Who was Frank arguing with? Had El Gato sent one of his men to take me out? Was it another psycho who got it in their head to track me down? I'd dealt with that not too long ago with Nick, but he was currently locked up in a high-security mental facility. It wasn't Jordan either, because he'd been checked into a mental health facility as well, though not one for the criminally insane like Nick was.

I should probably be concerned that all these mentally ill men seemed to target me, but then again, I knew how to handle myself. I was armed and wouldn't hesitate to pull the trigger if I needed to.

Grabbing my purse, I pushed open the door and got out. As soon as I was clear from my car, I put my hand on my weapon, ready to pull it at the first sign of trouble. I walked toward the two men. "Frank, everything all right?" I said, raising my voice slightly.

"This jackass reporter decided it was a good idea to stake out your house and lie in wait to ambush you as you came home. I caught him skulking around the side of the house, looking in the windows." The anger in Frank's voice was palpable.

I couldn't blame him. The idea that some random man, a reporter no less, was sneaking around my property had me very irritated as well. "I suggest you leave immediately and forget that you know where I live, or I'll call my co-workers to remove you. In case you've forgotten, I am a police officer, and I don't make threats that I don't follow through with."

"But, Detective Kendrick, I just want to ask you a few questions about El Ga—"

Frank didn't even give him a chance to finish saying the drug lord's name. His fist slammed into the reporter's nose.

The man cried out, and his hands came up to hold his now bleeding nose. "I can't believe you did that! I could sue you!"

"You're on private property. You were asked to leave. Count yourself lucky that I haven't pulled my weapon yet. Would you like to know what happened to the last person who stalked me?" I growled at him, thinking of Jordan, not that I'd been the one to shoot him, but this guy didn't need to know that. "Now get out of here. And don't think I don't recognize you, Overton. That hit piece you wrote on me? Yeah, I remember what you said. You're the last person I would ever give an interview to. And I will be filing a restraining order tomorrow morning against you."

"The public has a right to know—"

I pushed Frank into the house and slammed the door before Overton could finish. I didn't need to hear it because I knew exactly where he was going with that statement. He was one of those zealous reporters who thought I was a vigilante cop out to kill anyone who stepped out of line. If that were the case, I'd be calling the coroner instead of LAPD patrol to deal with him.

"911, what's your emergency?"

"Yes, I'd like to report a peeping tom and stalker. This is Detective Kendrick, and there is a man looking in my home's windows and claiming to be a reporter."

"I've got a patrol officer on their way to you, Detective."

"Thanks."

"Would you like to stay on the line until they get there?"

"No need. I've got my service weapon if he tries to break in."

"In that case, have a good night, ma'am."

I hung up. The reporter was still out there, shouting at me, but I ignored him and focused on Frank. His fists were clenched, and he was breathing hard, staring at the door like it was an enemy. I needed him to calm down before he had an aneurysm and I had to take him to the hospital. He was only in his forties and too young for that sort of thing, I hoped, but you never knew. Slowly, I moved toward him and put a hand out to stroke his arm.

His gaze flicked from the door to me.

"Frank? The situation is handled. Patrol is on their way. They'll deal with him."

His jaw worked, and he gritted his teeth. "How the fuck did he get your address?"

I shrugged. "He's a reporter. They have their ways of finding things out. Hell, he could have followed me here one day. Without asking him, we won't know. Would you like me to have patrol ask?" I kept my voice calm, trying to reason with him.

"I don't like it. He could have been one of El Gato's men. I don't like that any random person can find you. It's not safe."

"Frank, that's a moot point. El Gato already knows where I live. If you recall, he already sent his assassin here to try to kill me. He wasn't successful, and now that assassin is in the wind. I doubt any of his men are better than that guy. And I also doubt he wants to have me killed. At least not right now. If he did, he would have tried again before now."

Dragging a hand through his hair, he grunted in frustration. "TT, I don't like it. That guy is dangerous, and just because he hasn't tried anything yet doesn't mean he's not going to, damn it."

"I know he is, and you know I am fully capable of taking care of myself. I'm never without my weapon. On top of that, I have you here with me."

"What about when I'm not here?"

"Again, I have my weapon, and I'm not helpless. We've been over this multiple times now. You've got to let it go. I'm fine. I'll be fine."

"Maybe you should move."

I moved closer to him, grabbing hold of his arms and sliding my hands down to link with his. "Frank, I'm not moving. I love this house. It's the first place that has ever felt like mine, and I haven't even lived here very long. You're welcome to stay here with me, and I'm happy to go to Santa Monica to stay with you when I can, but I'm not selling my house. I worked too hard to get it. Giving it up would be letting them win, and that's not going to happen."

Frank closed his eyes and sighed. "Okay. I'm not happy about it, but I get it. I just worry about you so damn much. I can't lose you, babe. It would break me."

My lips quirked, and I reached up, cupping his cheek. "You're not going to lose me. I'm right here."

He covered my hand and then kissed my palm. "This wasn't how I imagined welcoming you home."

"Oh? Did you have something planned?" I asked, breaking into a full grin.

He nodded and started to tell me, but we heard the police sirens growing closer, and then Overton shouted, "You bitch! You actually called the cops on me! You're going to regret that!"

I shook my head. Had the delusional asshole thought I was bluffing? Of course he had. I opened the door and said, "Play stupid games, win stupid prizes. Enjoy your night in lockup." I saw Officers Min-Ji Kim and Julie Desmond getting out of their patrol car and pointed to Overton.

"You okay, Detectives?" Desmond asked as Min-Ji went for Overton.

"Now that you're here, yes. I want to press trespassing charges as well as stalking and unlawful peeking."

"What? No! I wasn't," Overton protested as Min-Ji read him his rights.

"Take it up with the courts," Julie said as she gripped Overton's arm and started taking him to the car.

"You sure you're all right? He didn't put his hands on either of you, did he?" Min-Ji asked.

"No, but I did punch him in the nose," Frank admitted.

Min-Ji paused and considered that. "Private property and

he was trespassing, so I think you're okay. I'll let you know if he tries to jam you up."

"Thanks, Min-Ji. Have a good rest of your night." I gave him a nod.

"You too, Detectives." He gave me a two-fingered salute and jogged back to his car.

Once they were on their way, I turned to Frank. "Now, where were we? What was it you had planned for our evening?" I arched a brow and gave him a sultry look.

A moment later, Frank swept me up in his arms and carried me inside while I laughed. He kicked the door shut, switched the lock into position, and then took me to my bedroom. For the next hour and a half, he proceeded to show me how much he loved me and desired me.

Wrapped in his arms after a romp between the sheets was my favorite place to be. In his arms, I could relax and pretend that all was right with the world. That there weren't bad guys murdering women in their homes. There weren't mobs of teenagers stealing everything in sight. There weren't pedophiles abusing children. There weren't awful people causing mayhem and chaos just for kicks and self-gratification.

Frank pulled me close and settled me against his chest. "You know I'd turn my life upside down for you."

I smiled and kissed his chest, then turned my head to look at him. "You've already turned my life upside down, and I don't know if I'd ever want it to go back to the way it was before."

"Then maybe it's not upside down, but right side up now." He smiled sleepily at me, then sighed. "Just for the record, TT, I know you're fully capable of protecting yourself, but you shouldn't have to. I just want to keep you safe."

"I know. And I love you for it, but you can't take over my life and direct it. I have to be able to make my own choices. You understand?"

"Yeah. I do. I'm not happy about the choice you've made to stay here, but I get it, and I'll work with it."

"Thank you." I scooted up and kissed his lips.

12

FASHION HIT
THE ENTREPRENEUR

Wednesday

"What the hell happened?" I stabbed my sharp, pointed fingernail at Moxie's chest.

Moxie wasn't her real name, it was the name I gave her, and it was what all the kids in the crew knew her as. If nobody knew her real name, then they couldn't finger her for the hits my crew did, and if they couldn't name her, they couldn't identify me either.

"I don't know," Moxie replied. "The guy came out of nowhere and pulled a gun. He just started shooting. He hit Walrus."

"Somebody's got to get him to the hospital; think we need someone else to stay behind?" I stared at the chaos taking place on the street. The man with the gun was hovering over the boy he'd shot, puttin' pressure on the stomach wound and shoutin' at everyone to stop, but they weren't. They'd all gone in different directions with the merchandise they'd grabbed, which was what I'd told them to do.

"Maybe he'll take care of him?" she said, gesturin' toward the man and the boy on the ground.

"Fine. Get in the car."

Moxie ran around the back and climbed in the passenger side. "Where are we goin'?"

"I'm droppin' you at the meet point. I've got other business to handle."

"For reals?" She stared at me like I was out of line.

"Bet. I'm makin' a future for us, for them. What? You think this is all for nothin'?" I started the car and pulled away from the curb.

"You just want to go on like nothin' happened? Walrus got shot! That's...we told these kids they would be fine; this wouldn't happen...and now—"

"Oh, grow up. Shit happens, okay? We need that merch, and you gotta deal with it." I pulled up at the front of the warehouse where her car was parked. "Go. You know where to bring everythin' later."

"Bet." Moxie forced the door open, pushin' it so hard it actually swung back at her as she got out.

She sounded annoyed, but I didn't care. "Chill, it'll be fine."

Givin' me a hard look, she slammed the door shut, rattlin' my car, then backed away.

The girl was askin' for me to throw hands, but I wasn't playin'. I didn't have time for her shit. Instead I pulled away from the curb, trustin' she'd do her job.

As I drove off, I hit the steerin' wheel. My crew weren't gettin' paid enough to get shot at over some merch that was drippin'. Maybe it was time I took matters into my own hands again. It had worked with Helena. The chick who'd asked for this last haul was a bitch with a capital *B*. She was some stay-at-home wife, livin' in a big fancy house, married to some nobody Richie Rich lawyer type.

Glancin' at the clock on my dashboard, I figured it would be the perfect time to hit her, take her business like I did Helena's. It was just after two, her man would be at work, she'd be alone...it was perfect. I turned the car around and headed back toward Hollywood Hills. She didn't live in the same neighborhood as Helena, but near Beachwood Canyon.

The house was nestled into a hill, with the front of it overlookin' the canyon. The view was incredible and so undeserved by the twat who lived here. One of these days I'd be the rich bitch livin' in a pad like this. I parked in the drive, which was large enough to hold three cars side by side. I grabbed the Glock from my glovebox, chambered a round, and then got out and walked up the cement steps to the house.

Ringin' the bell, I waited. I could do this. This was my future. I was doin' it for the crew. For me. For all of us. She was nothin'. A no one.

The door opened, and she stood there lookin' like a whole meal in her Givenchy dress. "You're not supposed to be here until tomorrow, peaches." She put her hand on her hip and tossed her hair over her shoulder.

"Yeah, I wanted to talk to you 'bout it. Can I come in?" I held the Glock behind my back. This wasn't somethin' I wanted to do on the front step.

She rolled her eyes, but stepped back and gestured for me to come in. "What is it? I've got plans in thirty minutes."

I gave her a tight smile. "Won't take long."

She closed the door and started down the hall. The house was full of windows, so many that you could see everythin' outside from every room. She went up the stairs, which were wooden, all the floors were, and I followed behind her, wonderin' where she was leading me.

"Something to drink?" she asked as we entered the kitchen. She picked up her wineglass, which had been sittin' on the table.

I glanced around the room, takin' in the windows. These windows faced the back of the house, so there'd be no one lookin' in. This would work. I moved my hand from behind my back and pointed the Glock at her. "Sorry, Mar, but this is the end of our business arrangement. I'm takin' over."

She gasped, and the wineglass slipped from her hand, shatterin' on the floor. "What the hell? What are you doing?"

"Bye, bitch," I muttered as I pulled the trigger, obliteratin' her face. She hadn't been all that pretty anyway, I thought.

I watched her body drop to the floor, then turned to leave the kitchen. So far, I hadn't touched anythin' in the house. Not even the handrail as we'd climbed the stairs. I needed to make sure I didn't touch anythin' but the merch I was carryin' out to the car, but first I had to find it.

The house was four stories, so it took me a minute to find the room she used to store the goods I'd brought her. Grinnin', I grabbed a handful of high-end designer clothes and headed back down the stairs and out to my car. I tossed the clothes in the backseat and then ran back inside to get some more. It was goin' to take me several trips to get it all.

As I was comin' out of the room with the third load, I heard a man call out, "Mariah? Who's here? That'd better not be JJ's car!"

I was standin' on the landin' outside the kitchen, where Mariah's body lay. The man was comin' up the stairs. There was nowhere for me to go, nowhere for me to hide.

"Who are you? Where's my wife?" he asked, reachin' the landin', a gun in his hand.

I couldn't help that my gaze slid to where she lay on the floor, bloody and dead.

He yelled and then lunged toward me, his silver gun flashin'.

I shoved the clothes at him, hopin' to confuse him, pulled the Glock from the back of my jeans, and shot at him. I didn't look back as I ran down the stairs and out to my car. I knew I'd hit him in the head and had seen him start to drop, but I didn't stick around to watch him land.

I needed to get out of there ASAP. It was a shame I hadn't gotten that last load of clothes to the car, but I didn't want to stop and get caught, so I jumped in my Toyota, turned it on and backed down the drive. I hit the gas as soon as I was on the street and didn't breathe proper until I was back on the 101, no cap. If I'd had more time, I'd have grabbed Mariah's laptop too, but it wasn't necessary, not really. I had Helena's, and I knew what I was doin' now.

As I drove, I couldn't help feelin' that killin' those two asshats had been easier than I'd thought it would be, and she fuckin' deserved it for what happened to the boy—what had Moxie called him? Walrus? Weird name, but if that's what he chose, then that's what I'd call him. Hopefully, he lived. The kid didn't deserve to die doin' shit for that rich twat.

13

TARGETED
MARCY

Thursday Morning

I rolled over and snuggled into my pillow. I was in that place between wakefulness and sleep. Something had disturbed me, but I wasn't sure what. Frank had left thirty minutes earlier to head back to Santa Monica, as he had an early shift today and had to be in by six. I didn't have to be in until seven, so I'd stayed in bed and slept a little longer.

Yesterday had been an uneventful day. We hadn't made any real progress on the Richards killing, but we'd gotten Lauren's alibi—she'd been to eat with a friend and spent the rest of the day at a spa, and she'd spoken with the bank, so we'd gotten Helena's financials too. After that, we'd spoken to Jessica, who hadn't known anything about Helena's business and had been shocked to hear that she'd been selling stolen goods. We'd also gotten with Tech about the websites

Stephen mentioned, and then went to see Lindsey, who told us the team came up empty on additional prints at the scene. We needed a break in the case. Something to lead us to the killer, but at the moment we were stuck. If something didn't break soon, this case was headed for the cold-case files. I hated not clearing my cases. It didn't look good.

The one good thing I'd accomplished was filing that restraining order against the reporter who'd shown up at my house. It had been the highlight of my morning. Unfortunately, the joy I'd felt in getting it didn't last. The day had gone downhill from there, and I'd been happy to leave for the day when our shift ended.

Frank and I had spent the evening shopping for the BBQ we were having this weekend, then came home to have dinner and a quiet night in. It had been nice to just relax with him. We'd even gone to bed early, not that we went to sleep right away. The thought of our bedroom escapades made me smile. He'd worn me out. In a good way.

Something buzzed to the left of me. I cracked my eyes open and glanced at the digital clock on my nightstand. It said it was not quite five thirty. I wasn't planning to get up for another fifteen minutes, so I closed my eyes. Then I heard the sound again, and I finally recognized it as my phone vibrating against the lamp. Sighing, I sat up and grabbed the phone. Looking at the screen, I saw it was Angel.

"What's up? Is this a friendly get-your-ass-out-of-bed call, or—" I started.

"We've got another home invasion homicide. Two victims, one is hanging on, don't know how, he's already on his way to the hospital."

"Shit. Okay, text me the address. I'll meet you there."

I jumped from my bed, ran to my bathroom, and started

getting ready. A glance in the mirror told me I needed a quick shower, but thankfully with this short haircut, it wouldn't take much to wash it, and it could air-dry on my drive. I raced through my morning routine, dressing in record time, and then headed out to my car.

I stopped short at the end of my walkway. My car, which was sitting in the driveway where I'd parked it the night before, now had four slashed tires, and the word "Bitch" was carved into the paint in multiple places.

"Damn it!" I didn't have time for this shit. I pulled out my phone, ordered an Uber, because I needed to leave as soon as possible, and sent Angel a text letting him know my car was out of commission, before calling Frank.

"Hey, TT, miss you already," he said, sounding happy.

I hated that I was about to ruin his good mood. "Frank, did you see anyone around my car this morning when you left?"

He didn't say anything for a moment, but then asked, "Why? What's happened?"

"Just tell me, did you notice anything...off?"

"No. Marcy, what's going on? Are you okay?"

I clenched my fist. "Someone slashed all four of my car tires and carved 'Bitch' into the paint."

"Motherfu—" he shouted, and I could hear him hitting something that sounded like a wall. "I'll head back—"

"No. I've got to get to a crime scene; you coming here won't do any good. I'll get a tow truck to come get it later and take it to Jimmy's. I've already called for an Uber. It was probably that dumbass reporter from the other night."

"Marcy, you don't know that. It could be El Gato—"

"Frank, we are not having this discussion right now. I don't have time for it, and the dude has more shit to worry about than me. I'm fine. My Uber's here. I won't be alone, and Angel will watch my back. Okay?"

Frank stayed quiet on the other end of the line.

I headed for the Uber, covered the microphone on my phone and gave the driver the address. Taking an Uber to the crime scene wasn't ideal, but I didn't have any other choice since Angel was already on his way there. I got in the backseat and then said, "Frank, I need to go. I'll see you tonight, right?"

"Yeah, yeah, but I don't like this, Marce. I don't like that someone's targeting you."

"I'll be fine. There's no reason to worry about me. I have to go."

"Okay, please stay out of trouble, and don't worry about your car," he offered.

I smiled. "I'm not going out looking for trouble, Frank."

"Good. Keep it that way. Stay safe."

He hung up, and I sighed again. My calls weren't finished yet. I googled a tow company and then called them. I made arrangements for them to pick up my car and take it to my mechanic, Jimmy, and then I called Jimmy and explained what was going on.

"We'll need the keys," Jimmy said over the phone. "And we'll probably have to give it a new paint job."

"I'll get them to you, and that's fine. I'm headed to a crime scene at the moment, but as soon as I can, I'll drop them by the shop."

"Okay, that'll work; see you after a while."

"Thanks, Jimmy." I hung up and met my driver's gaze in the rearview mirror.

"Did you say crime scene?" he asked, looking startled. "You a cop?"

"Yeah."

"And somebody slashed all four of your tires and messed with your paint?" His eyes widened and looked like they were about to pop out of his head like those googly eyes in the cartoons. "Who the hell did you arrest?"

I grimaced. "Not sure it was someone I arrested who did it. Might have been a pissed-off reporter I wouldn't give an interview to."

"Wait a minute. I knew I recognized you. You're the detective who caught El Gato," my driver replied, sounding awed.

"One of them."

"Damn, lady, you'd better be careful. That's a dangerous guy. I wouldn't want to be in your shoes." His head immediately went on a swivel as though he was looking for someone targeting us.

"He used to be. He's in jail awaiting trial and has other things to worry about than little old me."

"Right, right," he said, but he didn't seem convinced.

Maybe it was just me, but I wasn't going to live my life in fear because some asshole with an ego might be targeting me. I didn't have time to worry about anything other than doing my job and keeping people safe.

"You can pull up right here," I said, seeing we were close to the address I'd given him. I didn't want him rolling up on the scene and then getting blocked in by cop cars. Not that he would be; it seemed I was the last to arrive.

"You sure?" He slowed down and pulled over toward the curb.

"Yeah, I can hoof it the rest of the way." I paid him and gave him a good tip. "Thanks for the ride."

"Sure, no problem. Hope your day improves," he said as I got out of the car.

I gave him a nod and watched as he pulled into the closest driveway, then went back out of the neighborhood the way we'd come in. I glanced up the street and started walking. I'd had him stop about a block away. By the time I got to the right house, I was sweating. The sun was already pretty warm. It was going to be a long day.

"I can't believe you're late to your own crime scene," Angel said, smirking as I walked up the stone steps to the front door.

"Yeah, yeah, I'm such a flake." I rolled my eyes at his play on a quote from *Point Break*. "I hope that second cup is for me."

"Maybe." He gave me a smile and handed it over. "It's a messy one," he said, tilting his head toward the house.

"You said one of the victims survived?"

"Yeah, James Osgood," Angel said, getting serious. "It's pretty shocking since it looks as though the hit happened yesterday afternoon. Osgood was actually the one to call it in before he passed out again. Black thinks he was out for several hours after the initial attack. Woke briefly, dialed 911, but didn't say anything when the dispatcher answered. They thought it might be a crank call or a butt dial because the call hung up within seconds. That call was around eight p.m. He tried again around three a.m. and managed to say a few words before he passed out again."

"How is that possible?" I asked, sipping my coffee.

"Black spoke to the EMTs who arrived with patrol. They said Osgood took a gunshot to the head. It hit near his right temple, tore off his ear, basically shredded the right side of his head. He's currently in surgery."

"And the deceased?" I asked.

"His wife, Mariah Osgood. She wasn't so lucky."

I nodded. "Okay, let's go check out the scene." I swallowed the last gulp of my coffee and handed the cup to Officer Banks, who was on the door. I was sure his partner was around here somewhere, and I turned to look back at the street. I saw him a moment later setting up the yellow crime scene tape. "Pitch that for me, would you, Banks? And it's no comment when the reporters start asking questions."

"Yes, ma'am."

I patted his shoulder, and Angel and I entered the house.

14

CRIME SCENE CHAOS
ANGEL

Thursday Morning

Marcy's text this morning had worried me a bit. The last time her tires were slashed, it had been the copycat Face Flayer who'd had an unhealthy obsession with her. I worried that she was facing another stalker. Still, I didn't bring it up. She'd tell me when she was ready.

Instead, I'd greeted her with a movie quip, well, I'd substituted "crime scene" for "raid," but she got the quote. She was always good at trivia night. It dawned on me that we hadn't been to one in a while. I'd have to see when the next one was, and maybe she, Callie, Frank, and I could all go.

"It's up the stairs. James was found on the landing. The wife is in the kitchen," I offered, directing her to the wooden steps.

"How many levels?"

"Four."

"Do we think this is the same killer who hit Helena Richards?"

"It's possible, probably likely, but until we get some definitive proof..." I shrugged.

We reached the landing near the kitchen, and CSI was there bagging up all the clothes that were strewn everywhere.

Marcy took a moment to take in the scene. She glanced toward the kitchen, but Lindsey and Black were blocking the view of the body. "So what are we thinking?" she asked.

"The wife's phone had a detailed calendar on it. She was supposed to go to an afternoon charity event at three. Obviously, she missed it, so we're presuming she was killed shortly before she planned to leave, as she looked as though she was dressed for the event."

"Okay, so she was killed around two p.m.? Two fifteen?"

"Right. We—well, Lindsey believes she let the killer in, led them to the kitchen, where she picked up her glass of wine. It's shattered on the floor, the wine mixed with the victim's blood."

"And she was facing the killer when she—" Marcy waved her hand toward the body Damien and Lindsey were hovering over.

"GSW straight to the face. Probably took her completely by surprise."

"We have a gun!" one of the CSI techs announced after picking up a dress they were bagging.

"We need to test it for prints," Lindsey said from the kitchen as she rose to her feet.

"Are we thinking this is the weapon used to kill our

victim?" Marcy nodded toward the silver .357 Magnum on the landing.

"Can't be sure, but I don't think so," Damien said, also rising.

"We've recovered a .38 Special bullet from the wall here" —Lindsey moved toward the wall and pointed it out— "which can be shot from the Magnum. The gun used in the Richards shooting was a 9mm. Presumably from a Glock."

"Which would be consistent with the shot to Ms. Osgood's face," Damien added.

Marcy nodded. "Right, and no gun was recovered at the Richards scene. So either we have two killers and you're wrong about the caliber used on Ms. Osgood, or this hit didn't go as well as the killer intended."

"I'm not wrong," Damien said, "but I'll prove it once I get her to the morgue."

"I'm just speculating," Marcy replied, "playing devil's advocate, if you will."

"Yeah, okay." He nodded and went back to the body.

Marcy looked at me. "What was taken? Did our victim own her own business like Helena Richards?"

"Clothing. All designer. And yes, she did."

"But wouldn't it be odd to hit someone selling different product than the first hit?" Marcy frowned.

"No clue. Might be a question for R and H."

"Okay," Marcy said as she typed into her phone, taking notes. She turned and walked into the kitchen and looked at Lindsey and Damien again. "So what can you tell us about her death?"

"She was shot from about three feet away, so I'd put the killer in the doorway to the kitchen, gun drawn," Damien began. "From the angle of the shot, I'd say the killer was between five foot five and five foot seven. Ms. Osgood was in heels, which put her close to five foot ten. I don't think she was expecting any kind of trouble. There are no defensive wounds on her. She didn't even have time to raise her hands and attempt to block the shot. There are no glass fragments on her face, so either she was holding the wineglass down in front of her, at waist level when she was shot, or she dropped it before she was hit. There are splashes of wine on her legs as well."

"I think she dropped it before she was shot," Lindsey offered. "Imagine, she'd just taken a sip, lowered the glass and looked at the killer, who had to be someone she knew, someone she trusted, and then saw something that startled her. The gun pointed at her, maybe?" She made a gun-shooting motion. "I'll have the kitchen and the rest of the house dusted for prints, but if this is the same killer, they've probably wiped it down. We might get lucky."

"Okay, so if that's what happened with the wife, how do you see the rest playing out?" Marcy asked.

"Let's go upstairs," I suggested. "That's where all of the clothing for Ms. Osgood's business was."

Lindsey followed us out of the kitchen and up the stairs where more of her team were bagging and tagging.

"We're absolutely positive she had an online business? These weren't just her designer clothes?" Marcy asked. "Damn, I hate being late and seeing everything second-hand," she muttered under her breath.

I nodded. "Not only were the clothes in various sizes and multiples of the same thing, but we also found a desktop computer, with her business website on the screen."

"We'll want to make a note of the website, then get this computer packed up and taken to Tech."

"We're on it," Lindsey offered.

"What else do we know?" Marcy asked, looking around the room.

"We're thinking that the perp stood on the landing just outside the kitchen, murdered Ms. Osgood, then walked up the stairs to this room and began taking loads of the designer clothing down the stairs, probably out to a waiting vehicle. It looks as though they were coming down the stairs with an armload when Mr. Osgood entered the home and came up the stairs."

"Okay, that makes sense," Marcy said, following along as we returned to the landing near the kitchen.

"We believe that he was aware something was wrong, and he arrived with the .357 in hand."

Marcy paused and studied the scene for a moment. "So he came up those steps, saw the perp with an armload of clothing, and took a shot at what he thought was a thief?"

"Maybe, or he could have seen his wife dead on the floor from here and then taken the shot and missed, hitting the wall," I replied.

Marcy rubbed her forehead and pursed her lips. "Why not take another shot if you miss the first one?"

"Seeing as he was shot, maybe the perp tossed the clothes as a distraction and then shot him?" Lindsey offered.

"Yeah, that could be. How many bullets were fired from the Magnum?" Marcy asked, turning toward the CSI tech who had bagged the weapon.

"Only one bullet was missing. We bagged the bullets separately."

"And that bullet was recovered from the wall?"

"Which proves me right. Ms. Osgood wasn't shot with the .357," Damien said from the kitchen.

"But it doesn't prove it was a 9mm like with the first victim," I said to Damien.

"Not yet, but if it was the same 9mm, I'll prove it when I recover the bullet from her."

"Okay, let's get on that," Marcy replied. "If there's nothing else here, I'll release the scene to you and Lindsey to finish up." She was speaking to Damien, but looking at me.

"I think we've got everything we need for now. Need a ride to the precinct?"

"Yes, please."

Marcy and I walked out to my car, which was parked in front of the neighbor's house. As I stood at the driver's door of my car and looked toward the Osgoods' house, I realized I couldn't see much of it, nor could I see anything but the tail end of the driveway. There were quite a few trees blocking the view.

I moved from the driver's door and, looking both ways, stepped into the street, moving to the right side, where an oncoming car would be. I looked again and still couldn't see much. I stepped forward, walking up the street and looking toward the house. I had to be almost even with the driveway to see up it to the front walk and door.

"What's up?" Marcy called, watching me from the passenger side of my car as I came back toward her.

"Mr. Osgood wouldn't have known anything was off until he was ready to pull into the driveway," I said, joining her by my car.

"What do you mean?" she asked.

"I've been wondering why he came in carrying his gun. He had to have known something was wrong or off before entering the house, to have the gun in his hand. But if he thought he and his wife were being robbed, why didn't he call 911 immediately? Why enter the house at all?"

"That's a good point." Marcy nodded. "Maybe he thought he could strongarm whoever it was, not thinking they had a gun as well?"

"Maybe. Or maybe he saw the car in the drive and thought something else was going on?" I suggested.

"An affair?" Marcy asked.

"It's not an unrealistic theory, is it? I mean, guy comes home in the middle of the day, sees a strange vehicle in the drive..."

"No, you could be right. Let's run a check on Mariah, look into her life, see if that theory holds any substance. Could be she was having an affair with this guy, and he betrayed her. Maybe he was also having an affair with Helena?"

I unlocked the car, and we got in. "Could be how he got access to their houses so easily."

As we headed back to the station, I thought about giving Callie a call and asking if she knew Mariah Osgood as well. The pictures I'd seen of her around the house showed she often changed her hairstyles. And maybe Callie would know if either Helena or Mariah were seeing someone. Helena was divorced; was it possible that she was seeing someone who might have killed her? Had she been seeing them while she was married? Was that the reason for the divorce?

I knew I was making suppositions that I couldn't substantiate yet, but I couldn't rule them out. I couldn't rule them in either. As I considered calling Callie, my gut told me I shouldn't. She was already squeamish about me being a homicide detective, and I didn't want to drag her into our investigation. If she offered information, that was one thing, but I didn't want her to feel like I was interrogating her.

"Did the hamster go too hard on the wheel?" Marcy asked, a smirk on her lips.

"What?"

"I can smell your brain cells burning from over here. What are you thinking so hard about?"

I laughed. "It's nothing. Just thinking about the case. And —" I stopped, rubbed my jaw, and then gave her a sheepish look. "I was thinking about asking Callie if she knew Mariah Osgood."

"Why would Callie know her?"

I shrugged. "She knew Helena and her friend Jessica."

"It was a huge coincidence that Helena Richards and her friend Jessica happened to be regulars at Callie's salon. I highly doubt that we'd get that lucky again."

"Yeah, you're probably right. The odds aren't in our favor."

"Exactly." Marcy shifted in her seat, and her stomach grumbled loudly.

"Hungry?" I asked, laughing.

"Shut it. I didn't have time to eat before I was summoned." She glared at me. "How did you manage to get up and out the door so fast this morning anyway? Did you stay at Callie's last night?"

I chuckled. "Yeah, I did. She lives over in Larchmont Village."

"Which is fairly close to lower Hollywood Hills; that makes sense, her business is over there."

"How about we go brief Chenevert and the captain and then go to lunch? CSI won't have a report for us anytime soon, and neither will Damien."

Marcy agreed, but asked to make a stop at her mechanic first to drop off her car keys, and then we headed into the station. We'd been at the scene for about three hours, and it was now going on ten thirty. I wasn't starving, but I was hungry. Like Marcy, I'd skipped breakfast, gotten us coffee, and that was about it. I hoped these briefings would go quickly and we could go grab food.

"Sir?" I asked, knocking on the lieutenant's open door.

Chenevert looked up, his face serious. "Reyes, Kendrick, come in. What can you tell me about the scene?"

I explained how we'd found Ms. Osgood, that Mr. Osgood was currently at the hospital, and I wasn't sure of his current status, and that we had reason to believe we were dealing with the same perpetrator from the Richards case.

Chenevert nodded, his fingers steepled as he rested his elbows on his desk. "Okay, how long before CSI finishes? How long before Dr. Black can do the autopsy?"

"Stone was finishing up the scene when we left. Dr. Black was also getting the body ready for transport to the morgue, so hopefully we'll have something by later this afternoon."

"Good. Check in with the hospital, get a status report on Mr. Osgood. I want his interview conducted as soon as he wakes." He paused, and his lips pressed tight for a moment. "If he wakes. I want to know everything about their lives. What drew this killer to target them. If they have a connection to Helena Richards, you need to find it."

"Yes, sir," Marcy replied.

"We'll just go brief the captain," I started.

"No, that won't be necessary. I'll get him up to speed." Chenevert stopped and looked between me and Marcy. "Look, I know the two of you have had some past issues dealing with my predecessor, but that ended the moment I took this job. I have no problem if the captain asks you specifically for an update, but it's my job to know what my officers are doing, and to make sure you have everything you need to do your job. You shouldn't have to go to the captain for those things."

I relaxed a little. "It's nice to have someone in the position who's going to do the job properly. Marce and I have no problem following the chain of command, as long as we don't get jammed up for doing our jobs to the best of our ability."

"I'm aware that your former lieutenant seemed to have a grudge against the two of you and made it difficult for you to do your jobs well. I won't be interfering as long as what you do is by the book. I don't condone anything your former lieutenant did with regards to you, Detective Kendrick. You were cleared by IA on every occasion that you were investigated. That's good enough for me, and it tells me that I should trust you. So until you give me a reason not to, I'll do that."

"Thank you, sir," Marcy replied.

"Appreciate that," I added. It was a relief to know that we wouldn't be put under a microscope for every call we made.

"No problem. I'll let you get back to work." His gaze flicked to the clock, and then he added, "Or maybe take your lunch now, then check in with the hospital?" he suggested.

"That was our plan, sir."

"Okay, check back in with me before shift ends. I want to be kept in the loop on this case."

"Will do," I answered.

"And if you get a call from the coroner, I'd like to go to that meeting. I've yet to meet Dr. Black, and as this might be the beginning of a serial, I want to be in on the major aspects of the case so I can help."

"Sure thing, we'll let you know."

Marcy and I left his office and headed back to my car. I couldn't help but wonder about Chenevert. He'd been here a few days, and already things were different. Not that it was bad, in fact it was the opposite, but I couldn't help but wonder how long it would last.

Had we really gotten lucky with this guy? Or was he just biding his time until he could screw us over?

15

AN INCONVENIENT COMA

MARCY

Thursday Afternoon

Over lunch at Aloha Café, which was downtown and not too far from the Good Samaritan Hospital where Mr. Osgood had been taken, Angel and I discussed Lieutenant Chenevert and how nice it was to have a lieutenant who actually seemed to have our backs. One who would do his job. It certainly made our lives easier. Plus, with a good lieutenant, Captain Robinson would be less stressed, which he really needed after the past year.

I took the last bite of my Loco Moco, which was a hamburger patty and eggs over rice with brown gravy and onions, and sighed. We didn't often get to sit down at an actual restaurant for lunch, and when we did, it was usually at Alebrijes Mexican Grill, which was my favorite. "We should do this more," I murmured, wiping my mouth.

"What, eat?"

I laughed. "No, well, yes. But I meant go to places that we can sit down and eat a nice meal, not just a burger and fries in the car, or from a food truck at our desks."

Angel shook his head. "We normally don't have time for this, remember?"

He wasn't wrong. We often had to eat on the go or while we were working at our desks. "Yeah, I know. Still, I didn't even know this place was here. How did you find out about it?"

"It's been here for ten years. It's the best Hawaiian restaurant in Los Angeles; how have you missed it?"

I folded my arms. "Angel, how long have you known about this place?"

He smirked. "About a month. Callie loves this place."

I rolled my eyes. "Trying to gaslight me, you're a brat."

Chuckling, he grabbed the bill and pulled out his debit card. "Ready to go see if Mr. Osgood is awake?"

I nodded and dropped a cash tip on the table. It seemed only fair since he paid for both of our lunches.

We returned to his car and drove the couple of blocks to the hospital and parked near the main entrance. After showing our IDs to the front desk, we were told Mr. Osgood had been moved from Emergency Care over to Critical Care. The woman gave us directions, and we soon found ourselves at the nurses' station outside of Mr. Osgood's room.

"May I help you?" the nurse who was seated at the desk asked.

"Yes," Angel and I flashed our badges, "we're looking for Mr. Osgood's care doctor."

"Of course. That will be Dr. Bethel. Let me call him for you."

"Thanks."

A few minutes later, the doctor approached us. He held out his hand. "Detectives, I'm Dr. Bethel. I understand you have a few questions?"

I gave him a tight smile. "We do. What can you tell us about Mr. Osgood's condition?"

He held a clipboard in his hand in front of his waist and folded his other over it. "As I'm sure you're aware, Mr. Osgood suffered a gunshot wound to the right side of his head. We've reconstructed his ear, pulled several bone fragments from his skull, and put in a steel plate. Currently he is stable, however he's in a coma, and we're unsure when or if he will come out of it."

"So it's not a medically induced coma?" I asked, hoping I was wrong.

"No, ma'am. We attempted to wake him after the surgery. However, Mr. Osgood remained unconscious."

"Has his next of kin been notified?" Angel asked.

"His first emergency contact was his wife, Mariah Osgood; however, we were made aware upon his arrival that his wife was killed in the same attack. Luckily, Mr. Osgood had his mother down as his secondary emergency contact, and she's been here dealing with all the legalities regarding Mr. Osgood."

That sounded promising. If his mother was close enough to him and his wife, maybe she'd be able to help us with the investigation. "Is she here still?"

"I could not say for sure. If she's not in the room, perhaps she went down to the cafeteria?"

I'd glanced in the room while we'd waited for him to arrive, but I hadn't seen anyone. "Maybe so. Do you know her name or what she looks like?"

"Oh, right, Mrs. Carpenter, she remarried. She's probably in her fifties, dark brown hair, brown eyes, well-dressed."

"Thank you," I offered.

"Sure, if you have any more questions, you're welcome to ask the nursing staff. They're with the patients more than I am and may be able to answer." He turned and headed back down the hall.

"I overheard Dr. Bethel telling you about Mrs. Carpenter. She did go down to the cafeteria about ten minutes before you arrived. She's wearing a navy-blue dress," the nurse at the nurses' station offered.

"Thanks, we'll see if we can find her," I replied.

Ten minutes later, we saw her seated in a booth in the cafeteria and approached her.

"Mrs. Carpenter?" Angel asked.

She blinked up at us, her eyes red-rimmed and watery. "Yes? Has something happened to my James? Has he woken up? Has—"

I stopped her before she could speculate further. "No, ma'am. We're with LAPD. Detectives Kendrick and Reyes. If you wouldn't mind, we'd like to ask you a few questions about your son and his wife."

She sniffled. "Of course. Please, sit down." She gestured to the booth seat across from her.

I sat and slid toward the wall so there was room for Angel. "What can you tell us about Mariah and James?"

"I don't know what happened except what I was told when the medical staff called to tell me James was here," she replied, looking like she was going to burst into tears at any moment.

I put my hand up to stop her again. "That's okay, we're

aware of that. What I meant was, in general. What can you tell us about their life together?"

Mrs. Carpenter dabbed at her eyes. "Oh. Well, James is a very successful lawyer; he's made senior partner at his law firm and is working toward becoming a named partner and buying into the firm. Mariah has always supported him. She's on the board for several charities and runs a side business, though James wasn't happy about that. I didn't think there was anything wrong with her having a small business."

"Why was James not happy about her business?"

Her brow furrowed, and she replied, "Well, it was very odd. He said it was dangerous, but for the life of me, I can't see how. She sold clothing online, for goodness' sake. They had some horrible rows over it." She shook her head and then abruptly stopped, and her eyes widened. "Wait...was... is that why this happened? Is that how my James ended up here? Why Mariah was killed?"

"We don't know, ma'am. That's what we're trying to determine. Did James ever tell you why he thought it was dangerous?"

"Oh, no. Honestly, I thought he was just being stubborn because he didn't want her working. He said the charity work she did was enough, especially since they were trying to start a family."

It dawned on me that I hadn't relayed my condolences and that we still needed to inform Mariah's family of her death as well. "I am sorry for the loss of your daughter-in-law, Mrs. Carpenter."

"Thank you, dear."

"Do you happen to know Mariah's family? Is there anyone I need to contact?" I asked as my phone buzzed in my pocket. I pulled it out and looked at it as she answered.

"Oh, no. I don't think so. Mariah didn't have any family other than James and myself. Well, and my husband, Ty."

"I see." I pulled my card from my purse and handed it to her. "The hospital will let us know when James wakes. We don't want to overtax him, but we do have a few questions. However, if you can think of anything before that, feel free to call me."

"Yes, of course. Thank you for...for being optimistic about his condition..." She looked down, letting her words trail off.

Angel slid out of the booth and held a hand out to help me up. "Thank you for your time, Mrs. Carpenter."

As we walked out of the cafeteria, I told Angel about the text I'd gotten. "Damien's requested us at the morgue."

We got back in the car, and I called Chenevert to tell him about James' condition and what Mrs. Carpenter had said. "And, sir? Dr. Black has requested we join him down in the morgue. I've told him to give us thirty minutes to get back to the station. Should I tell him you'll be joining us?"

"Thirty minutes?" he repeated, then added, "Yes, that'll be good. See y'all there in a bit."

"So I was right," Damien said as we headed over to the body on the slab. "I recovered a 9mm bullet from the brain. It's with Lindsey now, she's checking the striation marks on it, but we are both pretty confident the bullet will match the one recovered from Helena Richards."

"Which means we're probably looking at a serial," Lieutenant Chenevert said, his jaw ticking. "I was hopeful that wouldn't be the case, but seems we should expect a few more deaths. Judging by the fact that less than a week has passed from Ms. Richards' death to Mrs. Osgood's, this perp is escalating pretty quickly."

Unfortunately, I couldn't disagree. "No, you're right. The first death seemed almost accidental in the way she was shot, since the angle was strange, and from the bruising on her from what had to have been a struggle, but this one was intentional. Almost an execution. Like the killer found their nerve after the first death."

"And if they're targeting home businesses," Angel began, shaking his head. "Well, there's a lot of them. Anyone could be the next target."

"Maybe we should put out a public statement? A warning to home business owners?" I suggested.

"I'll make the suggestion to the captain, but I can already guess what he's going to say," Lieutenant Chenevert replied. He looked weary, and he'd only been with us for a few days.

"You don't think he'll agree?" Angel asked.

"My guess would be no, but we'll see." He turned to Damien. "Can I get a copy of your report when you make one for Kendrick and Reyes?"

"Yeah, sure. No problem," Damien said, looking startled. "I hate to mention it, but she was three months pregnant."

My heart dropped hearing that. "That makes this a double homicide."

"Triple if James doesn't make it," Angel added.

"And don't forget about Helena Richards." Chenevert's lips went flat. "I want this guy caught ASAP. I don't know what magic you have to work, Kendrick, but you're our expert at catching serial killers. Find this guy."

16

PR PRINCESS

MARCY

Thursday Late Afternoon

A ngel and I returned to the detective pool, and just as I sat down, Police Chief Warren approached me. Warily, I stood up. "Sir," I acknowledged.

"Kendrick, just the detective I was looking for." He smiled, and I knew I was about to get assigned something I didn't want to do.

"What can I do for you, sir?"

"We've been contacted by *LA Women Magazine*. They want to do a piece on you and how you successfully brought down the biggest drug lord in Los Angeles. I told them you'd be happy to meet with their reporter, Harriet Sullivan, tomorrow morning."

"Sir—"

"Seven a.m., Detective, they'll expect you at their downtown office. I'll have Robinson's assistant text you the address. And, Kendrick—"

I sighed. "Yes, sir?"

"Make us look good."

I nodded. "Yes, sir." I watched him head back down the hallway.

"You gonna need a ride tomorrow?" Angel asked.

I glanced over at him. "I don't know. I need to call my mechanic and see if he got to my car yet."

Sitting down, I put my head on my desk and groaned. "Frank's not going to be happy," I muttered.

"What's wrong with Frank?" Angel asked.

I turned my head so I could see him. "He's not happy about all these interviews. He says it's painting a target on my back. He thinks El Gato has his men, the ones who are still free, aiming for me. I keep telling him the guy has bigger things to worry about than me, but he isn't listening."

"He knows you can take care of yourself. I bet he's just overprotective because of what happened with his brother and because El Vibora managed to get into your place. He probably feels like he almost lost you, which he did, but you overcame that assassin, like you always do." Angel smiled.

"Not sure I would have if it weren't for Jordan breaking my window." I shrugged. "It was a close call, but I can't live my life being afraid the bad guys are going to take me out for doing my job."

"I get it. Frank probably does too, but you'll need to be patient with him."

"Yeah. I know. Just not looking forward to the argument." I lifted my head and slid my chair forward, then clicked on my computer. "Let's start digging into Mariah's and James' social media. Maybe there's something there."

"I'll take James," Angel offered.

I began diving into Mariah's online life. An hour after digging and finding nothing, I took a break and called my mechanic to find out about my car.

"Jimmy's Garage, how may I help you?"

"Hi, this is Marcy Kendrick. I was calling to check on my car."

"Yes, ma'am. It was picked up an hour ago."

I sat there confused for a moment. "What do you mean?"

"Frank Maldon called about your car this morning and said to call him when it was ready. Jimmy called him around two, and he came in about an hour ago, paid the bill and picked up the car. He said he had your permission...please tell me—" the receptionist said.

"It's fine. He's my boyfriend, and he knows Jimmy. I just didn't know he was going to do that," I blurted.

"Oh dear, did I ruin the surprise?" she said, sounding upset.

"No, no. It's fine. Thanks so much for letting me know."

"Sure. Was there anything else?"

"Not that I can think of. Thanks again." I hung up and texted Frank.

> You picked up my car?

> Yeah, it was bugging me that I didn't notice it this morning, figured it was the least I could do to make up for it.

> You didn't have to. It's not your fault, you didn't slash my tires or carve that nasty word into my car.

But I should have noticed.

Frank, it might have happened after you left. It's not on you.

Still. I'll pick you up in ten minutes.

I glanced at the clock and saw it was nearly six. There was nothing else I needed to do at the moment, so I told him I'd be ready and then put my phone in my pocket.

"Frank picked up my car, so I don't need a ride," I said, looking at Angel.

"That was nice of him. Do you know who did it?"

"Pretty sure it was a nasty reporter I denied an interview to because he showed up at my house. I had him arrested for trespassing and stalking."

"When was this?"

"Um, night before last?"

"Wow. So what makes you think it was him?"

"He said I'd regret it, and I don't think I've pissed off anyone else lately."

"You don't think it was one of El Gato's goons?"

I tilted my head at him. "Do you really think El Gato's goons would vandalize my car? They'd be more likely to break in to try to kill me, *if* they were after me, which I don't think they are."

"Good point."

"Anyway, Frank's headed here to get me."

"You two want to meet me and Callie for dinner?" Angel asked, shutting down his computer.

"I thought she worked later on Thursdays," I said, closing my computer program and then turning it off.

"Normally, yeah, but she didn't have any clients scheduled tonight after six, so she's taking the night off early."

"When Frank gets here, I'll ask what he wants to do. Where are you going?"

"Just to Alebrijes."

"You know that's my favorite." I grinned at him.

"Which is why I asked if you two wanted to join us." Angel chuckled.

Frank walked through the door a moment later. "Hey, Angel, good to see you. You and your girl coming over Saturday?"

"For the barbeque? Yep. Good to see you too, by the way."

They shook hands as I grabbed my purse from the drawer. "Angel invited us to join him and Callie for dinner at Alebrijes, if you want to go?"

"Sure, that's fine." He wrapped his arm around my waist and kissed my cheek. "Missed you today."

I smiled. "Thanks for taking care of my car."

"My pleasure, babe. Ready to go?"

"We'll see you at the restaurant," I said over my shoulder to Angel.

"Just gotta pick Callie up, and then we'll be there."

Frank and I walked out to my car, which had all of the scratched words filled in, repainted, and buffed. The paint made it look as though the scratches had never happened.

"Jimmy did a great job; it looks as good as new."

"It does," I agreed. "Hopefully it will stay that way."

"I've been thinking about what you said," Frank said as we got into my car. He turned the engine on, but didn't move.

"What did I say?" I asked cautiously.

"About it being the reporter from the other night. You're

probably right, he was pretty riled, and you did have him arrested."

"I was justified."

"You were. The guy should never have been able to get to your home in the first place. Your address isn't public knowledge, and that's what has me worried."

"Frank, you know I don't advertise where I live, but it's not hidden information either."

"I know, I just worry." He pulled out onto the road.

I took a deep breath and prepared myself for his reaction to what I had to say. "I know you do, and I appreciate that. Really, I do. And I know you've asked me to stop doing the interviews, which I would really like to, but Police Chief Warren and the mayor have been persistent about it. In fact I have another one tomorrow for *LA Women Magazine*. I don't want to go, but I have to. I don't have a choice."

Frank's jaw ticked, and he stared at the road, his fingers clenching tighter on the steering wheel. "You always have a choice." His voice came out hard and brittle.

"You're right. I do. I can choose to do my job, follow orders from the police chief and keep my job, or I can quit." I stared at him. "Is that what you want, Frank? You want me to quit my job? A job I'm damn good at? All because PC Warren has ordered me to do another interview?"

"No," he growled and smacked the steering wheel. "Damn it, Marcy, no. That's not what I want. I know you're good at your job. You were meant to be a detective, not the damn spokeswoman for the LAPD."

"I get that. And you're right, I don't want to be the spokeswoman for the LAPD, but right now that is what my superior officers are demanding, and unless I want to be written up for insubordination, I can't just disregard their orders."

He sighed. "I know. I don't like it, but I understand."

"Look, I'll talk to Robinson. Maybe with these murders going on, I can suggest it's keeping me from doing my job to catch this killer and he'll agree."

"I just don't want anyone coming after you," Frank murmured. "And every interview you do puts you in the spotlight, and that's a dangerous place to be in our world. I can't lose you, TT. It would break me."

I laid a hand on his arm, and he looked over at me. "I'm not going anywhere, and for the record, I'm not enjoying any of this notoriety."

"I know that." He nodded as he pulled into Alebrijes' parking lot. "So what time is this interview tomorrow? Can you come to Santa Monica tonight?"

"I have to be there at seven in the morning, so no. Can you not stay tonight?"

"No, I've got an early meeting tomorrow." He sighed. "We'll have dinner, and then I'll bring you home and pick up my truck." He didn't sound happy about any of it.

"Frank—"

"Just leave it, Marcy; it's fine."

I bit my lip and kept my mouth shut. I could see he was struggling to keep his feelings about all of this tamped down. I hated when he did that. Sometimes I wished he'd just yell or blow up and get it all out, but he didn't. He'd probably go home and spend half the night hitting a heavy weight bag before falling into bed for an hour of sleep. He was going to therapy, but sometimes he fell back into old habits and took his frustration out on the bag. He didn't resolve his issues or talk them out. He just buried them. The problem with that was eventually it would all come out and in the worst way at the worst time.

"You know I'm not dismissing your concerns, right?" I offered quietly. "I respect your opinion, and I'm not trying to be reckless with my safety. I'm just trying to do my job. A job I am fully capable of doing."

Frank shifted in his seat and looked at me. He reached a hand out and caressed my cheek. "I know. This isn't me doubting your abilities. I know you're an amazing detective. You're smart, talented, and skilled. But even so, you aren't all powerful. You aren't all knowing. No human is. And I don't like you being put into a situation where you can't control the outcome."

"That's life, Frank. I can't control anyone else, but I can control what I do, what I say. I can minimize the threats to my life, make the bad guys think twice about coming after me, but I can't control their actions. What they *might* do. I can only react when they do come after me, and eventually someone might choose to do that. If that happens, I promise I'll be ready and act accordingly, but I'm not going to be afraid. I'm not going to let them control me and what I do just because they *might* come after me. That's not living."

Frank's hand slid from my cheek to behind my neck, and he guided me forward, kissing me. I leaned closer and wrapped my arms around his torso.

When the kiss broke, he leaned his forehead against mine. "I do trust you, TT. I trust your abilities. I just know what this world is like, and that's my issue to deal with. I know I frustrate you, harping on about safety, but it's because of everything I've seen, everything I know about this world. It's hard for me to not try to fix things so that you are always safe. Always protected."

I smiled. "I appreciate that about you. That you want to fix things and protect me, even when I can do that for myself. It's nice to be able to give that over to you occasionally, but you have to know that I can and will do that for myself when you aren't with me." I paused and then added, "And you also have to know that I feel the same way about you. I want to protect you and keep you safe as well."

"Yeah. I know." He sighed. "I can't promise I won't worry about you. I can't promise that I won't bring this up again. I can't promise we won't argue about this again, especially if I think you're acting recklessly, which you have to admit you sometimes do." His lips quirked in a teasing way.

I rolled my eyes. "Yeah, yeah. I can't say I've never acted recklessly, but I can promise to work on that. Not saying it won't happen again, but I'll think twice about it, knowing you will worry."

"Thank you." His gaze flicked to the car entering the parking lot. "Angel and Callie are here."

I followed his gaze, seeing Angel's SUV as he drove past us and pulled into a parking space a few spots down from us. "Ready to go eat?" I asked.

Frank kissed me again and then pulled his hand back and sat back in his seat. "I know being with me is hard, but I swear on all that I am, I'll make this relationship, I'll make *me*, worthy of your love."

"You already are," I replied, keeping my gaze on him.

He held my gaze for a moment and then nodded slightly before opening the door and coming around the car to open my door for me. He reached for my hand and helped me out of the car, then wrapped his arm around my waist as we headed into the restaurant.

. . .

THE NEXT MORNING, I was up at five a.m. to get ready for the interview. I arrived at the *LA Women Magazine*'s building at a quarter to seven and was directed to Harriet Sullivan's office. I wasn't nervous exactly, but it was the first interview I'd had to do on my own, so I was more apprehensive about it.

Again, Harriet wanted to get additional details about El Gato's capture, but I kept to the talking points that Angel and I had worked on. Realizing I wouldn't speak any more on that topic, Harriet moved on to some of the other cases Angel and I had worked on, and then she brought up Nick Pound and tried to get me to speak about my mother. That was when I shut the interview down. I couldn't do it. I couldn't keep doing these interviews. I was done.

Now I needed to make that clear to Police Chief Warren and Mayor Taylor. How I was going to do that, I didn't know, but it needed to happen and soon.

17

PHONE UNLOCKED
MARCY

Friday Morning

After leaving the interview with Harriet Sullivan, I arrived at the precinct around nine a.m. I felt as though I'd just wasted two hours that I could have put into working our current case. I was frustrated, hungry, and caffeine deprived.

I noticed the beignet truck parked at the end of the parking lot and headed there before going inside. I ordered two of the chocolate beignet boxes, as well as two large coffees. I wasn't about to walk in and not bring Angel anything. If he didn't want it, I would have them myself, so it wasn't a big deal.

I set the boxes and drink carrier on my desk and put my purse away. Angel was away from his desk, and I wondered where he was. Sitting down, I opened one of the boxes and took a bite of one of the beignets. I had eaten three of the four beignets in my box before Angel showed up.

"Hey, how did the interview go?" he asked, eyeing the closed box and extra coffee sitting on my desk.

I handed him the box and nodded toward the coffee. "That's for you. The interview was...annoying. She asked me about Nick Pound and my mother."

"Why did she bring all that up?" he questioned as he ate.

"I think she was pissed that I wasn't giving her any new information on El Gato. Just the same talking points we've given everyone. She wanted something juicy, so she went for the jugular."

"What did you say?"

"Nothing. I don't even know how she knew that Nick is still obsessed with me and still trying to contact me even though the facility blocks those letters from going out. Or that he was fascinated with my mother's murder. Let alone that I was there when she was murdered. She knew a lot about me; it was kind of creepy, honestly."

"You taking it to Robinson?"

"Yes, if he doesn't put an end to these interviews, I'll do it myself and tell the police chief and the mayor I'm done." As I spoke, my desk phone rang a couple of times, so I answered. "Kendrick."

"Detective, it's MacHenry. Can you come over to Tech? We've finally gotten Helena Richards' phone unlocked. You're going to want to see this."

"We'll be right there," I said, looking at Angel. I hung up and then said, "That was MacHenry. He's unlocked Helena's phone."

Angel dropped the beignet he was eating back in the box

and shut it. Putting the box on his desk next to his coffee, he stood up. "Let's go."

I closed my box as well, then got up to go with him, but I brought my coffee with me. I needed the caffeine. We reached Tech a few minutes later and walked in. I nodded to the commander and then headed for MacHenry.

"Hey, Mac, what have you got for us?"

MacHenry pushed his glasses up his nose and smiled. "Come take a look."

He pulled up some text messages between Helena and someone she named Village Idiot. "This thread has the most texts, but there are also some between Helena and someone she named Inbreeder and another she called Spaz."

"So she didn't use real names; do we know who the numbers belong to? Can we trace them?"

"We tried that, but they're all burner phones. Those monthly pay-as-you-go numbers."

"Great. So how does this help?" I asked, reading over the texts, which showed she was definitely buying stolen goods. In fact, she was placing orders with the person she called Village Idiot, demanding certain products be stolen and delivered to her.

"It doesn't, I guess, but we'll keep working on it. We've got the numbers, and even though several are deactivated, we're finding everything that person texted, every number they texted or called, and we'll cross-reference them to see if we can find someone with a name, and maybe we can find them that way."

"Good idea," Angel acknowledged, his eyes on the text thread. "You know, from the looks of it, Helena was a criminal. She should have been behind bars for what she was doing."

"You're not wrong, but we already knew she was a criminal from the fact she received and was selling stolen merchandise," I said. "This text thread just tells us she was a worse person than we imagined."

"Wonder if Mariah was the same," Angel questioned.

"We're still working on her phone. It would help if there was someone who could give us her code to unlock it. Didn't her husband survive the attack? Can we ask him?" MacHenry inquired.

"It will be one of the first questions we ask if and when he wakes up from the coma he's in. Right now, he's our only lead. He might have actually seen the killer, but until he wakes up, we're stuck."

"Right, well, we'll keep working on it," MacHenry said with a sigh.

"Thanks, Mac. Let us know if you discover anything else," I said.

Angel and I left and headed back to our desks.

"Was really hoping that would be the break in the case we needed," Angel muttered.

"You and me both. If we can link those conversations to the perp, the DA will be able to use them in court, so at least there's that."

"True, but that's a big if."

I nodded. I felt sick to my stomach because I knew this killer wasn't done. "I've got a bad feeling about this perp. Like they're growing empowered every moment they stay off our radar."

"You think they're going to kill again?" Angel asked.

"You don't?" I asked, but Angel didn't reply.

We returned to the detective pool and spent the rest of the afternoon going over both cases, trying to find connections. We set up an incident room with pictures from both crime scenes and waited for news that didn't come about the phones, the computers, anything that would help us pinpoint the killer.

I'd also gotten a call from Lindsey that she'd sent a CSI tech over to Jimmy's garage yesterday to take prints of my car, and they were still searching for a match. I hadn't told her about the damage to my car, but she'd found out and wanted to track down who'd done it. I thanked her and then went back to work.

At the end of the day, I headed home, glad it was the weekend. Unless something happened, Angel and I were off until Monday. My fingers were crossed that the killer wouldn't get a wild hair up their butt to go on a killing spree.

It would be just my luck that we'd get called out on our days off.

18

VENGEANCE IS MINE
CHAOS

Saturday Morning

I was fed up. They'd fucking stolen from me for the very last time. Nobody stole from Chaos and got away with it. Nobody.

I lived in the neighborhood. I knew the various crews that ran these streets. I'd even bought some of their boosted products over the past year because they were sticking it to the corporate powers. I couldn't care less about what these crews got up to as long as they kept their shit to the big corporations that could absorb the crap they pulled. They marked that shit up five thousand percent anyway.

But now, they were stealing from me, and that, I wouldn't let stand. I owned small discount shops, so I didn't have the kind of luxury the big assholes did. Everything I bought I only marked up a hundred percent. It was still a discount for the consumer considering I got everything wholesale or cheaper. But I couldn't afford to have these assholes targeting me and my businesses.

I'd tracked down Pretty Boy—that was what the kids called him, but I knew his real name was Jerimiah—to his hangout, which was in the back of an abandoned single-wide trailer in a crowded mobile home park on S. Western Avenue. I sat in my car, parked across the street, waiting for the little shit to stick his head up. I'd been here for hours, waiting for my chance to grab him.

I sucked my teeth as the asshole leader came out of the house on his own around seven p.m. I shoved open the door to my car, pulled my Smith and Wesson M&P 45 from my holster and approached him before he could get in his Mazda Miata. Probably bought it with the shit he stole off me. That just served to piss me off more. I moved up on him from behind and shoved the gun in his side.

"One word and I'll blow a hole right through your guts," I hissed in his ear.

"What the fuck, man?" He looked over at me, and his eyes widened. "Ch-Ch-Ch-Chaos?"

"Across the street. Get in the fucking car."

"Yeah, man. Sure...um...w-what's going on?" His voice squeaked as he stuttered. He started toward the passenger seat.

"No, you're driving." I didn't want to try to focus on the road and hold the gun on him. Too easy for him to get away.

"Oh-kay..." he said hesitantly.

I got in the passenger seat and kept my gun trained on him. As he buckled up, I put the key in the ignition and turned it on. "Drive."

"Where..." He gulped and looked at me, his expression frightened.

"Just drive. I'll give you directions."

We drove for thirty minutes, Pretty Boy getting more and more scared the longer we were in the car. I didn't care. We pulled up to one of my warehouses. It was currently empty. I didn't even have the electricity running on it at the moment. It was perfect for what I had planned.

"Get out."

"Chaos...I don't...what's going on? Why...why are we here? If...if this is about wanting more product...man, just say so..." The boy was obviously frightened.

He should be.

"Shut your fucking mouth." I backhanded him across the face. "Get out of the fucking car."

He scrambled to do what I said, his mouth bleeding from the blow I'd just given him.

I got out and kept my weapon pointed at him. "Inside." I nodded toward the door.

Pretty Boy stumbled as he headed for the door I'd indicated. He pulled on the handle and went in. As soon as he was inside, I clubbed him with the butt of my gun, and he went down. I grabbed the rope I'd prepared earlier and bound his hands and then his feet, then dragged him to the hook I'd set up. I hung him up on the hook by the rope around his wrists and waited for him to wake up.

"Know why you're here?" I seethed.

"N-no..." he stuttered.

I slammed my fist into his stomach. "Don't fucking lie to me."

"I swear...I don't know," he said between gasping breaths.

"Fucking liar!" I slammed my fist into his mouth this time. "You fucking stole from me! Me! Your crew hit my shop and ripped off every high-priced item I had for sale." I punched him again, this time in the gut. "And now you're going to pay the price." I continued hitting him, punctuating each word with a slam from my fist. "Nobody. Fucking. Steals. From. Chaos."

Pretty Boy wasn't so pretty by the time I was done with him. His face was swelling, he had two black eyes that were nearly swollen shut, his nose was broken, and I'd probably shattered a cheekbone as well.

I cut him down from the hook, dragged him outside to my car and tossed him in my trunk. He was semiconscious and still bound, so he wasn't going anywhere. It was dark now, as it was nearing midnight. I got back in the car and drove back to his hangout, where I opened the trunk, dragged him out and set him on the driveway by his car, then cut the bindings on his wrists and feet.

As he lay there, I kicked him in the ribs for one last reminder, and he grunted in pain. They were probably broken from the pummeling I'd given him earlier, and I didn't fucking care. "Spread the word, Pretty Boy. Nobody. Fucking. Touches. My. Business." I kicked him with each word. "Next time, I won't be so gentle. You hear me?"

His eyes fluttered, but he managed a nod.

"Bullet to the head next time someone steals from me."

I stared at him for a full minute and then got back in my car and drove home, feeling completely satisfied.

Vengeance was mine, indeed.

19

4 A.M. WAKE-UP CALL
MARCY

Sunday Morning

The barbeque had been nice. It was a pretty relaxing time with Frank, Stephen, his girl Yazmine, Angel and Callie. After they left, Frank and I had gone to bed. He'd been a little distant most of the day, after Yazmine had asked about the El Gato case. We'd talked a bit about it and moved on, but it seemed all it had done was remind Frank of his worry.

I was snuggled in his arms when my phone rang with the song "Ride Captain Ride" by Blues Image, because I'd forgotten to put it on vibrate before I went to sleep. I glanced at the clock and saw it was nearly four in the morning.

"What?" Frank groggily came awake. "What time is it?" he asked, waking up more, but sounding grumpy.

"Almost four. It's Robinson." I grabbed the phone and answered, "Sir?"

"Kendrick, sorry about the early morning call, but we've had a possible development in your case."

I rubbed my face, trying to wake up more. "A development? What is it, sir?"

"A teenager was brought into the ER by some of his crew. He's been beaten pretty badly. Jackson recognized him and floated the idea that there might be a connection to your case. We don't want to miss the opportunity to speak to him before he's discharged."

"Okay, what do you want me to do? Are you thinking he's the perp? Or a victim of the perp?"

"Not sure. He's not giving up any names as to who did this to him." Robinson answered my last questions first, then said, "I want you and Angel to give it a go. See if you can get a name from him. Treat him as a victim until we know otherwise."

"Yes, sir. What hospital are we headed to?"

"Good Samaritan."

"Have you called Angel?"

"He's next on my list."

"Okay, tell him I'll pick him up. He's on my way."

"Will do."

I hung up and noticed Frank sitting up in bed, his arms crossed over his chest, glaring at me. "What?" I asked, wondering if we were about to get into another argument.

"It's your damn day off, and he's calling you in because this kid might be connected to your case?" He sounded pissed, but whether it was at me or Robinson, I wasn't sure.

I got out of bed and started pulling on my work clothes. "Frank, this is the job. You know this. You deal with this too when you're on a case, or have you forgotten?"

"No. This is...reaching. Just because this kid is part of a

crew doesn't make him the killer or the victim of the killer. Do you know how many gangs there are in LA? Hundreds. This is ridiculous. A four a.m. call on your day off about a possible connection is bullshit. It's encroaching on your free time."

"Frank, I don't have time for this right now. This is the job. This has always been the job. If you can't handle me doing my job, then maybe we should rethink this relationship. I love you, but I can't keep doing this. I can't keep having this argument with you." I went in the bathroom and yanked a brush through my hair.

A couple of minutes later, I heard my front door slam shut.

My eyes shut, and a couple of tears slid down my cheeks. Had I just let go of the best relationship I'd ever had?

I PULLED up to Angel's, still feeling like I wanted to crumple and cry over Frank, but I didn't. "Hey," I said as Angel got in the car.

"What's the matter?" Angel asked, seeing my face.

I shook my head and pressed my lips together in a firm line. If I told him, I'd break down, and we had work to do. "Just an early morning."

Angel looked at me for a minute before he eventually said, "How about we grab coffee before we head to the hospital?"

I glanced at him as I backed out of the driveway, but I didn't say anything.

"It won't take that long. Just go through the drive-thru."

I gave him a slight nod and headed for our favorite coffee shop. I pulled into the drive-thru lane behind a large truck.

"I had a fight with Frank," I murmured, trying to keep my emotions in check.

"Why? What did Frank do?"

"He didn't do anything. Not really. He just..." I swallowed back the emotions that were threatening to spill out. Taking a deep breath, I said, "He was upset about the four a.m. wake-up call when we don't even know if this is related to our case, and it's my weekend off."

"I mean, he's not wrong, not really. If this isn't related, then we're out here for nothing. And we do deserve time off. Still, this is the job."

"Exactly." I pulled up and placed our order at the speaker. "I don't know what he wants from me. I love him, but I'm not quitting my job just to make him happy."

"Is that what he wants?"

I thought about it as we waited for our order. "Honestly, I don't know what he wants. Other than for me to be careful and stay safe in a bubble. Not put myself in the spotlight by doing interviews that draw attention to me, which could lead to me being targeted."

"Well, considering how many cops we've lost lately, what happened with his brother, and all of that, he does have cause to ask you to be cautious. I mean, we all should be. This isn't the force we joined ten years ago. We're targeted all the time. Not just here, but everywhere. Patrol can't even make a traffic stop for speeding without having guns drawn on them. You never know what you're walking into in any given situation. So I get that."

"I'm not saying I don't—" I started, getting frustrated as the barista handed me our coffees.

"I'm not accusing you of not being cautious, Marce. I know you are. You are generally pretty careful. You do tend to jump quickly when we're after a killer, and put yourself front and center when you have that suspect in your sights, but you're trained, and you know what you're doing. None of us know when we wake up in the morning if it will be our last. Things can go from a controlled situation to chaos any second, and all we can do is prepare the best we can. I think Frank just wants to make sure you're not doing anything that will add to that possible switch being flipped."

I nodded and then cringed as I drove to the hospital. "I told him that we might need to rethink our relationship because I couldn't keep arguing with him, and he left without a word before I came out of the bathroom."

"Wow. Okay, yeah, that's a bit more to unpack than the other."

"We just keep having this argument, and I was sleep deprived and frustrated. I didn't mean it. Not really. I just hate having the argument. It's not like I don't worry about him too. I just feel like he's trying to control me."

"Which is what Jordan attempted to do."

I nodded. Maybe that was what had me so upset. Frank hadn't been this way before El Gato, so why was he doing it now? Had he just been biding his time? Waiting for the perfect excuse to start?

"Wait...before you start spiraling out of control, I want you to think carefully about this question."

I glanced at him as I pulled into the hospital parking lot. "What question?"

"When you were with Jordan, was he trying to control you because he was concerned about your safety, or was it so he could have power over you? And then compare that to Frank."

I sighed. "Jordan was about the power. Frank just wants

to keep me safe. He's not trying to control me," I whispered. I knew it like I knew my own name. Frank didn't want to hurt me. He didn't want me hurt. His fear of losing me was making him act this way. Understanding that helped. How I could fix that though was another question.

"No, he's not. He's been through a lot this past year, and so have you. He's still dealing with his parents' trauma over his brother and dealing with his own trauma from that. You might want to cut him some slack."

I grabbed my coffee and got out of the car. "You're probably right." I sighed again, taking a sip of caffeine goodness. "We should go see what this kid can tell us. Maybe he's the killer we're after, and we can put this case to bed."

Angel raised his cup and said, "Here's hoping."

20

POTENTIAL SUSPECT IN SIGHT

MARCY

Sunday Morning

"We're here to see Jerimiah Robins," I said, flashing my badge at the nurses' station. Captain Robinson had texted me the details of the kid while I'd been picking up Angel. Frank and our relationship were still lingering in my mind. I'd thought by dating another detective, he'd be more understanding, but because he truly understood the job, he was more worried. It was a conundrum I didn't have the mind power to deal with at the moment. I had work to do.

"Yes, he's in room 314."

I was still so focused on my thoughts that it took me a moment to register what she'd said. I shook my head and blinked. "Thank you," I replied a moment after Angel did.

We walked into room 314 and saw a boy; his face was a

mass of bruising, red and swollen. His blondish-brown hair was spikey and messy, probably not how he normally wore it. I noticed multiple bruises on his arms and chest, at least the upper portion where the hospital gown had slipped below his collarbone. I had a feeling there was more bruising beneath the gown. He appeared to be asleep, but with his eyes so swollen it was hard to tell.

"May I help you?" a quiet voice asked from the corner of the room.

I turned to see a nurse dressed in blue scrubs standing next to a computer station. "We're Detectives Kendrick and Reyes. We would like to ask Jerimiah some questions. Is he capable of speaking?"

"Barely, he's been beaten pretty badly. He's got multiple hematomas and contusions, a broken nose, four broken ribs, one that was dangerously close to puncturing his lung, a dislocated shoulder, and a sprained wrist."

"Is he sedated?" I asked, looking at him.

"No, just sleeping. Not well, mind you. He's in for a rough time with all that."

"I hate to do it, but we really need to speak to him."

The nurse nodded and moved to the boy on the bed. She laid a hand on his arm, careful not to touch a spot that had bruising, and said, "Pretty Boy, wake up."

I arched a brow.

"It's his street name; he said nobody but his mom calls him Jerimiah," she said softly.

I nodded.

She shook his arm a little and repeated, "Pretty Boy, I need you to wake up."

"Water," he croaked a moment later.

"Sure, here you go," she said, holding a cup with a straw to his lips. "Some detectives are here to see you."

His squinted gaze moved to me and Angel. "What do you want?"

"Jerimiah—"

"Pretty Boy," he interrupted.

I gave him a tight smile. "What can you tell us about what happened to you?"

He shook his head, refusing to talk.

"We can help you. We just need you to tell us who did this, and we'll get him or her off the streets. You don't have to worry."

"Pretty Boy, tell them what you told me."

I tilted my head at her; something about the way she spoke to him seemed as though she knew him personally, not just as his nurse. "Do you two know each other? Aside from you being his nurse?"

"Jeanie's my sister's friend," Jerimiah answered.

"Your name's Jeanie?" I questioned, looking for a name tag.

"Yeah. Sorry I didn't introduce myself. Figured you'd read my name tag."

"You're not wearing one," Angel observed.

Her hand went to her chest, and she looked down, her eyes widening. "Crap." She moved back over to the computer and searched, then headed for the small bathroom. When she came back in, she had her name tag in her hand. "It falls off sometimes; the clip is loose. I didn't realize."

"It's fine. Back to the question. Pretty Boy, tell us who did this, and we'll get them off the street."

"He said he'd put a bullet in my head," he whispered, his voice strained and shaky.

"He who?" I asked, pushing him to answer.

"Chaos."

That didn't tell me anything. I had no idea who Chaos was. "Tell me what happened."

Jerimiah explained that Chaos had forced him to drive to a warehouse, where he was tied up and beaten because someone's crew hit his shop and took all his merchandise. Chaos thought it was him and his crew. Which he vehemently denied, but I suspected he actually had and just didn't want to get in trouble for the theft.

"Who is Chaos?" Angel asked. "What's his real name?"

"Carlos Renaldo," Jeanie answered, her arms folded across her chest as she frowned at Jerimiah.

"What can you tell us, if anything, about the home invasions where a couple of people have been murdered?" I asked him.

He rolled his head from side to side, but then winced. "Nothin'. My crew ain't involved in that kind of shit."

"Okay, but have you heard anything? What about this guy Chaos? Do you think he's involved?"

"He's crazy enough," he murmured. "Don't know anything about what happened though. Some of the crews are spooked, not mine, but some."

"You said Chaos forced you at gunpoint...did you see the gun?" Angel asked.

It was a good question, considering we were looking for a Glock 9mm.

"Not really. It was just a black and silver handgun. I don't do guns."

"If you think of anything else, let us know," Angel said as he handed Jerimiah a card.

. . .

As we headed to the precinct, I thought about what we'd learned. Robinson had been right. This could very well be connected to our case. Could it have waited a couple of hours? Maybe, but the sooner we got this guy off the street, the better.

"I think we need to check in with Jackson or Rice and see what we can find out about this guy Chaos. If he's got a street name, he could be part of a gang too."

"It's Sunday," Angel reminded me. "They may not be in."

"Shit. Yeah. Well, let's check anyway. Jill Rice gave me her number, so I can call her."

"You do that, and I'll start digging into his life. Look for any arrests or warrants in his name," Angel suggested as I parked the car.

"Good idea," I said, getting out and locking the doors once he was out of the car as well.

At my desk, I put my purse in the drawer and sat there thinking. Not about the case, but about Frank. I pulled out my phone and sent him a text.

> I'm sorry about this morning. I didn't mean it.

I waited a moment to see if he'd text back, but when he didn't, I sighed and put my phone away, then headed for R and H. I stepped into their detective pool and looked around for Jill and her partner, but didn't see either of them. I started to turn back, but as I did, I heard my name.

"Kendrick."

I looked over my shoulder and noticed Keith Jackson coming out of one of their incident rooms.

"Were you looking for me?"

I nodded. "We went to see Jerimiah Robins at the hospital."

Jackson motioned toward the room he'd just left. "Why don't we talk in here?"

I moved toward him and then paused. "You're not using the room for one of your cases?"

"Oh, no, I was just taking a phone call and needed some privacy."

I followed him into the room, and he shut the door.

"Can you tell me more about Jerimiah?" I asked.

"He's the leader of the Royal Boys. Mostly they're just suburban kids playing at being a gang. They aren't known to be violent...more like frat boys, honestly, who think it's cool to do some of this shit. They don't think they're hurting anyone with their shoplifting antics. They post a lot of videos of them doing these mob theft hits."

"Well, they may think twice now, considering what happened to him. Some guy named Chaos beat him up. He also said he'd put a bullet in his head. He didn't elaborate, but I suspected it was a threat against anyone who stole from him again."

"Chaos?" Jackson repeated. "That's a name I haven't heard in a while."

"His real name is Carlos Renaldo."

Jackson snapped his fingers. "Yep. Now I remember. Carlos, aka Chaos Renaldo, used to be a gangbanger back in the day. Did some time for armed robbery, grand larceny, and assault with a deadly weapon. For a while it looked as though he'd turned his life around. He's got a string of corner shops, small bodegas that sell a variety of items. Anything he can get his hands on cheap and resell at a massive profit."

An idea struck me, and I asked, "Think it's possible he was buying some of the stolen merchandise from these shoplifting crews?"

"Let me check with some of the other detectives here in R and H, and I'll let you know if there is any suspicion of that."

"I'm also wondering if he might be our guy for these home invasions. Given his history, it might not be too far-fetched."

Jackson nodded. "Absolutely could be. I'll see what I can find out for you."

"Thanks, I appreciate it. You've got my number?"

He grinned. "Sure do."

"Great." I opened the door to the incident room and headed back to HSS.

"I take it you saw someone?" Angel said, looking up from his computer.

"Yeah, Jackson. This Carlos guy has a rap sheet from a ways back. Jackson is going to do some checking with the other R and H detectives and see if he's under suspicion for anything, but it's possible he could be our guy."

"I think so too. I started looking into his businesses; he's got four shops here in LA, plus a couple of warehouses. His merchandise is pretty random, never sells continuous products, and each store sells different products. He's been amazingly lucky with certain items being in his hands at just the right time."

"What do you mean?" I asked, sitting down and rolling my chair next to his to look at his computer screen.

"Okay, so remember the pharmacy that was recently hit?"

"The one where the two workers were killed?"

"Yeah, that's the one. So one of the things those kids stole was the entire section of toilet paper. Well, this week, his shop that's closest to that pharmacy has a blowout sale on toilet paper. It's almost like their downfall is his windfall... you know?"

I nodded slowly. "The question is, was the toilet paper that was stolen the toilet paper that he's now selling?"

"Might be hard to prove without looking at his books, but it sure seems suspect to me."

"If Carlos isn't on R and H's radar, he should be, but I'm starting to think he might be our guy."

"Want to get a warrant?"

I paused and thought about it. "Maybe we wait for Jackson's report and then check in with Lieutenant Chenevert, if he's here?"

Angel nodded. "I'll keep digging. See if there's anything we can run him in on."

"Maybe we can look at some of the other robberies and see if we can match his sales to what was stolen?"

"That's a good idea. I'll call over to R and H again and see if I can get a list of items that were taken in some of these hits." I rolled back to my desk, picked up the phone and called the other department.

Within minutes I had the compiled lists of stolen merchandise emailed to me. I started looking through it and frowned. A lot of these products were designer or at the very least high-end cosmetics and perfumes.

I glanced over at Angel. "Does Carlos sell anything designer or cosmetics?"

"No, not really. Mostly it's closeout stuff. Everyday household items, some food, products that have been clearanced at other shops...dog food, pet toys...that kind of thing. Looks like he'll occasionally have name-brand things. Oh, and he has quite a bit of random electronics."

"Okay, so we can probably cross off the designer clothes, handbags, cosmetics and perfume, right?"

"Yeah, I would think so."

"Does he have a frozen food section at his shops?"

"Two of them have both frozen and chilled sections, why? Was frozen food something that was taken?" Angel questioned as he typed.

"Yeah, looks like several of the supermarkets have been hit over the last month and have had entire sections cleaned out. Ice cream, French fries, frozen pizzas seem to be popular. And the meat departments have been hit heavily."

"Funny the two shops with those sections...he's had sales on all those items. He's got twelve-ounce ribeye steaks advertised right now at one of his shops. Damn, he's selling them for fifteen dollars a pound. Whole Foods has them for twenty-four a pound. That's a hell of a price difference. There's no way he got those steaks through legal channels."

"Interesting. Six cases of twelve-ounce ribeyes were stolen two days ago from one of the supermarkets on Whittier Blvd."

We spent the rest of the morning going through and matching products. Jackson finally called and let me know that he'd spoken to a couple of R and H detectives. They were watching Carlos Renaldo because they suspected he was receiving stolen goods, but they weren't sure how he was acquiring the products from the crews that were stealing them from various other shops around LA.

"Thanks, Jackson. I appreciate you looking into that for me."

"No problem. Let me know if you need anything else."

"I will." I hung up the phone. "Let's go see if Chenevert's in his office."

21

ONE STEP FORWARD, THREE STEPS BACK

MARCY

Sunday Noon

"Sir?" I said, knocking on the lieutenant's door when I noticed he was there.

"Kendrick, Reyes, have you had a break in the case?"

"We've got a potential suspect, sir."

"Come in." Chenevert motioned to the chairs facing his desk.

After Angel and I sat down, I told the lieutenant about our talk with Jerimiah "Pretty Boy" Robins and Carlos Renaldo's possible connection to the shoplifting mobs.

Chenevert steepled his fingers, his elbows resting on his desk. He looked deep in thought for a couple of minutes and then looked up at me and Angel. "It's all circumstantial. How about bring Renaldo in on the assault charge to question him and then press him to see if he slips up, gives us something more on the home invasions."

I smiled. "We'll still need a warrant for his arrest on the assault, and we can also get him on a felony firearms charge. He's a former felon, and according to Jerimiah, he's got a gun in his possession. Maybe we can get a search warrant to find it?"

He nodded. "Probably going to be limited search; do we have an address?"

Angel blew out a breath. "He spends time at all four of his businesses, and then he's got a house in Angelino Heights, plus two warehouses, and his vehicle as well."

"So seven properties and a car? That's going to be an expensive raid. Can we narrow it down?"

"I don't think so, sir. He travels between his shops and home every day. The warehouses he visits less, maybe once a week or so. There's no way to know where he's stashed his gun," Angel replied.

"Okay, I'll run it by the captain, see what he thinks."

"Did you ask him about the warning I wanted to put out to the public?" I asked. I hadn't heard back, and I hadn't heard anyone give the public a warning about this killer.

"I did, and he ran it by the police chief, who shot the idea down. They want this kept quiet as much as possible."

I nodded. "Thanks for trying."

"It wasn't a bad idea, Kendrick. The police chief was just afraid it would make us look incompetent when we're still struggling to get back in the public's good graces after the past year."

I sighed. I could see his point, but that just brought up another subject I needed to address, only not with him. He

wasn't the one who'd been pressuring me to do those interviews. Still, I wondered if maybe he could step in. "Sir?"

"What is it, Kendrick?"

"Any way you can do me a favor?"

He glanced at Angel and then back to me, a wary look on
his face. "That depends. I don't normally do favors."

"Right, well, it's not exactly a favor, I just...can you intervene and let Police Chief Warren and the mayor know I'm
unavailable to do any more interviews?" I wrinkled my nose
and sighed. "They don't seem to be listening to me when I
try to talk to them about it."

I swear he swallowed a grin and schooled his face into a
serious expression. "I can do that. It's taking you away from
more important things like catching this killer anyway." He
glanced at Angel. "Do you want out of these interviews too?"

He nodded. "If at all possible, sir, that would be great. I
just want to be able to do my job."

"I'll see what I can do." He smiled. "Why don't you two
knock off for the day. Even if we can get the approval for the
arrest warrant and search warrants, it's going to take some
time to get a judge to sign off. It will probably be tomorrow
morning before we can even get that to happen."

"Thank you, sir." I smiled and stood up.

With the afternoon free, I decided to head to Santa
Monica. I needed to fix things with Frank, one way or
another.

"WHAT ARE YOU DOING HERE?" Frank said, coming to the
door, his arms crossed over his chest as he stared at me. "I
thought you were done with me."

"I don't want to be done with you. I never did. I was just

tired of arguing, Frank. I'm sorry I said something I didn't actually mean. And I'm sorry for my part of the argument. What I'm not sorry for is doing my job."

He dragged a hand through his hair and then pushed the door open. "Come in."

I hesitantly followed him into the living room and sat down on the couch so we could talk. "Frank?" I said after a moment.

"You were right about a few things this morning. I thought I could handle this. Us. You being on the job. I know you're a great detective. I'm not questioning your abilities, TT." He paused. "I just don't know if I can handle things if something happens to you. Maybe I'm not in the right place for a relationship right now. I don't know. I think I need some time to figure that out. Figure myself out."

My heart felt like it was being rent in two and demolished. I could feel tears building, and I'd be damned if I let him see me cry. Not now. I took a breath and stood up. "I understand. I'll go."

"I do love you, Marcy," he said, his voice coming out broken and lost.

My lip quivered as I turned away from him. "I love you too. Goodbye, Frank."

I walked out of the house and across the lawn to my car. I didn't look back as I got in and then backed out of his driveway. I didn't glance in the rearview mirror as I drove away. I couldn't. The tears that I'd felt building were now spilling down my cheeks, and I had to pull over once I was out of his neighborhood because I couldn't see well enough to drive.

I don't know how long I sat there sobbing, but it was long enough for a patrol officer I didn't recognize to come to check on me. I quickly dashed the tears from my cheeks as he approached my car window, and put a tremulous smile on my lips, then rolled down the window.

"Ma'am, are you having car trouble?"

"No, Officer. I'm sorry, I just got some bad news and needed a few minutes to collect myself. I'll be on my way."

"It's fine, ma'am. Take the time you need to drive safely, or would you rather I call someone to come get you?"

"No. Thank you. I'm all right now."

He studied me for a moment and then said, "Okay then. Be safe."

I rolled my window back up and pulled back onto the road, heading back to my house. All I wanted to do was sleep. Maybe it would all be better in the morning.

IT WASN'T. I'd spent the entire night tossing and turning and fighting off nightmares. By five a.m. I was up, showered, and ready for work. My appetite was nonexistent. I did need coffee though, so I fixed a pot, sat down at my kitchen table, and opened my laptop. I logged into the group therapy site and waited for some of the others to show up. Eventually they did, and then Dr. Fellows' face popped up in one of the squares.

"Welcome, Detective Kendrick," he said.

"Hi, Dr. Fellows."

"Is everything going well?" he asked, giving me a wary look.

Sucking my lips in between my teeth, I shook my head. "No. No, it's not."

I spent the next hour talking and sharing what was going on with me and Frank and how I was feeling about it all. It wasn't all about me, everyone shared during that hour, and it helped me to put things in perspective. At least enough that I was in a better frame of mind before heading in to work.

"Thanks, everyone. Thanks, Dr. Fellows."

"Of course, that's what we're here for. Why don't we schedule a one-on-one session for later this week?" he offered.

"I might call your office to make an appointment," I said before signing off and closing my laptop.

A moment later my phone buzzed with a text from Katrina asking if I wanted to get lunch. She had been in the group meeting as well. Because I had no idea what today was going to look like, I told her I was on a case and would have to play it by ear. She told me to just message her when I knew, and we'd go from there.

Grabbing my car keys and my purse, I locked up and headed in to work. Maybe we'd even get lucky and get Carlos to confess today. I could only hope.

22

DENIAL ISN'T JUST A RIVER IN EGYPT
MARCY

Monday Midmorning

"We've got it," Lieutenant Chenevert said, jogging out of his office and down the hall toward me and Angel. "I've already organized with Myers, head of Patrol; he's got officers ready to roll out. Do you have eyes on Renaldo?"

"Yes, sir," I said with a sharp nod. "Kim and Desmond called in. Said he's at his shop in Koreatown."

"Okay, you and Reyes head there, get him arrested. Hummel, Vance, you take the shop in Skid Row. Carter, Sands, you take the one downtown. Ferris, you and Bridges take the one in Lincoln Heights. Bailey and Clark, you take the warehouses."

"Sir, what about his house?" I asked.

"I've borrowed a couple of detectives from Robbery and Homicide; they'll take care of Renaldo's house. They've already got their warrant to do the search. Go ahead and head out. I'll be here to coordinate things as needed."

Angel and I took the paperwork for the shop in Koreatown along with the arrest warrant and headed for Angel's car. "I can't believe how much more smoothly things run with a competent lieutenant around," I said, getting in the passenger seat, hoping he wouldn't bring up Frank or anything related to him. I didn't want to talk about him.

THREE HOURS LATER, back at the station with Carlos Renaldo in custody, I gathered up what I needed to go to the interview room. The raids on his businesses, his warehouses, and his house had gone well; we'd recovered a Smith and Wesson M&P 45, but no Glock 9mm. That didn't mean he didn't have one, just that he didn't have it where we could find it. Forensics was going over his vehicle, and if they recovered anything, they'd let us know.

"You ready for this?" Angel asked, studying me.

I gave him a tight smile as I sent Katrina a text telling her today wasn't good for lunch. "Yep." I knew he knew something was up with me, but so far, he hadn't asked. I really wanted it to stay that way, but he was my best friend, and eventually, he'd press me for information. I just didn't know how much I actually wanted to share. "Let's go." I put my phone away and gestured toward the hall.

"Marce," he said hesitantly, "is everything okay?"

I shrugged. "Yeah, just ready for this to be over."

Angel didn't say any more, and I was grateful. We made our way down the hall to the interview room.

I put on my game face before we entered. I needed to focus so I could get this guy. Looking at Angel, I opened the door and stepped into the room. "Good afternoon, Mr. Renaldo."

"What's so good about it?" he said, staring daggers at me and Angel.

I kept my expression flat, not wanting to give anything away. "Would you care for some water? A soda maybe? Or coffee?"

"No. What's all this about? Why are you hassling me when these mobs of kids are robbing everybody blind? Do you know they hit my stores seven times in the last month? I'm so sick of having them take my stuff. Something needs to be done about them."

"Sir, some serious allegations have been made against you for assault. And with your past felony, you are now up on a weapons charge as well. Would you care to comment on that?"

"It was self-defense. And the gun was just for show. It wasn't loaded. You didn't find any bullets, did you?" He huffed and looked mulish.

Sal, his lawyer, leaned in and whispered something to him that I couldn't hear.

"Kidnapping, tying up and beating a person isn't self-defense, sir," Angel interjected.

"He's the one behind all the stuff being stolen from my shops! I was just doing what I had to do because you all won't do your jobs and stop these maniacs."

We were getting nowhere fast with him. I decided to change tactics. "Let's talk about that. What has been stolen from your stores? Do you have proof of purchase? Do you have surveillance video evidence of them taking specific items?"

Carlos nodded to the mousy little man he had on

retainer. "He's got the tapes."

"VHS?" I questioned with surprise, seeing his lawyer pull actual VCR tapes from his briefcase.

"I haven't upgraded my systems; the VCR works fine; why fix something that ain't broke?"

"It's going to take a few minutes to find a machine. If we even still have one." I got up and walked to the door. I found the lieutenant in the viewing room with the captain. "Sirs?"

Lieutenant Chenevert was on the phone, but Robinson said, "Chenevert is trying to track down a VCR."

"Thanks."

"I'll let you know when we find one."

I nodded and returned to the interview room. "They're working on it. In the meantime, what do you know about these shoplifting mobs?" I questioned.

"What? Nothing. Other than they're a bunch of stupid-ass kids doing stupid-ass things."

"Do you know any of the leaders of these crews?"

Carlos shrugged.

"What can you tell me about the goods they've stolen, and you appear to have?"

His eyes widened, and he looked momentarily stunned. "I don't know what you're talking about. I don't."

"So it's just a coincidence that you happen to have the exact quantity of Edy's ice cream in the exact flavors that were stolen from Jessops Supermarket yesterday in your freezers at your Koreatown location?"

"I can carry that brand if I want to; what's it to you?"

"You can indeed carry that brand, but not if it's stolen merchandise. Do you have a proof of purchase from the wholesaler for that ice cream?" Angel asked.

"I don't know, probably. Yeah, sure," he stuttered, looking a little panicked.

A knock on the door a moment later had me getting up from my chair again. Opening it, Lieutenant Chenevert rolled a cart into the room that contained a TV and a VCR. He gave me a nod and then headed back out without a word.

I took one of the tapes from Sal and put it in the VCR. We watched several minutes of grainy, unidentifiable people with hoods and masks run around his shop, grabbing things.

"Are they all like this?" I asked.

"Yeah, you can see how they mob the place and grab everything they can get their hands on. They're like a plague. You pigs need to do something about them," Carlos spat at me.

I shut down the useless videos. "We can't do anything with these, and they have nothing to do with why you're here today."

"Why am I here?" he pouted.

"A couple of reasons, the first of which is assault; the second is a violation of your parole by possessing a firearm—"

"You can't prove that it's mine."

"It was found in your shop, under your counter, and your prints are all over it."

"It's a glorified paperweight; there's no bullets for it."

"That doesn't matter. Mr. Renaldo, do you own a Glock 9mm?"

"No. The Smith and Wesson you took from me is the only potential weapon I own. I'm not stupid, you know."

"I think you're lying."

"Detective, you've asked the question, and my client has answered."

I flicked my gaze to Sal, then turned to Carlos. "Let me tell you what I think, okay? I think that you're wanting to expand your business, maybe start selling pricier merchandise. But there's a lot of competition out there, so you decided to take matters into your own hands."

"What are you talking about?" Carlos asked. "Sal, what's she talking about?"

Sal shook his head. "Are you asking my client if he's involved in the recent home invasions where a couple of businesswomen were murdered?"

"You're good," Angel said sarcastically.

"I think we're done here. My client has nothing further to say."

"Wait, yes, I do!" Carlos sputtered. "I didn't off nobody. Especially not some stay-at-home wives with their own businesses. You checked my shops; did it look like I sold the kind of shit they did?"

While that was a good point, I still couldn't help but think his denial rang false. What the hell else was he hiding?

23

GETTING NOWHERE FAST

MARCY

Monday Evening

"**R**eyes, Kendrick, you did good today," Lieutenant Chenevert said as he walked down the hall toward us. "You might not have gotten Renaldo to confess, but we're checking out everything he said, and it's only a matter of time before we know the truth. You've been at it all day, not to mention yesterday when you should have been off, so go home. Take a break. Relax. You can jump back into the fray tomorrow morning."

"Yes, sir," I offered, but there was nothing for me to go home to. Frank was gone. We were over, and I didn't know if there was any going back. If Frank would want to. Hell, if I would want to.

I could once again feel my eyes stinging from unshed tears. Clicking off my computer, I scooted my chair back and pulled my purse from the drawer. I glanced over at Angel. I still felt guilty because I hadn't told him that Frank didn't want to see me anymore. But he did know something was up with me. I could tell in the way he was acting around me. Like he was handling me.

But I didn't want to lean on Angel. Not this time. He had Callie, and he was happy with her. The last thing he needed was me being all weepy on him because my boyfriend didn't want me anymore. So I put on a smile and pretended I was fine as I said, "Night, see you tomorrow," in as happy a voice as I could muster.

"Night, Marce. See ya."

I could tell he wanted to push me to talk, but he was holding back, like he was waiting for me to spill my guts to him. I wasn't going to do that.

I hurried out of the building to my car before he could catch up to me. I had to get out of there. I drove home without stopping. Normally—well, before Frank and I got together—I would have swung through a drive-thru and gotten dinner. I'd been cooking a lot more with Frank around, or he would, but I wasn't hungry. I hadn't been hungry since Frank pretty much dumped me. My stomach was too unsettled for me to eat.

I pulled into my driveway and parked next to Stephen's truck. I figured he was probably here using my exercise room. He did that occasionally. I went inside and called out, "Stephen? I'm home," as I set my purse and keys on the table by the door and then turned the lock on the handle of the doorknob.

Stephen came out of the living room, a towel around his neck. "Hey, hope you don't mind me using the equipment."

"You know you're always welcome," I said, turning to the kitchen before he could get too good a look at me.

Either I wasn't quick enough, or he'd heard something in my voice, because he asked, "What's wrong?"

I hesitated just a moment too long.

"Marcy?" He grabbed my arm and turned me back to face him.

Without meaning to, I burst into tears. I'd been so good about holding them back, shoving my feelings away and into a corner all day, but now, here in my house, I couldn't contain them anymore. Stephen immediately pulled me into a hug and let me cry all over his sweaty shoulder. I was glad for it, honestly. At least I wasn't ruining a nice shirt with my tears.

"What happened? Are you okay? Is Angel? Is Frank?" he rambled.

The moment Frank's name came out of his mouth, my sobs increased.

"Is Frank okay? Did something happen?" He rubbed my back and led me to the sofa in the living room.

I was too upset to answer. Eventually, I said, "I think he broke up with me," but it came out a bit jumbled.

"You and Frank broke up?"

I nodded and wiped my nose with the back of my hand. "I think so."

"Tell me what happened."

I told him about our arguments and what I said, and how I went to apologize, but Frank said he needed time and didn't want to see me. "I didn't want that. I didn't mean what I said," I said, hiccupping between sobs.

"Marcy, it doesn't sound like he actually broke up with you. Just that he needs time to figure things out, how to handle you doing the job you do. He'll come around. Just give him time."

"What if he doesn't?" I murmured, shaking my head. "Maybe I'm just unlovable. This always happens. Jordan—"

"Was an asshole control freak who turned stalker, you are not responsible for him, and you aren't unlovable."

"Bobby."

"What...that boy in high school?" Stephen scoffed. "He was a jerk, and I told him to stay the fuck away from you."

I blinked. He was the guy I'd pined after who had finally asked me out, but then stood me up. I shook my head, dismissing him. "Henry..."

"He was a good man, and if what happened hadn't happened, you probably could have been happy with him."

I sighed and wiped my cheeks. "I just—"

"Stop. This isn't like you. Even when you were married to Jordan and it was all falling apart, you didn't get like this. You've always been confident, if a little neurotic." His lips twitched in amusement. "Stop anticipating the worst. What's going on that's making you think like this?"

He wasn't wrong. Something had shaken my confidence in myself. My emotions were all over the place, and I couldn't put my finger on why. "I don't know."

"Well, figure it out. Maybe Frank's not the only one who needs to take some time to work on themselves."

I sniffled. He could be right about that, but I wasn't about to admit it. "Did you get a psych degree when I wasn't looking?" I frowned at him.

He chuckled and shook his head. "I've been in intense therapy for a long time. I've learned a few things."

I gave him a sour look. "You're not the only one going to therapy though. I talked to the group this morning. Thought I was handling things well, but..."

"But you broke down the minute you saw me?"

Shrugging, I said, "Yeah."

"Maybe you need a one-on-one with Dr. Fellows."

His words reminded me that Dr. Fellows had requested that as well. "Yeah, maybe."

"Look, I'm going to get out of your hair." He stood up and drew me up too, hugging me. "You work a high-stress job, Marce. Your superiors are asking you to go beyond your normal routine to put yourself in front of the camera and be the face of the LAPD, which is adding to that stress. On top of that, you're trying to make a relationship work with someone who is also in a high-stress job. It's bound to take its toll, and you look like you aren't getting much sleep."

"I'm not." At least I hadn't the night before, and the past couple of weeks hadn't been great sleep-wise either.

"You need to decompress, take a relaxing bath, and get some rest. Then tomorrow, call Dr. Fellows and set up an appointment. Frank loves you. I know he does. He just needs to figure some shit out. He'll be back here being your over-protective boyfriend again before you know it."

I seriously hoped Stephen was right because I wasn't ready to let Frank go. I wasn't ready to not have him in my life.

After Stephen left, I did what he suggested, took a long, hot bath, and then went to bed. I hoped I'd get the rest I so needed, but considering how emotional I was, I didn't think it was going to be possible. It took hours for me to finally fall asleep, and the last thought I had before I drifted off was that my heart would never recover if Frank and I didn't make it.

24

MOVING UP IN THE WORLD
THE ENTREPRENEUR

Monday Night

Three days ago, my crew had pulled off a jewelry heist for a client, but we hadn't been paid by her yet. I was sick of these "clients" takin' advantage of us. I needed to do somethin' about it. In fact, I was in the process of makin' sure we never had to rely on one of these asshole clients again.

My new online shop was up and runnin' and doin' really well, in fact we'd practically sold out of everythin' I'd taken back from Helena, and all the designer clothes I'd been able to grab from Mariah's were nearly gone as well. My crew had already been out to grab the shit we needed to keep things goin', and I'd brought Moxie and some of the others in to help get things shipped.

I'd been thinkin' about things as I looked at the money comin' in from the cash apps for the products we were sellin' through my website. "Hey, Mox?" I called from the desk I'd set up with Helena's laptop.

"Yeah? What's up?" she asked, movin' from the box she was fillin' to come over to me.

"Get me everyone's cash app address. The crew needs their cut of what's comin' in on the products we're movin'."

"Yeah?" she asked, her face lightin' up like it was fuckin' Christmas.

"Bet." I nodded. "You heard from Bella?" I asked, thinkin' about the client who hadn't paid us yet.

"Naw."

I sucked my teeth in anger. "Looks like we're gonna be addin' jewelry to our product line." I stood up, picked up the leather gloves I'd acquired recently, and started toward the roll-down door of the storage warehouse we'd rented to hold all the shit we'd started movin'. "Stay here, keep workin', and get me those addresses."

"Bet."

Soon I'd have enough to replace my piece-of-shit car for somethin' more upscale. Somethin' that suited my position. I grinned thinkin' about what ride I'd get. I pulled the Glock from its spot in my glovebox and checked it. I was done waitin' on Bella. The bitch had a gamblin' addiction, and I knew that was why she hadn't given me our money. She'd said she needed to wait till she sold more, but I knew it was just a fuckin' excuse.

I set the Glock on the passenger seat next to my gloves. It was dark out, so I wasn't afraid of anyone lookin' in my car and seein' it. I turned the car on and drove over to Bella's house. She lived in Westwood Village, just outside of Beverly Hills. It took more than a minute to get there.

It was nearin' eleven p.m. when I pulled into her short

driveway by her detached garage, which sat at the back of her property on the corner lot. Her house wasn't anywhere near as luxurious as Helena's or Mariah's. It had a great address though, bein' so close to Beverly Hills, so it was still probably worth more than two million.

There was a fence between Bella's house and the house next door, so I wasn't too worried about bein' seen by anyone as I headed for the kitchen entrance with my gloves in my hand and the Glock in my waistband. The house was dark, so I assumed Bella was already in bed. I didn't think it would be hard to get in through the back door; it had a glass window above the door handle. I used my elbow to break it. It sounded loud to my ears, but it probably wasn't.

I took a moment to pull on my gloves and look around, waitin' for Bella to come see what the noise was, but she didn't. Reachin' in, I turned the lock and let myself in. I'd been here several times before and knew the layout. Of all the "clients" we had, Bella had been the most laid-back, but also the flakiest. I knew where she kept the shit we boosted for her, and I knew where her bedroom was. That was where I headed.

My sneakers squeaked just a little as I moved through her house in the dark. I pushed open her bedroom door and saw her sleepin'. She hadn't woken, hadn't heard me come in, probably because she had two box fans on high in the room. I didn't know how she slept through that noise. I walked up to the bed, aimed at her temple, and pulled the trigger.

Smilin', I left the bedroom and went into the room next door that she used to sell the jewelry. It had tables with mannequin heads and plastic necks to show off the necklaces and earrings. There were also several white, ceramic hands displayin' rings. I could use all of it, and I had plenty of time, so I started gatherin' things.

I'd been smart this time, wearin' the gloves. Now I could touch shit and not leave prints behind. Most of the jewelry was in boxes, so that made it easy to pack up. The stuff on display I had to be more careful with. I was out of there with everythin' by one a.m.

"Should have done this sooner," I muttered, backin' out of the driveway. "Definitely movin' up in the world."

ON THE WRONG TRACK

MARCY

Tuesday Morning

Unfortunately, my sleep had been punctuated by nightmares from my past, and when I was woken up by my phone playing "Send me an Angel" by the Scorpions, I had to wonder if I was just not meant to be happy in this life.

"Yeah?" I mumbled into the phone groggily. I didn't even know what time it was, but my alarm hadn't gone off, so it had to be early.

"Hey, Marce, we've got another victim."

I blinked and ran a hand over my face as I sat up in bed. "Where?"

"Westwood Village. Edge of Beverly Hills."

"Great." I sighed and then wondered why it wasn't the captain calling me. "How come you're the one calling me this morning?"

"You must have been dead to the world, because this is the third time I've called, and the captain tried to call you before he called me." Angel paused and then quickly added, "You aren't in Santa Monica, are you? Because if you are—"

"No. I'm home. I was just asleep." My head was still fuzzy from the nightmares I could barely recall. I knew they'd been dark, had involved several of the serial killers I'd interacted with over the years, and had also involved Henry, Frank, Jordan, and even Bobby and a few other boys from my high school and college years. I tried hard to let the images fade from my mind as I got out of bed.

"Okay, good. I mean, it's good you aren't in Santa Monica since we've got a crime scene, and you won't be so far away and have to deal with a lot of traffic." He rushed through his words. "Anyway, I'm already dressed, so I'm headed out. I'll text you the address and see you when you get there. I'll have coffee waiting for you."

I could hear the promise in his voice and how he was trying to keep from asking me any questions about my night, which I was grateful for. "Okay, I'll see you there."

I hung up and went to get dressed. Once I was ready to go, I put a call in to Dr. Fellows' office. As I'd gotten ready, I decided I needed way more therapy than I'd originally thought, considering how things were going. "Hello? Dr. Fellows? It's Marcy Kendrick...I need to make an appointment."

I PULLED up to the corner lot and parked on the curb. There were several patrol cars all around the property as well as the coroner's bus and the CSI vehicles. A black Honda sat in the driveway, with a couple of stickers on the back window claiming the owner was a fan of the LA Dodgers and the Calvin and Hobbs comic.

There were also three news crew vans parked on the street, and patrol was doing their best to keep the reporters and their cameramen at bay, as well as the neighbors who were out on their porches, watching all the activity.

I ignored the shouts from the reporters as I got out of my car and headed to the front of the house. Looking at the property, I could see the house had seen better days. The green trim of the house was peeling, and the wooden steps up to the porch looked as though they might not survive the day. Cautiously, I went up the three steps.

I flashed my badge at Officer Braun, not that he didn't know who I was, but it was protocol. He opened the door for me and said, "Morning."

I didn't bother saying anything, just gave him a nod before going in. "Angel?" I called.

Angel stepped out of a room into the hallway with two cups in his hand. "There you are. Everything okay?" he questioned, seeing my face as he offered one of the cups.

"Thanks, and yeah. Just didn't sleep well, had some nightmares." It wasn't an unusual occurrence. I'd had them pretty often before I started seeing Frank, but they'd become rarer with him spending a lot of nights with me. Now that he was gone...I guessed they were coming back in full force. Not that I shared that part.

"Well, even with the nightmares, you had a better night than our victim." He tilted his head toward the door he'd come through. "Shot in her sleep, almost execution style."

"So are we thinking this is the same killer as Helena and Mariah?"

"Looks that way. Bella Jones had an online jewelry business. The room next door looks like where she conducted her business, there's shipping supplies and the like in there, but no jewelry. She was cleaned out."

"Who found her?" I asked.

"Her sixteen-year-old son. Brendan lives with his dad. He came over here because, apparently, Bella had promised to give him something for his birthday, which is today." He kept his voice down.

I frowned. "Some birthday present," I muttered, keeping my voice low as well.

"Yeah, I feel bad for the kid. Said he got here at six, found the back door broken and came in to find his mom dead. He immediately called us," Angel said as we walked toward the bedroom.

As I stepped through the door, I saw two box fans on TV trays that were both pointed from different angles toward the bed. The woman on the bed was partially blocked from my view by Damien, but I could see she was on the plump side, with long red hair. "Were those fans on?"

"Yes, and they're kind of loud when on full blast. Probably why she didn't wake when her killer broke the glass in the back door."

I nodded as I walked forward, moving to where I could see the victim. "Did she wake before she was shot?" I asked, looking at Damien.

"I don't think so. See the way she's positioned? Take away the bloody mess of her temple, and her body looks relaxed, peaceful. I'd say she was completely asleep when she was shot."

"What time are we thinking?" I asked, wondering where our suspect was at the time. Did we still have him in custody?

"Judging by liver temp, how cool the room was, and the amount of rigor, I'd say between ten p.m. and midnight."

I glanced at Angel. "Do we know if Carlos was still in lockup?"

"He wasn't. He was arraigned at five, and his lawyer posted his bail around eight last night."

That surprised me. "So he could still be our guy," I said.

"Unfortunately, no," a Southern voice said from behind me.

I turned to see Lieutenant Chenevert in the doorway. "Sir?"

"I sent Hummel and Vance to pick him up after we got this call. Turns out, the Royal Boys were waiting for him when he got home and beat the crap out of him for what he did to Pretty Boy. He's been at Good Samaritan since eleven last night."

"Well, shit." I dragged my hand through my short bob in frustration. We had been on the wrong track, and now our killer was getting bolder.

"Exactly. Y'all've got to start over. Find me a new suspect," Chenevert said, obviously frustrated. He looked at Lindsey, who seemed flustered by Chenevert's gaze. "I want this whole house dusted for prints."

"Y-yes, sir," Lindsey stuttered, flushing like a schoolgirl.

I arched a brow at her.

"Carry on. I'm going to give the press a statement, and then I'll see y'all back at the precinct," Chenevert said, turning to leave.

"Yes, sir," I replied.

"Wonder what he's going to say," Angel said, half under his breath.

"Not the foggiest, but I'm glad he's going to do it, so they'll leave us alone."

"Good point."

"Damn, he's hot," Lindsey said, moving closer to me and keeping her voice to a whisper so only Angel and I heard her.

I smiled. "And that accent, woo boy."

"I know, right?" She shook her head, blew out a breath and fanned herself.

Angel rolled his eyes. "Anything else you can tell us, Damien?"

"About the new lieutenant? No, pretty sure Linds and Marcy just covered it." He snickered.

A laugh burst from my lips, and I quickly turned it to a cough because the time and place were completely inappropriate for that. I noticed Angel's lips twitch in amusement as I attempted to get my giggle under control.

"Right. How about with the victim?" Angel asked.

"Not right now. I'll know more once I get her back to my lab."

"Okay, we'll release the scene to you," I said.

"Sounds good. Hopefully, Lieutenant Hotty will get the news crews moved on so we can get her out of here," Damien replied.

I had to swallow hard and press my lips together to stifle another burst of laughter. I was generally more in control of myself, but the last several days had me on an emotional rollercoaster that made me feel as though the belt had come loose and I was two seconds from flying out of the seat into the ether.

I had to leave the room and work hard to get my composure back. I couldn't go outside in front of the reporters like this. They'd have a field day if they saw me smiling and laughing at a crime scene.

"Marce, you all right?" Angel asked; his voice was laced with concern.

I nodded. "Fine." I drew in a deep breath as I stuck my head in Bella's office. "Did we find a computer?"

"It's already been boxed up by CSI. It was on the desk. It, along with the flat boxes and bubble wrap, are all that was left in the room."

"We'll want Tech to get on that immediately."

"I know." Angel stood next to me, patiently waiting. "You sure you're okay?"

I started to nod, but then stopped and looked at him. "No. I'm not, but I also don't want to talk about it right now. Okay?"

He searched my face for a moment and then said, "Okay. Let's go talk to Brendan Jones."

26

THAT'S WHAT BEST FRIENDS ARE FOR

ANGEL

Tuesday Morning

Something was wrong with Marcy. I wanted to fix whatever it was. But it wasn't my place. It was Frank's. At least I was pretty sure it was. She hadn't mentioned him since the other day, when she'd said they'd argued.

Now I had to wonder if something else had happened. I thought back to the conversation in Bella Jones' bedroom between Lindsey and Marcy. Did she have a crush on our new lieutenant? Was that the cause for her mood? Had it caused problems between her and Frank? Did she break up with him?

Too many questions loomed in my mind, and none of them were really any of my business. I wasn't her romantic partner, just her best friend. But Marcy normally told me everything damn near immediately. Why wasn't she this time? If she couldn't tell me what was going on, then it had to be bad, right?

I'd asked her if she was okay, and she'd said she wasn't but didn't want to talk about it. Not that a crime scene was an appropriate place to have that conversation, but her mood was all over the map, and I wasn't sure I should push her for a real answer here. Instead I'd suggested talking to Brendan Jones, whom we were now headed to talk to.

He was seated on a wooden rocking bench in the backyard with Officer Garcia. His father was standing, his arms crossed, at the corner of the bench. He didn't seem upset at his ex-wife's death, but concerned about his son's emotional state. I couldn't blame him. It sucked the kid was the one who'd found her. That wasn't a trauma I'd wish on anyone, but it happened all too often.

"Sir, would you mind if we ask your son some questions?" Marcy asked.

"I'm not leaving him while you question him." His voice was deep and harsh.

"That's fine; you can be with him," Marcy replied, keeping her tone soft. She was good at speaking to the deceased's loved ones. "Brendan?"

The boy looked up, his eyes glassy.

I gestured for Garcia to get up so Marcy could sit with him, which he did.

Marcy sat down and turned her knees toward Brendan, facing him the best she could on the bench. "I wanted to ask you a few questions about when you arrived here this morning. Do you think you're up to answering?"

Brendan shrugged, looking miserable.

Marcy pressed on. "Were you and your mom close?"

"They were barely on speaking terms. Bella had just

started contacting him and his sister about a month ago, trying to get back into our lives," Mr. Jones answered.

Marcy flashed her eyes at the man and then repeated the question for Brendan. "I want to know what your thoughts are, Brendan."

"She left us about six years ago," he said, his voice soft. "She saw me at a gas station and approached me about six weeks ago."

"Six weeks...you said it was a month," his dad interjected.

"Sir," I said, putting my hand on his arm. "Please let my partner speak to your son without interrupting."

"Fine." He didn't seem happy about that.

"So she came back into your life six weeks ago? What brought you to her house this morning?"

"It's my birthday; she said she would have something for me. Told me to come over for breakfast."

"When did she tell you this?"

"She texted me last night."

Marcy glanced up at me, and I leaned in as she whispered in my ear, "Did we recover her phone?"

I shook my head. We hadn't found one, as far as I was aware.

"We need to find it," she murmured. "Text Lindsey."

I nodded and pulled out my phone.

"So you were in contact with your mom via text messaging? Do you know what time she sent that message?"

Brendan pulled his phone out, pressed a couple of buttons and handed the phone to Marcy. I looked over her shoulder and saw the message was timestamped at 9:58 p.m.

"May I take a picture of this message?" Marcy asked. "It will help us establish a timeline."

He nodded.

"Thank you." Marcy also made sure we had a picture of his mother's phone number so we could get all of her contacts, messages, and voicemails from the phone company if we couldn't find the phone.

"What can you tell me about your mother, Brendan? I understand she had her own business?"

"Bella was a gambling addict, sure she had her own business, but she was flat broke," Mr. Jones interjected again.

I took note to check Bella Jones' finances. If she was a gambling addict, this might not be connected to our home invasion perp. "What kind of business did she run, Brendan?" I asked.

"She sold stupid jewelry," Mr. Jones cut in. "I don't know where she got the money to sell anything worth anything. She was about to lose this house, and her car was repossessed last week."

"Dad, Mom's dead! Why are you dragging her?" Brendan shouted.

"It's her own damn fault!" Mr. Jones argued. "If she wasn't involved in all that gambling shit and paid her debts, she'd probably still be alive, and you wouldn't have walked in to find her brains splattered all over her pillow!"

I got between the father and son and guided Mr. Jones away from Marcy and Brendan so he could cool off. "Mr. Jones," I said softly once we were across the yard, close to the sidewalk, "I understand you're angry right now, but your son just lost his mom. And I know from what the two of you said, she hadn't been in his life for a while, but in the end, she was still his mom, and he was trying to have a relationship with her. You need to respect his feelings."

Mr. Jones looked like he was at the end of his rope. He

clenched his fists, and it seemed like he was looking for something to hit, but there was nothing around us except for me, and I wasn't about to allow him to hit me.

"Sir, you need to calm down. Violence isn't the answer. I know you want to expel that energy by hitting something, but you need to contain yourself." I kept my eyes on him and my voice calm.

He gritted his teeth and took a couple of deep breaths. "I just can't believe she did this to him. Coming back into his life, fucking with his head, making him think she loved him. She didn't. She just wanted something from him. Money probably." His eyes were shiny, but he didn't cry.

"What makes you think she didn't love him?" I asked.

"She left, didn't she? Abandoned him and his sister when they were just little kids. What kind of mother does that?"

"A troubled one who needs help?" I suggested. "Maybe she was getting that help, and that's why she reached out. She was making an effort. You're assuming she wanted money from him, but you could be wrong."

He sighed and dragged a hand through his hair, leaving it ragged and messy. "I doubt it. I told you she was about to lose the house; she'd already lost her car. She probably wanted Brendan to drive her to a casino this morning. Did you see any kind of gift in that house for him? No? I didn't think so." He sounded bitter, and I couldn't blame him after what she'd done to him and the kids.

"We didn't, however, her business was robbed, so it's possible that what she got him was stolen as well."

He shook his head. "No. I know Bella. Knew Bella. She didn't buy him crap. That woman was poison and destroyed everything she touched; it's why I divorced her and got custody of the kids. I'm lucky the kids are as happy and healthy as they are. If she'd stayed, they'd probably be as screwed up as she was."

I couldn't argue with him, I hadn't known Bella Jones when she was alive, so there was no point. "Look, I know your feelings about her, but you need to understand your son needs your compassion right now. He lost his mother, and no matter how shitty you think she was, she was still his mom. He's going to need you to be more understanding. I'm not saying let him put her on a pedestal, but also don't talk badly about her in front of him because all you're going to do is push him away. I've seen it happen."

I could see the grief in his eyes as he looked across the yard at his son. "I just hate what she did to him, and then for him to be the one to find her...it's not fair."

I shook my head. "It rarely is." I patted him on the shoulder. "Come on, I'll take you back over there, but no more derogatory words about her, okay?"

"Okay. I know you're right. I'm just so mad at her."

"And that's okay. You're allowed to be mad at her. You can even tell your son why you're mad at her. You don't have to sugarcoat what she was like, but also be understanding that he probably has memories of her that are good, so don't destroy that."

He stared at me for a moment and then nodded. "Yeah. Okay. I'll do that."

I hoped they would be okay as a family. It sounded like Bella had really done a number on him, and he held on to a lot of resentment, but he also loved his kids, and he didn't like seeing them hurt, especially by her.

"You mentioned you were divorced; do you happen to know how she started her business? Was it from a divorce settlement?" I asked.

"No idea where she got the money, probably gambling, like always. She would win big and then blow it." He scowled. "All she got from me was enough for a down payment on her house, and even that wasn't much, so I'm surprised she managed to hold onto it long enough to even buy the place."

"I see," I murmured as his gaze flicked back toward his son and Marcy.

As we walked back over to the bench swing, Marcy stood up. "Take care, Brendan, Mr. Jones. We'll be in touch."

Mr. Jones took Marcy's place on the bench as we walked back toward the street. "Did he say anything after I moved his dad away?"

"Just that his mom said she'd done some things she wasn't proud of and was about to lose everything. She didn't give him any details, so we need to do a deep dive into her life and see what she meant. Jones mentioned she had her car repossessed last week and she was going to lose the house, so she must have been in some deep financial debt. I want to know everything. If she had an online jewelry business, where did she get the money to start it? It didn't sound like she had all that much."

"I was wondering the same. Mr. Jones suggested it was from gambling." I glanced at her as we reached her car. "It's possible this isn't the same perp. Could she owed someone money and they took the jewelry as payment and put a bullet in her as an example to others."

Marcy nodded. "Maybe. Let's wait to see what Damien and Lindsey can tell us later in their reports."

"I'll see you at the station," I said, moving to my own car a few spaces away.

. . .

I HUNG up the phone and looked over at Marcy, who seemed to be in her own little world, staring off into space. It wasn't like her. She was usually very focused and tenacious. Today she seemed almost depressed and down. I reached out and touched her shoulder to get her attention.

Turning her head to look at me, she asked, "What's up?"

"That was the hospital. James is out of the coma."

"Can we go talk to him?" she asked, her voice sounding dull and unengaged.

"Not yet. He's still sedated. The nurse is going to call when he's stable enough to speak to us."

She nodded and turned back to her desk.

"Marce, is everything okay? You seem..." I hesitated to go any further in my question.

"Remember the other day when I told you Frank and I had a fight?"

I nodded slowly.

"I tried to fix things." She shook her head and looked upset. "But he...he's rethinking our relationship."

My heart jumped with joy for a half a second. Not that I was happy she was upset, but that those old—okay, not so old—feelings I had for her came flooding back. I knew in my head that it would never happen, but for that half a second I had hope that it might. I quickly shut that down.

"What do you mean? What exactly did he say?" I asked.

"That he thought he could handle me being on the job and all that it entails, but he's struggling. Said he needed to figure some things out."

"That doesn't sound like a bad thing. Think of everything he's been through, everything you've been through together.

I know having El Gato send someone after you and him not being here really did a number on his mind. I'm sure he's afraid El Gato's going to try again."

I couldn't say I wasn't concerned about that too, but it was Marcy, and I knew she'd be okay. She was very well trained, and while sometimes in the heat of the moment, she ran headfirst into danger, she could handle herself. It wasn't anything that either of us wouldn't do. It was ingrained in us as cops to charge toward that danger instead of running away. Marcy would never run away; she'd never be the kind of woman to hide from danger. She'd confront it head-on, her safety be damned if it meant saving someone else.

"But what about the next killer? And the one after that? I'm not going to stop doing the job; it's part of who I am. I can't change that."

"I'm sure he knows that too. It's one of the things he admires about you; he's said so. I don't think he wants you to stop being you or to quit the job." I rolled my chair closer. "I think he's worried about losing you because one of these crazies might target you."

"And one of them *might*, but that doesn't mean they'll succeed. Just because I'm a woman doesn't mean I can't protect myself."

"Marce, I don't think it's about you being a woman. I think it's about you being someone he cares for. Someone he loves. Look at how he worried about his brother and what happened to him. Things happen. Sometimes we can't protect ourselves from everything. I think he just wants you to acknowledge that."

"I *do* acknowledge that, but I'm just so damn frustrated to keep having to."

"And he's probably just as frustrated at not being able to

let it go. He wants to, I'm sure, but the loss of his brother is still fairly recent, and he's still dealing with it. Just give him some time."

"In the meantime, I get to feel like shit because I'm the one who's making him feel like he's not in control of things. I'm the one who doesn't get to have him in my life because of it."

I could see how upset she was, her eyes were watery and her cheeks pink with anger, but she wouldn't cry. Not here. "I'm sorry you're feeling frustrated by it all, and you know I'm always here for you if you need a shoulder to cry on."

She nodded and gave me a grateful look. "Thanks. I'm sorry to have dumped on you. I'm just struggling to deal with this. It's different than what I went through with Jordan. I thought Frank would be more understanding because he's on the job too. I worry about him getting hurt as well, but I'm not harping at him daily to stop putting himself in danger. And I'm not even doing that, not really. Yeah, these interviews are annoying as heck, but of all the things I do in this job, they're probably the safest. And I don't even want to be doing them!"

I laughed. I could see her point. Sitting with a reporter in front of a camera was pretty harmless. It was just the part where some psycho might get it in their head to come after her because of who she was that had Frank worried. It was like we were challenging every criminal out there to come after us. To be the one to take out the cops who took out their hero, a criminal who'd escaped justice for the last ten or so years until we came along.

"You know it's not the interviews he's upset about. It's the ideas that the interviews might give to the killers out there."

"I know. And I know it's more that he's afraid to lose me,

but now he's pushing me away, trying to protect his heart from heartbreak, and in the end, he's just causing us both heartbreak by keeping us apart." She looked down at her hands and then whispered, "I don't know if I can go back into a relationship with him after this. Even if he wants to try. He's already hurt me. My heart is already broken. I'm not sure the pieces will fit together right again."

I nodded. I knew Frank was very close to losing her forever if he didn't come around soon. That window was going to close, and she wasn't going to open it again. Right now she still had some hope, but it seemed to be fading, and I didn't want that for her. I loved her, and I wanted her to be happy. It was what she deserved. She was the best woman I'd ever known.

"Whatever you decide, you know I'll be here for you."

Marcy reached for my hand, and I took it, squeezing her fingers. "Thanks, Angel." She gave me a tremulous smile and let go. "We should get back to work."

"We should. Before we got off track"—I smiled—"I discovered that Bella has been spending weekends in Reno. Almost every weekend for the last three years. She always stays at the Ramada at Wyndham. Her credit cards are maxed, but nearly all the charges for the hotel rooms are on them."

"So maybe whoever did this to her is out of Reno?"

"Maybe. It's a hotel and casino, so I was planning to check with them and see if they can tell me anything about her habits while she's there."

"That's a good idea. Maybe they know what kind of gambling she did," Marcy suggested.

"And if she was known to borrow from anyone there."

"Like a loan shark?" Marcy looked skeptical. "Are there

even any still around in this day and age? And if there were, wouldn't they want some sort of collateral?"

"Betting there are, especially around there and Vegas. There's always those gamblers who think they just need that little boost and they'll hit it big."

"I guess that's true, it's sad, but yeah."

"I'll call and see what I can find out."

"I'll keep going on her social media. She didn't post a lot, mostly anytime she had big wins, which were very few and far between judging by the Insta posts."

I picked up the phone and called the Ramada's front desk. It didn't take me long to learn that Bella usually stuck to the one-dollar slots, but occasionally she played black-jack. The staff liked her and were sad to hear that she'd died. They didn't know of her interacting with any kind of bookies or loan sharks, though they did have one who hung around outside. They'd had to kick him off their property more than once. I'd asked if they'd ever seen Bella with him, but they'd never seen them interact.

"Okay, well, thanks for your time. If you can think of anything else that might help us with Bella's case, please let me know," I said.

"Of course, Detective, and if you're ever in Reno, I hope you'll come and stay with us."

"I'll keep your hotel in mind if I'm ever out that way." I hung up and shared what I learned with Marcy.

"So I'm leaning toward probably not a loan shark from Reno coming up here to make an example of her. Besides, what good would it do to kill her here in LA? Not much of an example to anyone who would borrow from that kind of scum, right?"

"True, and if she was there every weekend, why not just

wait until she was back to kill her? Then you wouldn't have to travel."

"Exactly."

"So we're back to this being our home invasion perp. Only they've gotten smarter. More bold."

"Too bad we had to rule Carlos out," Marcy said with a frown. "He was a great suspect, and now we're back at square one."

"We need those phone records," I murmured.

"I'll call and see if we can't get them to move faster." Marcy picked up her phone and dialed.

I really hoped we'd catch a real break soon. If not, I was afraid our killer would grow even more daring and bold, and we'd have several more bodies to deal with.

27

LIFE IS MORE THAN A BOX OF CHOCOLATES

MARCY

Tuesday Evening

I knocked off at five, thirty minutes early, but I had cleared it with Lieutenant Chenevert. I hadn't mentioned it to Angel, but Dr. Fellows had agreed to squeeze me in for an appointment this evening before he went home. I hated doing that to him. Making him stay later than normal, but he was the one who'd suggested it when I'd called.

I drove to his office downtown and parked, then walked into the red-brick building. His secretary was already gone for the day, which made me feel even worse. "I didn't have to come in so late, Dr. Fellows. I could have—"

"Marcy, it's fine. You didn't ask; I suggested. I figured it would be better to get you in sooner rather than later." He sat down and gestured to the chair across from him. "Now, how are you? How was your day?"

I sat down in the leather cushioned seat, dropping my purse to rest against the chair leg by my foot. "I'm barely hanging on. Today was stressful. We've got a case that's increasingly frustrating, a new lieutenant who is expecting me to catch the perp before anyone else is killed, and I feel as though I'm letting him down. I've got the mayor and police chief pimping me out for interviews that I don't want to do, and my relationship with Frank is in the toilet."

Dr. Fellows stared at me. "That is a lot to unpack."

"I know. I'm sorry."

"Let's start with what you said first. The case you're working on. I know you can't give me details on it, I'm not asking for them, but maybe you can tell me what's frustrating you about it?"

"We thought we had a good idea of who was behind the murders, but he's got an unbreakable alibi for this last one, so now we're pretty sure it's not him. He could be working with someone, but after looking at everything, I don't think he's our perp. So we're back at square one, and I'm not sure how to proceed. I wanted to put out a public warning, but the Brass nixed that idea. They don't want to do anything to cause the public to lose any more faith in us."

"Go back to the beginning. Look at your first murder. Compare it to this last one. Find the pattern. Isn't that what you've told me before?"

I smiled. "Yes. And you're right. I'm just feeling the pressure. I think because of the various other things going on."

"Okay, let's talk about that. You've got a new lieutenant you're wanting to impress?"

I paused. Did I want to impress him? "I guess I do, actually. He's good. And maybe it's not so much that I want to impress him, more that I want to..." I searched for the right

words to describe what I was thinking, "live up to his expec-
tations of me."

"And you like him."

"I do. I respect him. He's fair, competent, and has a good
handle on the job and all it entails."

"I think you wanting to close this case, show your skills
off, and do your job well is fine. Just don't put additional
stress on yourself because of him. Keep doing what you do,
and you'll be all right."

I felt a little bit of the pressure on my shoulders ease. It
wasn't that Dr. Fellows was telling me stuff I didn't already
know, but having him confirm and validate my feelings
made it an easier burden to carry.

I nodded. "I'll try not to stress myself out about it."

"Now, I'm not going to lie, I've seen a couple of your
interviews. It does seem as though you've been in the news
cycle a bit more than usual, especially with the capture of El
Gato. Is his capture the only reason you're doing these
interviews?"

I sighed. "You know what the LAPD has been going
through for the past year with all the negative press, right?"

Dr. Fellows nodded, his pen poised over his notepad.

"The mayor and police chief are using me and Angel to
bring more positive press to the LAPD. If it were just about
the El Gato capture, I guess I'd be okay with that, but they
consistently ask questions about it that I'm not allowed to
answer. On top of that, they ask personal questions about
me. They've brought up Nick—"

"Nicholas Pound?" Dr. Fellows interjected, knowing he
was the copycat killer who'd been obsessed with me.

"Yes, as well as Jordan—"

"Your ex-husband...are they bringing up the fact you were married to him, or why he was fired?"

"Both, and I don't answer questions about any of that, so I leave the interviews frustrated and angry. It's not like the public is interested in that. At least I don't think they are." I frowned, wondering if they really were so nosy they'd want to know about a cop's private life.

"I've found that the public in general is very nosy and loves gossip, so not sharing probably does make them more intrigued with you."

"So I'm just making them more curious by not telling them?"

"Unfortunately, yes. You might consider giving boring answers to those questions, and eventually they'll stop asking."

"Well, if I have to do any more of those interviews, I'll give that a go."

He smiled. "Now, tell me what's going on with you and Frank."

I told him everything, including the chat I'd had with Angel earlier. I explained how I was feeling as though I was already heartbroken and unsure if I wanted to continue a relationship with him if he was going to do this to me.

"Marcy, it was just two days ago when he asked for some time, correct?"

Had it only been two days? I wondered. It certainly felt as though a lifetime had passed. I nodded, but didn't say anything.

"And you did tell him in the midst of your argument on Sunday morning that maybe you needed to rethink your relationship?"

I bit the inside of my bottom lip. I had said those words. "I did but—"

Dr. Fellows shook his head. "Listen, I know you said it in the heat of the moment. You were frustrated with the argument, and tired, but deep down you were having a moment of doubt about your relationship. You wouldn't have said those words if some part of you wasn't considering it, so let's talk about that."

He wasn't wrong. I'd said it, and at the time, I had been feeling that way. "I was just so tired of feeling attacked. Of feeling like he thought I was incapable of doing my job, of protecting myself, and I lashed out. By the time I got to work, I knew I didn't actually want that. I didn't want to rethink our relationship. I didn't want to break up with him. I just wanted him to stop attacking my abilities to protect myself, to do the job."

"So you said it as a threat to get him to back off. That's not healthy. You and Frank aren't communicating properly. I'm not a couples' therapist, but you might consider going to see one if you want this relationship to work long-term."

I pursed my lips. Again, he wasn't telling me anything I didn't already know. Granted, couples' therapy wasn't something I'd considered, but for Frank, I'd do it. If we were going to make this work, then we had to figure out how to communicate our needs to each other better.

"I think you need to be thankful that Frank actually took your words to heart and is taking the time to figure out where his fear is coming from. You need to give him however much time he needs to do that. You said he told you he loves you, correct?"

I nodded and looked at my folded hands.

"Then I don't think he's going to drag this on. He wants a

relationship with you, and he knows there's something wrong with how he's feeling, so he's trying to deal with it in the best way he knows how. Give him that time. And *you*," he said, waiting for me to look up.

I lifted my gaze and met his eyes. "Yes?"

"You need to learn how to share your feelings better. Saying the words I love you aren't enough. You need to communicate with Frank. Tell him how he's making you feel when he holds on too tight out of fear. And really listen to his concerns and explain to him what precautions you will take against his fears, so he doesn't have to worry."

Sighing, I said, "I think part of it stems from him being in Santa Monica while I'm here. Granted, it's less than an hour away, but he blames himself for not being there when my house was broken into, and I was nearly killed. As if him being there would have stopped the guy from breaking in. He'd have just been in danger too. And things might not have turned out as well as they did if he had been. I may not have heard the guy breaking in. I might have assumed that it was Frank I'd heard and just gone back to sleep. If he had gotten killed because of me, because of one of my cases... like...like Henry..." I stopped speaking, and tears filled my eyes. Suddenly I couldn't breathe properly as overwhelming emotion filled me at just the thought of losing Frank in that way.

"It's okay, Marcy, take a moment, breathe with me, inhale...exhale...again..."

I did as he asked, trying to calm my racing heart.

"How you're feeling right now is probably how Frank feels as well. And while you have learned how to move beyond that fear, that panic, he's still working on it."

His words put everything into perspective for me. The

thought of losing Frank in the same way I'd lost Henry was terrifying. Henry's death had wrecked me, and we'd only been together a short time. I hadn't even been fully in love with Henry, just more in love with the idea of us. Frank was completely different. If that happened to Frank, I'd never recover. It would ruin me. I'd burn the world down if I lost him because of a killer I was after. It wouldn't be much better to lose him because of his job. It was a minute difference. A fine line that my head and heart could distinguish between.

If something happened to Frank because he was a police detective and it pertained to the job there in Santa Monica, I would still be devastated, but I *might* survive that. I'd avenge him, find his killer, if there was one, and not stop until they were dead or in jail for taking him from me. But that was the job.

We both put ourselves in the line of fire every day to save other people. We both knew the risks to our own lives. I respected his decision to do that, just as I expected him to respect my decision to do it. What I wouldn't be able to handle would be losing him because of a mistake I made. Because a killer I was after went for him to get to me, or because of me. That was a bridge too far. If that was ever crossed, I'd lose myself, and there would be no survivors.

Thinking about it that way, I knew I needed to give Frank the time he needed to figure this out. No matter how long it took. I now understood his fear because it was a fear I had too, but I had already made my peace with it, so to speak. He needed to figure it out for himself.

"You're right. I'll give him time."

Dr. Fellows smiled, but it was hesitant. "I have a feeling

you just had a sort of breakthrough, an epiphany, but by the look in your eyes, I'm not sure I want to know what conclusion you came to."

"I'll just say, it finally dawned on me how someone could potentially destroy the world because they lost the one person who meant everything to them."

Dr. Fellows gave me a look I couldn't decipher. "I think we'll leave that for next time."

I smiled. "It's okay. I swear I'm not planning to destroy the world." *At least not right now.*

"Good to know."

"Okay, I'll see you soon." I picked up my purse and headed out of the office to drive home. I wasn't hungry, so I didn't bother stopping for food. Instead I went straight home, only when I got there, a familiar truck was sitting in my driveway. My heart began to race. Frank was here.

I pulled into my drive and parked next to his truck, then slammed the door open, got out, swept it closed, and practically ran to the door, shoving my key in the lock, and called, "Frank?"

He stepped out of the kitchen. "Hey, TT." He smiled as he wiped his hands on a kitchen towel.

I could smell something cooking, but at that moment I didn't care. I soaked in his presence, taking in every bit of him. "What...I..." I started, but I didn't even know what I wanted to ask.

"I thought we could talk." He gave me a wry smile. "My therapist suggested our problem might be a communication issue, along with my fear of losing you."

My hand flew to my mouth, and I nearly laughed. "Sounds like our therapists are on the same page." I held my hand up, not wanting him to say anything until I got out what I needed to say. I took a deep breath and then blurted, "I get it. I understand your fear. I mean, I have that same fear for you, but because of my past, I've learned how to deal with that anxiety. You haven't yet, and I need to give you time to do that."

There was a light in his eyes as he came toward me, pulling me into a hug and just holding me. "Thank you. And you're right. I am still figuring things out, but I missed you, and I wanted to see you."

"I've missed you too."

"Come on, I made us dinner."

I followed him into the kitchen and took a seat at the table. He'd made a steak and vegetable stir-fry over rice. "This looks great."

"Thanks." He brought the plates and sat down next to me. "You look good."

I snorted out a laugh. "No, I don't. I'm a mess."

"You look amazing to me. I'm sorry I've been distant these last couple of days, TT. I haven't been dealing with things the way I should have been, and I'm not going to lie and say I've got it all figured out yet, because I don't. But I don't want you thinking that I don't want to be with you, so I promise I won't shut down communication between us again."

I paused with my fork halfway to my mouth. "It's okay, Frank. If you need to take time to figure things out and you need to be on your own, I'm okay with that. I'm not saying I like it, but if that's what you need, then tell me."

He swallowed his mouthful of food and set his fork down, then reached for my hand. "I love you. I need you in my life, and yes, I am afraid of something happening to you because you present a challenge to a certain criminal element. That's my problem to deal with. That fear. I know that. It's not your fault. It's nobody's fault. Fault isn't even the right word, but I don't have a better one at the moment." His brow furrowed, and he met my gaze.

"I need to tell you something. You can tell me if you can relate to it."

The furrow in his brow deepened as he studied my face. "Okay."

"I realized while talking to Dr. Fellows that were something to happen to you because of me, something like what happened to Henry—" I paused, trying to gather myself to get the words out as I held his gaze. "I would lose my mind. I would go to the ends of the world to avenge you and not give a single fuck who I hurt along the way. That pain I felt with Henry's death would be multiplied by a billion, and I would shatter the world in my attempt to bring you back, even knowing that wouldn't be possible, I wouldn't care. Nothing would matter." I squeezed his hand. "So I understand, Frank. I understand that fear you have for something happening to me. But you need to understand, I have that same fear for you."

He let go of my hand to cup my cheek, drawing me in for a kiss. "I love you so much, Marcy. And you're right, that is how I feel or about as near as you can get, but I haven't figured out how to be okay with that fear yet. I haven't figured out how to let go of it."

"I know. I don't think it's about letting go of it, it's about living with it and learning how to overcome it, to let it temper your actions, but not keep you from doing what needs doing."

His slight nod told me he agreed, but he looked down at

his plate and didn't meet my gaze. "I'm struggling with that. I promise I'll figure it out, but it may take me a little bit, and in the meantime, I may be a bit grumpy about you having to do things that threaten your security. Like with that reporter who showed up here and then slashed your tires and keyed your car. That never should have happened."

"You're right, it shouldn't have. I didn't know it until the other day, but Lindsey heard about what happened, and she sent one of her CSI techs to have a look at my car while it was at Jimmy's. They took prints from the wheel well. She told me yesterday that they found a set that matched the reporter. He's been arrested and charged with vandalization and intimidation of a police officer. And I've been informed that the *LA Times* has fired him."

"That's good to know, but it could just make this guy even more vindictive," Frank replied, sounding worried.

"Well, right now he's in jail, waiting to be arraigned. I will be cautious, Frank. I'm keeping tabs on him, and Patrol is doing additional drives through the area to keep an eye out for him."

"That's good. Especially since I'm not going to be here tonight." He sighed.

I leaned back in my chair and stared at him. "You're not?"

"No. I've got an early appointment, and well, I think I need to be home and figure this out. As much as I want nothing more than to crawl into bed with you and hold you all night, I think it would be healthier for both of us for me not to right now. I know I'm holding you too tight. I'm smothering you and making you crazy with my worry. I don't want to do that. I don't want to drive you away from me."

"Frank, it's okay. I understand; you don't have to explain." I wished things were different, that he could stay, and things were easy between us again, but until he could learn to control his fears, maybe this was best.

He leaned in and kissed me, and it was desperate and sad. I really hoped that despite his words, this wasn't good-bye. At least not for good.

28

BRAINSTORMING AND BEERS
MARCY

Wednesday Night

At Dr. Fellows' reminder, I'd gone back to the beginning and looked at our first victim Helena Richards and how she'd died. I compared her death to that of Mariah Osgood, to James Osgood's injury. And then looked at Bella Jones again. Except for James, who seemed more like collateral damage, they all had two things in common. First, they were all businesswomen who ran online shops. The second was that they had all been killed with a 9mm weapon.

It didn't look as though the victims knew each other, nor interacted in any way. None of them shopped in the same place, attended the same church, lived in the same neighborhood or went to the same yoga class. But something had plunged them into the same category.

I just needed to figure out what it was.

My desk phone rang, and I picked it up as I glanced at the clock. "Kendrick," I said into the receiver. There was only twenty minutes left on our shift, and I really didn't want to be sent out on another case. This one was taking up all my brain power at the moment, and I didn't want to set it aside.

"Hey, it's Lindsey. Wondered if you had plans after work?"

"Angel and I are headed over to the Short Stop for a drink; you wanna join us?"

"I was gonna ask if you wanted to get dinner, but drinks would be good too."

"Great, wanna ride with us or meet us there?"

"I'll meet you there, that way I don't have to come back to the precinct, and neither do you."

I smiled. "You sound like me. I said the same to Angel earlier."

"Great minds and all that. I'll see you there after work."

I hung up and turned to Angel. "Lindsey's going to join us."

He glanced up from his computer and nodded. "Is Frank coming?"

I shrugged. He'd texted me that morning, and I'd replied, but neither of us had mentioned plans for tonight. I had been hesitant to push him to come see me, and I didn't want to drive out there and impose myself on him. "I can ask."

I grabbed my cell phone from next to my keyboard and began to type.

> Hey, miss you. Going for drinks with Angel and Lindsey at the Short Stop, want to join?

I waited, staring at my screen to see if he'd answer immediately, but he didn't. With a sigh, I set it down and looked back at Angel. "I don't know if he will or not. We'll play it by ear."

"We'll just get a bigger table in case he does come." Angel turned back to finish whatever it was he was working on.

I was sure it pertained to the case, but after feeling like I was just treading water with this case all day, I didn't want to focus on it anymore. I shifted papers around and slid them back into their file folders and then locked them up in my desk. I cleared the tabs on my computer, ran my cleaner program and then shut it down.

At five on the dot, I grabbed my purse, stuck my phone in the pocket of it and stood up. "Ready to go?"

Angel chuckled as he looked up at me. "Somebody's anxious to get out of here." He shut down his computer. "Go ahead. I'll see you there."

He didn't have to tell me twice. I was out of there faster than an F-14 aircraft out on maneuvers. I wasn't hanging around longer than I had to. This case was driving me mad. And even though I knew without a doubt that the case would inevitably come up tonight over drinks, I didn't want to be at the station anymore, looking at all the nonexistent evidence again for the thousandth time.

I pulled into the Short Stop thirty minutes later and headed inside. The hostess greeted me, and I told her I was meeting several co-workers and needed a table for at least five. I didn't know if I actually needed one that big, but figured better safe than sorry. She brought me to a large rectangle table, and I set my purse down on the table, then pulled out my phone.

"Your waitress will be over in just a minute," she said before leaving.

"Thanks," I murmured as I looked at my phone. Frank hadn't messaged me back. I wasn't worried. Not really. He could be tied up on a case. Of course, there was a small chance he was avoiding me, but I shoved that thought to the back of my mind. I set my phone on the table as I saw Angel walk in, followed by Lindsey and Damien.

"Hope you don't mind me crashing the party," Damien said, giving me a smile.

"Of course not. The more the merrier," I replied, glad I'd gotten a larger table.

"Hi, I'm Susan. I'll be your waitress this evening. What are we drinking tonight?" a cute brunette in an LA Dodger's jersey and white shorts asked.

"I'll have a Heineken," I said, and then the others all placed their orders.

"Would anyone like an appetizer?" she questioned. "We've got some killer wings, or maybe some pulled-pork BBQ nachos?"

My stomach took that moment to grumble. "I'll have the nachos."

"Make it two, and bring out an order of wings too," Damien said, then added, "my treat."

"Thanks, Damien, you can come to every after-work drinks night if you're gonna buy us treats," Angel said with a laugh.

"Gee, can I?" he deadpanned.

My phone shifted on the table as it buzzed with a text message. Thinking it was Frank, I picked it up to look, but was slightly disappointed to see it wasn't him, but my brother.

Hey, sis, got a minute?

I quickly texted him back.

> At the Short Stop with Angel, Lindsey, and
> Damien, what's up?

Less than a minute later, he replied.

> Mind if I join? I've got something to show
> you and Angel.

"Stephen's coming to join us too," I said as I texted him that was fine. "Says he's got something to show us."

"Sure, no problem. Should we get some more food?" Angel asked. "I mean, it's on Damien."

"Hey now, I'm not feeding all of LA," he replied with a laugh.

I shook my head and grinned. "I'll get the next batch of wings."

We started talking about the case. Lindsey mentioned how little evidence was at the Bella Jones scene and how it had almost looked like a professional hit in comparison to the other two scenes. I agreed, but to me it read more like our perp was getting better at killing and not a different perp altogether who'd committed the crime.

I was on my second beer by the time Stephen arrived.

"Hey, Stephen. I've got more wings coming; have a seat," I said, nodding toward a chair.

He had a laptop under his arm as he sat in the empty chair next to me. "Hey, thanks. Let me get a drink, and then I'll show you what I found." He waved to the waitress, and she came over with a smile.

"Hey there, handsome, what can I get for you?"

"Club soda with lime?" he said hesitantly.

I was glad he wasn't drinking. He'd been through a lot,

and alcohol wasn't really the best for him, considering his history.

"I'll have that to you in just a few." She gave him a wink and then sauntered over to the bar.

"So what did you want to show us?"

"You know how you were telling me about those women who were killed and how they had some online shops?"

I nodded. I hadn't given him anything that wasn't printed in the papers, so I wasn't too worried about him talking about it. "Sure, yeah."

"Okay, so I got curious and started doing some digging." He opened his laptop and started pulling up his web browser.

"Wait!" I stopped him. "Is this something that I'm going to have to question how we came by the information?"

His brow furrowed, and he shook his head. "I didn't hack anything, if that's what you're concerned about. It's all just there to look at, if you know what you're looking for."

"Then go ahead." I leaned in to see his screen, and Lindsey did the same from her chair, which was on his other side.

"Wait, I want to see too," Damien said, getting up and squatting down between Lindsey and Stephen.

Angel got up and moved to stand behind me so he could see as well. "So what did you find?" he asked, taking a swig of his beer.

"So I've been keeping track of the case, and I started looking at the three women's shops, just to see what kind of products they were moving, that kind of thing. They all say they're shut down, but you can look at previous products they've sold or had for sale on this website."

"Okay, I'm pretty sure that Tech has been all over that. I don't—"

"Yeah, I'm getting to it," Stephen said, pulling up several tabs on his browser. "Okay, so look at this." He pointed to a couple of products on Helena's site. Then clicked the tab, which showed Mariah's site. "And these," he said, pointing at a couple of designer outfits, then clicked the third tab, "and these pieces of jewelry from Bella's site."

"Okay..." I prompted him.

Stephen moved to the fourth tab, opening it to another shop. "So I put in those product details, and this shop popped up. Look...if I go back to just after Helena's murder, this site only sold cosmetics. Then after Mariah...you can see it began selling designer clothing...and then yesterday, they added jewelry. The items I showed you from the three other websites, they're all here on this one website now."

"So...it looks like all the stolen merchandise has ended up with the same online retail shop?" Lindsey observed.

"Yes. I think whoever owns this website might be your killer or, at the very least, knows who the killer is," Stephen shared as Susan appeared with his club soda and lime.

"Um...killer?" she said, looking pale. "What..."

Stephen glanced up and took the glass before it slipped from her hands. "It's okay; they're all cops."

"Oh, okay, I was concerned for a minute there," she said, smiling. Her eyes landed on me, and then her smile broadened. "I thought I knew you from somewhere. You were just on the *LA Morning Show*...you"—her eyes flicked to Angel and lit up—"and you were the ones who caught that drug lord, right?"

I gave her a tight smile. "It was a whole team, but yes, we were part of it."

"That's awesome, you getting him. Hopefully, it will get all that fentanyl off the streets."

"We can only hope."

"You know what, next round is on me," she said, her smile brightening even more. "Give me a minute."

"You don't have to do that—" I started, but she was already headed for the bar.

"I'll take this over being spit at any day of the week," Angel murmured.

"Yeah, I'd prefer to go back to anonymity, if at all possible," I replied.

"I'm sure you'll go back to that before long," Lindsey replied with a chuckle. "As soon as you stop doing the media circuit. When's Warren going to hire a new PR person, anyway?"

"It won't be soon enough to suit me," I said, my tone sour.

"Hey, Stephen, can you send me all those links so we can get them to our Tech department? MacHenry can dig into it and see who's behind that site, and then maybe we'll finally be able to close this case," Angel said, still staring at the computer screen.

"Yep, I can do that," Stephen said, pulling up his email. "Though I'll tell you, I haven't been able to find the owner of it. Not for lack of trying, but what I got was under a business name, not a person. I'll put it in the email for you."

"Thanks," Angel replied.

I really hoped this would be just the thing that helped us break the case wide open and we were able to finally catch the bastard before they killed anyone else.

29

MOVING FORWARD
MARCY

Thursday Morning

L ast night, after I left the Short Stop and headed home, I checked my phone and saw Frank had texted me back, but I'd missed it. I'd almost forgotten that I'd invited him to join us, so at first, I'd been confused by his text. Especially since he hadn't shown up.

> Hey, TT, I'll go, but I'm going to be fashionably late.

Sitting in my driveway, I'd texted him back.

> If you're still on your way, just come to my place. I've already come home.

I'd hit send, but then realized it looked almost harsh. Like I didn't care, which I did. So I'd added to it.

Miss you.

I had sat in my driveway for another five minutes, hoping he'd text me back, but didn't get anything, so I'd gone inside. When he hadn't texted back or shown up, I had called, but it had gone straight to voicemail. I'd tried to go to sleep, but I kept worrying about what was going on, why he hadn't texted or called. Finally, I'd fallen asleep at about two a.m.

I was up, dressed, and sitting in the drive-thru at the coffee shop when my phone rang with "Adore You" by Harry Styles. I immediately answered.

"Frank? Are you okay?" I asked, my heart racing.

"Babe, I'm so sorry I didn't make it last night and didn't answer. I was halfway there when I got pulled in on a case."

Relief swept over me because I'd been imagining all kinds of awful things happening to him, but now I knew he was okay.

I handed the barista my debit card to pay for my drink and mouthed that I was sorry I was on the phone.

She smiled and held up a finger to let me know it would just be a minute.

"I started a text to you, but forgot to hit send," he said. "I didn't get home until after one and figured it was too late to call or text."

I sighed. "It wouldn't have been. I was up."

"Why were you up?" He seemed taken aback. "Did you have to go to another crime scene?"

"No, I was up because I was worried about you. I don't care what time it is, please, in the future, text me back so I at least know you're okay."

"Damn, I'm sorry, babe. I didn't think. Yeah, of course. And I miss you too, by the way."

I smiled at his words.

The barista reached through the drive-thru window and handed me my debit card with the receipt, then gave me my coffee.

I mouthed, "Thank you," to her and gave her a wave. I'd have to remember to give her a big tip the next time I went in.

"So is it a big case?" I asked.

"Triple homicide, we've got some leads, but it looks like I may be working late today."

"So no dinner tonight?" I asked as I pulled back onto the highway.

"Not looking that way. I'm sorry."

"It's okay, Frank. I get it."

"I know you do. Listen, I've got to go, but I'll text you later."

"Okay, love you."

"Love you back. Be careful."

"You too," I murmured before hanging up. I tossed my phone on the passenger seat and grabbed my drink from the cup holder, taking a sip.

Ten minutes later I pulled into the precinct parking lot and headed inside. As I reached my desk, MacHenry walked up.

"Hey, Mac, what's up?" I pulled open my desk drawer and dropped my purse inside.

"We've got some news on the home invasion killer case," he said.

"What is it?"

"The phone companies finally came through, and we've got some sketchy text messages for you to take a look at."

I followed him back toward the Tech department. We

were halfway down the hall when Angel caught up to us. "Morning. Mac says he's got some text messages for us to look at."

"Great, maybe we'll finally be able to catch this asshole," Angel replied.

"It's a lot to sift through, but I've highlighted all the relevant messages from all three victims." MacHenry typed something on his computer, and the big screen on the wall lit up for us. "These are the ones between Helena Richards and someone using a burner phone, one of those monthly pay-as-you-go phones. It's the most current number she texted about this, but there are multiple numbers that go back about three years. It changes monthly, but judging by the content, I'm pretty confident it's the same caller she's talking to on each number."

"From these, it looks like she's ordering merchandise," I said, reading some of the texts.

"Exactly."

"And if you look at how the burner number person replies with a particular slang and use of emojis...well, you're going to see the exact same format from that number on Mariah Osgood's phone as well as Bella Jones' phone, not that we have her phone. Her son gave us her number, and we were able to get some of her messages from the phone company."

"That's great," Angel replied. "Can we see those?"

"Yeah, sure, here you go," he said, and pulled up the email with the texts between Mariah and the burner phone and then the ones from Bella and the burner.

"Can you email all this to me?" I asked. "I want to go over it and see if we can figure out who it is. Oh, and I've got a website I want you to check out. My brother found it yesterday, and I had him email it to me, so I'll send it over once I'm back at my desk."

"What kind of website?" MacHenry asked.

"It's a retail website that looks like it's selling the products stolen from Helena, Mariah, and Bella. He found a business name attached to it, but couldn't get farther than that."

"I'll see what I can find."

"Thanks," I said, and then Angel and I headed back to our desks.

"So what happened to Frank last night? I thought you invited him?"

"I did, and he was going to come, but he caught a triple homicide."

"Oh, damn. That's unusual for Santa Monica. He have any leads?"

"He said he did. He'll solve it, I have no doubt." I smiled as I sat down and turned on my computer.

Angel sat down and then rolled his chair over next to me as I pulled up my email and forwarded the one from Stephen to MacHenry. Then I opened the email from him and realized it was pretty massive.

"Why don't you send me the email; then we can both go through different aspects of it and compare things?" Angel suggested.

"Yeah, okay. Though it might be easier to just print it all out?"

"Waste of trees, let's try online first."

He wasn't wrong. "Okay. It would save paper to only print the necessary things we find."

"Exactly."

"You take Bella, and I'll look at Mariah. Let's see if we can find anything that will tell us who this perp is."

Angel rolled back over to his computer, and we started reading the texts.

I noted that Mariah was very specific in what she was looking for when requesting product.

Sizes 0-8 Anne Fontaine Tournesol Skirt; Sizes 0-8 Anne Fontaine Varly Vest by 8 p.m. Tuesday. No later, peaches. Come to the house.

Dioriviera Toile de Jouy Sauvage Dior Silk Top at least 10, by 9 a.m. Friday. Don't be late like last time, peaches, or I'm not paying you.

Jimmy Choo Etana 80 sandals in all three colors, gold, matcha, and silver, sizes 4-9, at least twenty pairs. $300 Bonus if you can get a silver pair in size 6. I want them for an event. Need them by Thursday at 5 p.m. Don't be late, peaches.

They all read pretty similar to those. The answering messages sounded as though they were written by someone younger, less educated, but that could just be because they wanted to sound that way. I knew many well-educated people who spoke like they grew up on the streets, and it was from whatever media they consumed, be it videos, music, or movies. Either way, it sounded as though whoever this burner account belonged to was the head of a shoplifting ring.

"Hey, Angel?" I said, staring at the messages.

"What's up? Did you find something?"

"Maybe. I'm looking at these messages, and Mariah never calls the burner phone person by name, but has in many cases called them 'peaches.' To me, that isn't generally how a woman refers to a man...or a kid...but another woman or a friend?"

"Are they all that way?" he questioned. "Do they ever get...more rude?"

I scrolled farther down, closer to when Mariah was killed..."Oh, well, yeah...in the last couple there is an exchange where she tells this person to 'stop being such a bitch,' and another she calls them a 'skank' and accuses them of keeping some of the stolen merchandise."

"Okay, because I've got several from Bella telling whoever this is that they're a 'bitch,' as well as a 'Slutty McSlut.' Pretty sure those terms aren't used toward a man."

"So we're looking for a woman as our perp?" I sat back in my chair, a bit floored. Women in general didn't normally commit this particular kind of murder. Not that it didn't happen, but it was unusual.

"You know, let's relook at the scenes with that in mind. Maybe we'll be able to figure out how it started," Angel suggested. "I'm thinking that whoever this woman is, she's the leader of one of these shoplifting rings."

I nodded. "You could be right." I hit print on the page with those first text messages on them, then added the ones where she used derogatory terms as well. "Can you print out the ones you found where Bella called the perp a name?"

"Yep."

"I want to add them to our incident board. Maybe we'll pick up on something else."

He did as I asked, and we went into the incident room we'd set up with all of the photos and information about the case.

"Look at us, moving forward in the case," he said snarkily.

"Hey, don't knock it. This was a good find. We're getting closer."

"Now we just have to find a needle in a haystack of shoplifters."

30

REPORTERS, RANTS, AND REQUESTS

MARCY

Thursday Afternoon

Realizing it was nearing noon, Angel and I had gone out to get lunch. We'd gotten away from the station, headed to Maccheroni Republic for some Italian food, which was quite filling. I'd had the polpette di manzo, which was beef meatballs, while Angel had chosen the lasagna di carne. We hadn't lingered though because both of us wanted to get back to the station to continue digging into our case.

Unfortunately, the moment we entered the HSS detective pool, Police Chief Warren was waiting for me. Lieutenant Chenevert was standing with him, not looking very pleased.

"Detective Kendrick, would you mind joining us," Lieutenant Chenevert said as we entered the room.

I walked over and gave the police chief a tight smile. "Yes, sirs?"

"Kendrick, just the detective I was looking for. Where have you been?"

I was slightly taken aback. We didn't have to account for every second of our workday, and we were allotted an hour for lunch like everyone else, which on many occasions we had to skip because of the case we were working on, so what he was asking was concerning. "Has something happened? Do we have another related death on our home invasion case? Nobody called," I started, pulling out my phone to make sure.

"You're fine, Detective." Lieutenant Chenevert stopped me. "Police Chief Warren is aware you were on your lunch. He's got a request."

I flicked my gaze from him to the police chief. "Yes, sir?" I asked warily.

"As you are aware, Kimber Michaels has hit the best-seller list on numerous occasions with his hard-hitting true-crime books. He's requested our cooperation in the book he's currently working on and specifically requested an in-depth interview with you, Detective, about your capture of El Gato."

"Sir, I'm flattered, but—"

"I've told him you would be happy to and will meet him at his office in"—Police Chief Warren checked his watch—"forty-five minutes." He smiled as he handed me a business card with the address. "You should get going."

"But, sir, I'm on a case—"

"Lieutenant Chenevert said he could spare you, so don't worry," he continued as though I hadn't even spoken.

I glanced at the lieutenant, who again didn't look happy. "Sir?" I was practically pleading for him to intervene.

"I'll have Reyes call you if anything comes up, Kendrick."

I realized his hands were tied and gave him a slight nod. "Alright, thank you."

"Best get a move on, Detective. Don't make us look bad by being late," Police Chief Warren said.

Turning on my heel, it was all I could do not to scream in frustration. I glanced at Angel on my way out, and he shook his head at me. This wasn't what we'd planned for the afternoon.

I was beyond angry about it, so I wasn't in the best of moods when I walked into Mr. Michaels' office.

"May I help you?" a woman seated behind a wooden desk asked.

"I'm Detective Marcy Kendrick. I'm here to see Kimber Michaels."

"Oh yes, he's been expecting you." She picked up the phone and said, "She's here," then hung up.

A moment later, a weaselly-looking man with thinning brown hair, wire-rimmed glasses and a slender frame came out of another room. His gaze traveled from the top of my head to my feet and back up again. "You're the detective who caught El Gato?" he asked with disdain.

I gritted my teeth. "I'm one of them, yes. I was told you specifically requested to speak with me?"

"Well, yes, but you seemed larger on TV. I suppose the TV does add ten or, in your case, thirty pounds and four inches."

I arched a brow at him. "Look, I have another case to get back to, so if you're just going to insult me, I'm going to go."

"I wasn't insulting you. Just stating facts. Come in." He blocked my escape and gestured to his office.

Reluctantly, I headed in with him, and he shut the door behind him. I was slightly uncomfortable about that, but I was wearing my weapon, so it was fine. "I'm not sure what I can actually help you with," I said, sitting down in the chair he indicated.

"I'm working on a true-crime book based on El Gato and his organization, and I wanted to get some information on his capture as well as about the detective who brought him down."

"First of all, I wasn't the only detective who was involved—"

"But you were the one in charge."

"Well, yes," I acknowledged.

"That works for me. I understand El Gato actually sent his assassin after you as well?"

I paused. Not many people were aware of that fact, and I wondered how he'd come across that information. "How—"

He smirked. "I always find out the information I'm after, Detective."

The way he said it made my skin crawl. "Very well, yes. He did send someone after me, but as you can see, he was unsuccessful."

"Yet he managed to get past a group of Long Beach officers to murder another detective with the LAPD. Are you just lucky, or...?"

I arched a brow at him. "*Or* what?"

"You tell me."

My eyes narrowed. "You're the writer; ask what you really want to know."

"I'm just curious. You've managed to take on multiple serial killers, now El Gato and his assassin; how have you managed to survive? Take the Face Flayer copycat; how did you survive that?"

I folded my arms and stared at him. "I thought this was supposed to be an interview about El Gato. Not about me."

"Call it background." He tapped a pen on his desk. "Tell me about the original case. I've read that you witnessed the original Face Flayer murdering your mother...how did you keep quiet so he didn't come after you?"

I stood up and shoved the chair back. "We're done." I stormed toward the door and yanked it open, slamming it into the wall so hard it bounced back and caught my elbow, but I was so angry I didn't even gasp.

The woman behind the desk out front jumped as Mr. Michaels called out, "Stop her!"

I had no idea how he was planning to stop me, but I sped up my steps anyway. In the end, she was too slow, they both were, as I slammed out of the building and strode to my car. I was pulling out of the parking lot as they made it out of the building. Fury didn't even begin to cover how I felt after that. I was so done.

Hitting speed dial on my phone, I called Frank. I needed to talk to someone who would talk me out of quitting. Maybe he was the wrong one to call, but I figured he would have the right words.

"Hey, babe, everything okay?" Frank said, answering after the first ring.

"No." I was breathing hard, I was still so angry. "Warren sent me to another interview, and before you say anything, I didn't want to go. I'd even told the lieutenant that I was done, but Warren was adamant that I do this one because it was for an author writing a true-crime book on El Gato."

"Marcy, I'm done getting angry about the interviews. I know you aren't out there requesting them, and you're just doing what you're told to do. Now what happened? Did he hit on you?"

I snorted a laugh because that came out of left field. "No. That might have made things better. The asshole insulted me right off the bat and then proceeded to bring up my track record and asked how I escaped both my mother's killer and the copycat. I mean, who the hell asks that?"

"Want me to kick his ass?" he asked, sounding almost amused, but there was a level of seriousness there.

I laughed, feeling a bit better. "Listen to you sounding all gangster."

"Everybody has a little bit of gangster in them," he said, chuckling.

"I think I've heard that before somewhere..." I said, wondering where I'd heard it. "Is that from a movie?"

"No, it's a paraphrase of a quote from a guy named Binya-vanga Wainaina, who was a writer from Kenya. I saw it in a meme and thought it was pretty true, so I looked it up."

"I guess it is fairly true. Just depends on the context, I suppose." I sighed. "Listen, I'd better go. I'm almost back to the station."

"Okay, babe. I'll text you later."

"Bye," I said as the call disconnected.

Back in the station, I headed straight for Lieutenant Chenevert's office. I didn't even bother to knock, but the door was open.

"Sir?" I said, stepping in and standing in front of his desk.

"Detective, is everything okay?"

"No, sir. It's not. I was this close"—I held up my finger and thumb together so barely a sliver of air could pass between them—"to handing in my resignation over this last interview, and it was definitely my last. I am not going to be treated the way that"—I bit my tongue to keep from saying something inappropriate and then continued—"man treated me. My life is not fodder for the masses to devour. There was enough of that when I was a kid, and I couldn't stop it. There was enough of it when it was brought up during the copycat case. I'm done."

He nodded. "I told Warren you weren't interested in doing any more interviews and that you were working a major case. He was insistent that this would be the last one, so I acquiesced. In hindsight, I shouldn't have. I apologize."

"Thank you, sir. I appreciate that. I know how he gets. Robinson usually runs interference for us, but it looks like he's bypassing him and coming to you to get to us."

"I'm wising up to things around here. I've got your back, Kendrick."

My shoulders relaxed. "Well, just so you know, I didn't give the guy what he wanted, and he's probably going to call and complain to Warren."

He snickered. "I'll make sure he doesn't come at you." He smiled. "By the way, while you were gone, a Dr. Zellers over at the hospital called. Reyes headed over there."

I hadn't even looked over at the detective pool when I'd come in to see Angel wasn't there.

"Dr. Zellers?" That wasn't the doctor we'd spoken to before.

"That was the name I was given."

"Okay, I'll call Angel to see what's up."

"Hey, Kendrick?"

"Yes, sir?" I said, turning back toward him.

"Just so you know, I appreciate the work you and Reyes are putting in on this case. I took a look in the incident room earlier, and I think you're close to getting it solved."

"Thank you, sir. I hope you're right." As I walked toward my desk, I pulled my phone from my pocket and called Angel.

He answered almost immediately. "You finished with the interview?"

I gave a derisive snort. "The interview was a joke. What's going on with James? Is he talking? And what happened to Dr. Bethel?"

Angel sighed. "James is currently sleeping, and Dr. Zellers, who has taken over James' long-term care, asked me not to wake him. Not that I actually could, the medication keeps him pretty out of it, so it could be a while before he does wake up again. But we've got a bigger problem."

I stopped my progression toward my desk. "What's wrong?"

"We've got a leak."

"A leak? Another one? But we found who was doing that. Robinson is going to lose his shit," I murmured, keeping my voice down.

"Yeah, I don't think it came from us, well, not from the LAPD anyway. Pretty sure it was from someone here at the hospital."

"Okay, back up; what was leaked?"

"That one of the home invasion victims is alive and the police are interested in speaking to them. And now there's a bunch of reporters camped out here."

"Do they have a name?"

"Of the victim? No. At least none of the questions shouted at me included his name."

"Okay, that's good. Let me talk to the lieutenant and captain and see if we can get an officer on his door to keep those reporters at bay."

"Good idea."

"I'll call you back." I hung up and turned back around, returning to Chenevert's office. "Sir, I'm sorry to interrupt you again."

"What's up, Kendrick?" he asked, looking up from the report he was working on.

"We've got a situation down at the hospital. Someone leaked that we have a living survivor from the home invasions, and a bunch of reporters are over there, trying to get information."

He ran a hand over his brow. "Great."

"I was hoping we could get an officer on Mr. Osgood's door. Just to keep them from getting to him before we can talk to him or to ensure they don't come back to finish the job."

Frowning, he asked, "Hasn't Reyes already spoken to him?"

"No, sir. The doctor requested that he wait until James wakes up again, and it might be a while."

"Let me speak to the captain." He stood up from his desk.

"May I join you?"

He shrugged. "Sure. Don't see why not."

Together we headed for Robinson's office, and Jason waved us on, not making us wait, which was nice.

A minute later we were seated across from Captain Robinson.

"How's the case going?" he asked, barely looking at the two of us.

"We've made some progress, sir. We have a strong reason to believe our perp is a woman. And we know she more than likely leads one of the shoplifting crews."

"Good, good...so what is this? Why aren't you out there with Reyes, identifying our killer?"

Lieutenant Chenevert explained the situation and my request. "Is that going to be possible? Should I speak with Myers?"

Robinson pursed his lips and then slowly shook his head. "No. Without knowing if he even knows anything, we can't afford to have an officer posted over there. The hospital has security, so they can keep the reporters from him."

"But, sir, what if the killer realizes that James survived and is capable of talking? They might decide to go after him before we can identify her," I said.

"We don't even know what this person looks like. And right now, the less attention we call to him, the less likely the reporters will identify him, and they won't know who to look for."

"But—"

"Get his story, Kendrick, and once we know more, then we'll revisit this."

"Yes, sir." I nodded, but I was disappointed. "If you'll excuse me, I'll go let Reyes know."

Robinson nodded.

I left his office and reached for my phone again. "Hey, Robinson says no, not right now. We'll just have to keep an eye on the reporters and what they say or publish. If James' name goes on the record, then maybe we've got call to get him a guard. Or if he talks to us and gives us something useful, we can get him one. Whichever comes first."

"Damn. I guess I should get comfortable, then." He sighed.

"We can take turns, or have one of the staff call us when he wakes again," I suggested.

"Okay, that works. I'll stay tonight, and if anything kicks off, I'll call you."

JUST AS I was about the leave the precinct for the night, my phone rang with an unfamiliar number. I swiped to dismiss the call, but it immediately started ringing again, and I wondered if it was Angel calling from the hospital for some reason.

Just in case, I answered, "Detective Kendrick, how may I help you?"

"Marcy? It's Desk Sergeant Glenn from SMPD."

The seriousness of his tone had my heart plummeting to my stomach. "Is Frank okay?"

"He's been shot."

31

THE STREETS ARE DANGEROUS
MARCY

Thursday Night

"**I**s Frank okay?" I asked Glenn again.

"As far as I'm aware, he's alive and in surgery. He's at UCLA Santa Monica Medical Center."

"I'm on my way; tell them I'm on my way," I said, running for my car.

I dialed Lieutenant Chenevert's number as I jumped in my car. "Sir?" I nearly shouted.

"Kendrick? What's wrong?"

"Sir, my...my boyfriend, Detective Frank Maldon, has been shot in Santa Monica. I'm headed to the medical center—"

"Be safe; use your siren if you have to. I'll get the details from Robinson, who I'm sure can talk to his captain. Go."

"Thank you!" I couldn't use my siren without permission

if it wasn't for a case, which was why I called. I slammed my foot down on the gas and gunned the engine.

Forty-eight minutes later, I pulled into the parking lot at the medical center and rushed inside. Gasping, I said, "I'm here to see Detective Frank Maldon." I flashed my badge.

"Marcy, over here," Frank's dad called from the waiting area.

I nodded at him and looked at the receptionist, desperate for any information she would give me.

"He's in surgery. The doctor will be out to speak to you after."

He was still in surgery? How bad was it? I wondered as fear filled me. I hurried over to Mr. and Mrs. Maldon, who pulled me into a three-way hug. "Glenn said he was okay; why is he still in surgery?" I mumbled.

"The shot tore something in his upper chest that needed repairing. They can't just do stitches, from what I was told," Mr. Maldon replied.

To me that sounded like a downplayed answer, but I didn't want to say anything more and worry him. Frank should have been wearing a vest, so if a bullet hit his chest, it was worse than anyone was saying, and I was terrified. I sat down next to Frank's parents. There were several SMPD officers and detectives there as well, but I didn't do much more than share a look with them. They all knew that this was worse than what his parents had been told, but wouldn't say anything either. Not until the doctor came out to tell us what was going on.

I folded my hands and started praying. I didn't know if it would help, if God was listening, but I really hoped he was. I wasn't a religious person. I barely believed there were more than a handful of good people in the world, but Frank was one of them, and I needed him to be okay, so I would do anything to put the odds in his favor, including praying.

Half an hour later, a doctor emerged from the double doors and said, "Who's here for Frank Maldon?"

Frank's parents stood, and so did I and half the waiting room. Frank's parents moved forward while the rest of us hung back, just in case. My heart had stopped beating in my chest, and I was still, waiting to find out what was going on.

The doctor spoke in a hushed tone to them, and then Frank's mom smiled as tears trailed down her cheeks. She turned to me and nodded.

My heart kicked back into action and began to race.

"When can we see him?" she asked the doctor.

"He's in recovery, and once he's completely stable, we'll move him to his own room. Then he can have visitors, but no more than three at a time and only for a short time."

"That's fine. When?" Frank's dad asked.

"I'd say within the hour."

"Thank you, Doctor," Frank's mom said and then came over and hugged me. "He's okay."

I held on to her tightly. I was so grateful he was going to be okay.

I needed to know what had happened. I didn't really know the detectives in the waiting room, but I saw Officer Kemp, and as I started toward him, Captain Stafford strode in, and I changed course.

"Captain," I said, drawing his attention.

"Detective Kendrick, how is he?"

"The doctor says he's in recovery, and we should be able to see him within the hour."

His shoulders relaxed, and he nodded. "Good, that's good to hear."

"Sir, what happened?" I asked, keeping my voice low. "Was this the suspect from the triple homicide?"

"No, different case. The suspect barricaded himself in a house, took some hostages. Frank was one of the detectives who went in to help get the hostages out. The suspect was attempting to shoot one of the kids, and Frank got between them and the bullet. Frank was damn lucky he was only hit once. Apparently, the perp nearly emptied his gun before he was killed. Two of the four hostages were also shot; one is in critical condition."

"So he's dead; someone took him out?" I wanted to make sure because I was feeling extremely vengeful.

"Yeah, basically suicide by cop. He wasn't giving up, and it seemed he wanted to take as many as he could with him on his way out."

Overwhelming emotion filled me, and I was very shaky. "Frank was wearing a vest, right?"

"Yeah, but it was like he was wearing nothing because the suspect had armor-piercing bullets. I've got some detectives looking into where they came from."

I knew he couldn't have come by them legally, not here in California. "Will you keep me updated? If there's someone selling those here in Santa Monica, you know they're on the streets in LA too."

"I'm already working with Robinson on that; he's got Vice looking into it."

"Good."

Stafford went to join a couple of his detectives, and I returned to Frank's parents.

Thirty minutes later we were allowed to go see him. I hung back as he hugged his parents, but he could see me, and while he talked to them, he kept his eyes on me. Once they were done hugging him and speaking to him, I moved to his side, and he reached for my hand, holding on to it tightly. Or maybe I was holding on to him tightly; either way, I wasn't going anywhere.

We still didn't say anything as his parents left and allowed a few SMPD officers in to see him. They too didn't stay long, and after an hour, it was just the two of us. His parents had left, saying they'd return in the morning.

"TT, you didn't have to come, but I'm glad you did."

I stared at him as I sank down in the chair next to his bed, my hand still in his. "You thought I wouldn't come?"

He shrugged his good shoulder. "I didn't know if you were working a case."

Shaking my head, I replied, "Frank, working a case or not, I would have moved mountains to be here. You were shot, and thank God you're okay and that perp is dead, because—" I stopped and took a deep breath. "You saved a kid's life today."

He scratched the back of his neck with his good arm. "I guess, yeah. I wasn't expecting to actually be shot this badly. I was wearing a vest. The kid had nothing."

"How are you? I didn't hear what the doctor told your parents; what kind of damage are you looking at?"

"Had some internal bleeding, some destroyed blood vessels, a shattered rib bone. That's why they did the surgery to repair that damage. I'm okay. I was awake until they put me under for the surgery."

"What are your doctor's orders?" I needed to know how best to support him.

"Can't use my right arm for a few weeks, so probably riding a desk for a bit, but I can head back to work once I get discharged. Not sure I want to."

I paused. "What do you mean you don't want to? You want to take some time off?"

He wouldn't look at me but continued to hold my hand tightly. "I don't know. Just seems like no matter how hard we try, how many criminals we get off the streets, they just get more and more dangerous. Maybe I'm just burnt out, but I don't know if I want to keep doing this."

Frank was a lot like me. That was one of the things that drew us together. I knew that deep down he really didn't want to quit, but he was probably right about one thing. He needed a break. A vacation. Something to help him reset. At least I was pretty sure that would be the case.

"I know how this incident can mess with you, Frank. I've been where you are. I think maybe taking some time off will help you decide if stepping away is something you really want to do or if you just need a break."

He nodded slowly. "What are you thinking?"

"Maybe we take a real vacation? Not just a weekend to Vegas, but a good week or two away from here."

He leaned back into his pillow. "I've always wanted to take an Alaskan cruise. What do you think?"

I covered our joined hands with my free one. "I think that sounds amazing. I have to wrap this home invasion case up, but I think we should book it. I'll clear the vacation time with Robinson." I put my hand on his cheek and leaned in to kiss him. "You had me so worried."

"I'm sorry, babe, it wasn't my intention to worry you."

"Frank, you're on the job, I'm always going to worry, but I also know you'll do your best to always come home to me."

"Always." He leaned forward, and I met his lips in another kiss before he yawned. "Sorry, I'm wiped."

"Get some sleep. I'm not going anywhere." I smiled at him.

"What about your case?" he murmured, his eyes half closed.

"It can wait until you're discharged. It's not going anywhere." I really hoped that was the case, because there was no way I was leaving Frank's side until I absolutely had to.

FRANK WAS DISCHARGED at six a.m. the next morning, and I drove him home. I took a quick shower and then changed into a spare set of clothes I'd left at his place, while he took a shower, being careful of his right shoulder. I had to leave for work soon—I'd put in a call to Robinson before we left the hospital, and he'd told me I could take the day, but I wanted to get back on the case and solve it—so I hurried to the kitchen to fix us some coffee.

I noticed Frank coming into the kitchen as I poured us each a mug. "You sure you're going to be okay here on your own?" I asked, feeling guilty for wanting to go back to work now that I knew he was going to be fine.

He chuckled. "Babe, I'm fine. I'd love for you to stay, but the sooner you get this case solved, the sooner we can take that cruise. I'm going to spend the day looking things up and seeing what, if anything, we need for it."

I grinned. "I'm looking forward to it," I said as my phone rang with "Send Me An Angel" by the Scorpions. I picked it up from the counter and answered, "Hey, Angel."

"Turn on channel 5; we've got a big problem."

I glanced at Frank. "Can you turn the TV on to channel 5?" I said, since he was standing nearest the remote.

"Sure," he grabbed it, turned the TV on and put it on channel 5. "What's going on?"

"Not sure," I said as the reporter's image appeared on the screen.

"—invasions that have been taking place here in Los Angeles. It turns out one of the victims of these invasions has survived, and the police have been keeping his identity quiet. However, we here at Channel 5 News have discovered that James Osgood, the husband of Mariah Osgood who was killed last week, is the survivor. Originally it was reported that both Mr. and Mrs. Osgood had passed away at the scene—"

"Are you freaking kidding me?" I said, slamming my plastic travel mug down on the counter with a bang. "Angel, get to the hospital, make sure James is okay. I'm on my way. I'm out the door right now."

"Already on my way there. I'll see you when you get here."

Hanging up, I started rushing through the house. "I've gotta go. They just put our only witness on blast."

"I'm coming with you," Frank said, grabbing my mug along with his and switching off the coffee maker.

"Frank—" I started because I knew he had to be hurting even with the pain meds.

"Don't argue, TT. I'm at least a good set of eyes, even if I can't aim a weapon at the moment."

"Fine," I tossed over my shoulder as we ran out of his house.

He climbed in the passenger seat and barely had his seatbelt on when I pulled out of his driveway. I didn't have to ask him to toss the siren on the dash; he did it automatically.

I didn't even want to think about what might happen if we lost this witness.

32

IT'S HIM OR ME

THE ENTREPRENEUR

Friday Morning

I entered my storage warehouse and sat down at the desk to check on my website. Orders had been pourin' in, and we were sold out of a lot of stuff already. I'd sent the crew out last night to pick up some new merch, and Moxie would be deliverin' it soon. I'd need to get pictures of everythin' and get 'em up on the website so we could bring in more cash.

My stomach rumbled because I hadn't taken the time to eat. Pickin' up my phone, I sent Moxie a text message to grab us some sandwiches and sodas. It was almost nine thirty, and the storage warehouse was kind of stuffy and quiet. It was climate controlled, or so they said when I rented it, but with the door closed, it felt like the walls were closin' in on me.

Ten minutes later, Moxie texted that she was on her way

with food and the merch. I decided to open the door halfway so she could get in but also because I was feelin' like a prisoner in there. I sat back down and was emailin' a customer when Moxie finally pulled up in her car. Her windows were down, and the radio was on a bit too loud. They were doin' some sort of news report.

"Hey, you should hear this," she said, gettin' out, but leavin' her car door open.

"What?"

"Listen."

"*—survived? I mean, the dude was shot in the head, and the cops reported he'd died at the scene. How can they get away with that?*"

A sliver of fear raced down my spine. What kind of podcast was Moxie listening to? What were they talking about? I glanced at Moxie, who looked pale.

"*I think the real question is, why did they keep it from the public? I mean, these home invasions are worrisome, and they've had this witness they've been sitting on? Why not share that? Why keep it a secret?*"

"He's fuckin' alive?" I shrieked, losing my cool.

"I thought you said you killed him; what the hell?"

"Look, he went down; I thought I fuckin' did. Fuck. He knows who I am."

Moxie shook her head. "You gotta get to him, stop him from talkin' to the cops."

"Yeah, you fuckin' think I don't know that? He's gonna fuck this all up for us. Stay here, get that merch logged on the site and finish doin' the orders. I'll go fix this." I ran out of the storage warehouse and headed for my car.

I didn't even know what hospital he was at, but that was the least of my worries. I needed to get in and out of the place without bein' seen. I switched on the radio, hopin' they'd say more as I headed for Walmart. I could pick up some scrubs and blend in. Then all I'd need was a hospital ID.

Luckily, I didn't have to wait long for some stupid reporter to give the name of the hospital. They were so helpful, those reporters. They probably hated the cops as much as I did, considerin' they were always reportin' the crappy stuff the cops were doin'. I parked, rushed into the store, and took a couple of sets of scrubs into the changin' room. I put one set on and then put my own clothes on over them. It felt a little bulky, but it would let me get out the door.

Now I just had to get an ID. That would take a little longer, but I wasn't gonna give up. I had too much at stake.

Twenty minutes later, I parked in the staff parkin' lot at the hospital, took off everything but the scrubs, and started wanderin' between cars, lookin' in windows. I knew somebody had probably left their ID in their car; people always did. Sure enough, after checkin' a bunch of 'em, I saw one on the passenger seat of a small hatchback. The car was locked, but that didn't stop me. I had one of those pry bars for windows in my car, so I went to get it.

Several nurses came out and got in their cars and left, but I made sure I wasn't seen as I made my way back to the car with the ID. It was quick work to get the door open and for me to snatch the ID. It was on a lanyard, and I slid it over my head as I returned to my car, puttin' the pry bar back in the trunk.

I entered the hospital through one of the staff doors, and after studyin' the board on the wall about the different floors, I went to one that said recovery. I found an empty nurses' station with a computer that was already on. After lookin' around to make sure no one was watchin', I typed in James Osgood's name. Smilin', I saw what room he was in. I was on the wrong floor, but that was okay.

I got on the elevator and pushed the button to go one floor down. I wanted to rush, but I didn't wanna draw attention to myself. I wasn't sure what I was gonna do once I got to his room, but I couldn't let James speak to the cops. He'd damn well better not have yet.

I found his room and looked up and down the hall. There were people everywhere, includin' a couple of security guys who were dealin' with a patient who was havin' some sort of fit. I couldn't help but think this was my opportunity. It was meant to be...so I went in. James was on the bed, his eyes closed. I couldn't tell if he was asleep or in a coma, but either way, he wouldn't be wakin' up.

I thought about smotherin' him with a pillow, and I started to reach for one when I noticed the IV bag hangin' next to him. Wasn't there a way I could put somethin' in the IV line that could kill him? That would give me time to get out before he started thrashin' and callin' for help. I moved to the cabinets by the computer and used the scan card on the ID to open it. Jackpot. Inside, there were some fresh syringes in plastic wrap. There wasn't any kind of liquid medication I could use, but I knew I'd seen some movies where the killer put air in the IV line and killed people. I could do that.

I opened the packagin' and filled the syringe with air, then headed for the line that went from the bag to James' arm. There was even a convenient place to insert the needle of the syringe about halfway down the line. Smilin', I picked it up and inserted the syringe.

The door opened, and three people walked in.

I stopped, the line and the syringe held up in front of me.

"What are you doing?" the woman asked, comin' forward.

"I—" I started, but I knew I sounded panicked, because I was. I dropped the line and syringe, slammed my fist into the woman's face a couple of times, yankin' on her black blazer, and swung her toward the cabinets. I ducked beneath one of the guys' arms who tried to grab me and brushed past the other guy, who had his arm in a sling but was attemptin' to block the door, then raced down the hall toward the stairwell.

I could hear them chasin' me. Where the fuck was I gonna go? I wondered. Cause I wasn't about to get myself caught. I'd die before I let that happen. And I wasn't dyin' today.

33

FRUSTRATION ABOUNDS
MARCY

Friday Morning

I winced as the doctor stitched up the cut over my right eye. I couldn't believe we'd let the perp get past the three of us and disappear without a trace. Granted, even though we'd been expecting the perp to try to get to James, she'd taken me by surprise when she'd punched me in the face. None of us had expected to walk in on her attempting to tamper with James' IV line.

We'd chased after the woman, but she had a good lead on us and was suddenly gone. By the time we got security to check for her on the cameras, she was no longer in the building. At least we didn't think she was. Just in case, we'd returned to James' room to be sure he was protected. I'd looked at the line and syringe, which was full of air, but it didn't look like she'd had a chance to push it into the line when we walked in.

I'd called immediately for James' nurse to come in and check his vitals to be sure he was okay, and they'd done some tests to ensure our perp hadn't managed to inject anything into him. The nurse also informed me that despite what we'd seen in the movies, shooting air into an IV line wouldn't necessarily harm someone. It would have to be a lot of air for it to kill. I was glad that was the case, but it just meant this woman had made a second attempt at killing James, which had to mean something. We'd left two hospital security guards on his door while I was being seen.

"I want you to ask security to get a still shot of this woman so we can show James and see if he can ID her," I said to Angel and Frank, who were standing off to the side while the doctor stitched up my eyebrow.

"I'm on it. You sure you're okay?" Angel asked.

"Yeah, I'm fine. Just battered."

He shook his head, looking between me and Frank. "Just couldn't let Frank be the only injured one, could ya, Marce," he teased.

I glared at him. "That's not funny."

Frank guffawed though, but quickly turned it to a cough as I turned my glare on him.

"Sorry, too soon?" Angel grimaced.

"Way too soon," I agreed.

He shrugged and headed out the door.

"You're all set," the doctor said, patting my leg. "Try not to get into any more fights, okay?" he suggested, then looked at Frank. "Either of you."

"I'll make sure she doesn't," Frank replied.

I rolled my eyes. "Can we go back to Mr. Osgood's room now?"

"Sure, that's fine."

Frank and I headed back to his room, and I pulled out my phone to call Lieutenant Chenevert. "Sir? It's Kendrick. Our suspect was just here at the hospital. She tried to murder him, but we stopped her. Unfortunately, she got away—"

I had to pull my phone from my ear as he shouted, "What? How did y'all let that happen?"

I explained how she'd escaped.

"Are you okay?" he asked.

"Had to get a couple of stitches, but other than that, I'm okay, sir. I'd like to have a patrol officer here to guard Mr. Osgood now that she's made a second attempt on his life. Can you talk to Robinson?"

"Yes, I'll take care of it. How is Mr. Osgood? Is he awake yet?"

"Well, the commotion in his room didn't wake him, the medication is keeping him pretty out of it, but I'll see if we can get Dr. Zellers to give him something to pull him out of it."

"Good because the sooner we find out what he knows, the safer he'll be."

I had to agree. I wasn't going to relax until then. I hung up and turned to Frank, who was looking a bit shaken up again. I frowned. "Frank?"

"Yeah, sorry. Just thinking about what happened and how bad it could have been. We were lucky that woman didn't have a gun. You know she's got one."

"You're right, it could have been worse, but it wasn't. Don't borrow trouble, Frank. One of us getting shot within twenty-four hours is enough, don't you think?"

His lips quirked as he pulled me into his arms. "It is. That vacation can't get here soon enough. I'm not sure I can wait too much longer," he murmured into my hair.

We spent several more hours at the hospital, and then Frank and I went home to my place. It had been a long and exhausting day, and James had remained too groggy to answer any of our questions. I had been glad to see him wake, but I wished he'd been more cognizant of what was going on so he could help us.

I sent Frank into the living room to sit while I fixed us a light dinner. I warmed up some frozen fajita chicken strips and added them to a salad with hard-boiled eggs for added protein. It wasn't much, but I didn't have a lot that was ready to eat, everything was frozen, and we hadn't stopped at the store because we were both tired.

"You know, I could order a pizza," Frank suggested, eyeing the salad I'd handed him.

I laughed. "What, rabbit food isn't filling enough for you?"

He shook his head and pulled me to him with his good arm. "Not if I want to keep my stamina up for after dinner."

I raised my uninjured eyebrow. "You sure that's a good idea?"

The grin that spread over his lips was rakish. "Making love with you is always a good idea, and it's been far too long since I've held you in my arms." He captured my lips in a searing kiss, and I sighed at the pleasure of it.

"Order the damn pizza," I murmured a few minutes later and took a bite of my salad. I was going to need the protein.

FOR THE SECOND night in a row, I'd gotten very little sleep. This time though it wasn't due to stress, but to the release of it. Frank and I had come up with some interesting positions to accommodate his injured shoulder and ribs, and now I wasn't just exhausted, I was sore in places I hadn't been in a long time. Still, I wouldn't have traded last night for anything in the world.

As I headed in to work, Frank had called his dad to come get him from my place. He was planning to go into work because they still hadn't found the perp responsible for the triple homicide he'd been working on before he'd saved the kid from their estranged father.

I'd finally gotten the full story of what went down during all of that, and it just made me sick. The perp had taken his ex-wife, her new husband, his own daughter, and her step-sister hostage, planning to kill them all.

The perp's daughter had been extremely brave, calling 911 the moment her dad had broken in. She had her phone in her pocket, but he hadn't known about it. By the time Frank and the others arrived, he'd already shot the stepfa-ther in the stomach and was yelling and screaming at the mother about how she'd stolen his life from him. They didn't wait for a negotiator to get there; instead they'd broken in as the guy shot the mother, his ex-wife, and was aiming at his daughter. Frank had jumped just in time. Both the woman and her husband had survived, but just barely, and both kids were uninjured, at least physically. I knew they'd have a lot of mental trauma from that.

I walked into the precinct and saw Angel on the phone. I sat down and caught the tail end of the conversation.

"What time did they say?" he asked as he stood and picked up his keys.

Wearily I stood back up, as it looked like we wouldn't be staying here. "What's up?" I asked as soon as he hung up.

"That was Keith. They got an anonymous tip about the next store one of these shoplifting crews is going to hit. The caller said it was the same crew whose leader was involved in the home invasions."

That sounded suspect to me. "They just gave that away? Is this some sort of trap to kill cops?"

Angel paused and said, "Good point. I think we need vests and backup. We don't have a lot of time; let's go give Chenevert a heads-up and have him talk to Myers about sending patrol."

Fifteen minutes later we were heading to Rodeo Drive. Patrol was already on the way, and so were Hummel and Vance. They were our backup, unfortunately. I was worried what this crew would do if they saw all of the patrol cars, so I told them to head for the nearest streets and wait for me to call them in. I parked my car a few stores down from Splendor, in front of Tom Ford, and headed for the shop. Hummel and Vance parked behind me and followed behind us, planning to hang outside, looking inconspicuous. I doubted they could pull it off, but that was the plan.

The caller had said they would hit the store just before eleven thirty, and it was already ten after. I walked in and asked for the store manager.

A woman in a white dress came forward, looking haughtily down her nose at me. "May I help you?" she asked.

I showed her my badge and explained what was going on. She seemed startled, but agreed to let us handle things. She directed me to the women's side, and Angel to the men's side, so we'd look less noticeable when the crew stormed the shop.

When they came in, completely overwhelming the store with their numbers, I nearly froze. They were like a plague of locusts, swarming various areas, filling bags, shouting, and laughing, their faces all covered with neck gaiters and matching black hoodies.

"LAPD! Freeze!" I shouted into the chaos, but it didn't even seem to faze most of them. "Patrol!" I said, pushing the button on my radio to alert them.

I heard a loud bang and then screaming from my right side and realized one of the teens had a gun and had just used it.

34

THE TIP-OFF
MARCY

Saturday Morning

I turned to see the teen had pulled the trigger, but had aimed at the ceiling, thankfully. I trained my weapon on him and shot him in the shoulder of his gun hand. He screamed as he dropped the gun and fell to the floor, clutching his shoulder.

There was more screaming as the teens realized one of their own had been shot; then they scattered. A slew of them ran back through the glass doors and out to the sidewalk. I was hopeful that Hummel and Vance were grabbing as many of them as possible and passing them off to patrol to be charged.

I moved toward the downed teen and put pressure on his shoulder where he was bleeding as he whimpered and cried. "Reyes!" I yelled.

"Here!" he called back. "You good?" he asked, seeing me on the ground.

"Bag his weapon," I replied, nodding toward it.

Within seconds the teens were gone as fast as they'd come in, and the store manager came over, looking irate. "What the hell was that?" she demanded. "I thought you were going to stop them!"

I glanced up at her, but ignored her ranting. "Call a bus; we need to get this guy to the hospital so he can be patched up before we book him."

Angel spoke into his radio, but it was at least fifteen minutes before an EMT entered the shop. Once the teen was being seen to, I told Angel to stay with him while I checked on everyone else.

I found Hummel and Vance standing together on the sidewalk, their hands in their pockets as they stared at numerous dropped bags of merchandise. "Did you catch any of them?" I asked. "See where they went? See anyone directing them?"

"They just appeared, jumped out of cars, came from around the buildings, and poured into the shop before we knew what was happening," Hummel said. "Couldn't even tell them apart. They were all wearing those black hoodies and had their faces covered."

"Did you stop any of them coming out with stolen goods?"

"Well, we tried, I mean we got our hands on one squirmy teen, but they got away," Vance said. "Little bitch kicked me in my junk."

I pinched the bridge of my nose and said, "So you're telling me that you caught nobody?"

"Patrol got a couple of them, but they'd all tossed the

bags by then, so not sure they can be charged with anything," Hummel said with a shrug.

I gritted my teeth. "Get all these bags of clothes picked up and brought back to the store. I need to know what, if anything, they got away with." I shook my head at them, wishing I could do more than that.

Angel followed the medics out of the store with the teen on a stretcher. "I'm going to ride with them. I'll meet you at the hospital."

"It's gonna be a minute before I can get there. I have to deal with this." I gestured toward the mess.

It took me nearly an hour to get the shop manager calmed down and to clear the scene. I'd had several texts from Angel giving me updates as I headed to join him at the hospital.

The best news I'd seen so far was that James was awake. I couldn't wait to get there and talk to him. I just hoped he knew the woman who had attacked him.

I was ready to put this case to bed.

35

RECOGNIZING HIS ATTEMPTED MURDERER

MARCY

Saturday Afternoon

I pulled into the parking lot of the hospital and headed into the ER, where the boy I'd shot was being seen. Angel had gotten his name and age, Malcom Washington, age fifteen, and my stomach twisted at the news. Fifteen and he'd had a Taurus GX4 in his possession. Used it in a robbery. The boy was already in a lot of trouble with just those charges. I really hoped it hadn't been used in any other crimes because it was very likely he'd have those charges brought against him as well.

I found Angel outside the curtain, waiting for the doctor to finish with him. "He doing okay?"

"Yeah, your aim was good; hit the fleshy part and missed the bone. Doc dug the bullet out and is patching him now."

"Good. Guess I'll have to turn in my weapon once we're back at the precinct." I hated having to use my weapon, but it seemed more and more over the last few years, I'd had no choice.

"Think IA is going to get involved?" Angel asked.

"God, I hope not. At the very least I hope the video evidence will show it was a clean shoot."

"It will. If you can see anything in that madhouse."

I sighed. That had better not be an issue. Either way, I decided I needed to press forward. "You said James is awake?"

"Yeah, when I came in with Malcom, Dr. Zellers was here in the ER. He said that James is doing well and more aware today, so they lowered his medication, and he should be up to talking to us now."

"That's great news. I'll see if we can get a patrol unit here to take Malcom to the precinct; then we can go talk to James. I've got the picture of our suspect that you got from hospital security in my car. I'll go get it while I make the call."

"Good idea."

As I returned to my car for the picture, I called it in, and twenty minutes later, Officers Min-Ji Kim and Julie Desmond showed up. I saw them coming through the door and went to join them. "Hey, Min-Ji, Julie. So the kid is still with the doctor, but he should be close to being discharged."

"Get a name out of the kid?" Min-Ji asked.

"Malcom Washington, age fifteen. We've got him on a weapon charge as well as armed robbery, reckless endangerment, and a handful of other charges."

"Okay, we'll get him in and processed." Julie shook her head. "These kids, ruining their lives before they even start."

I wished there were something we could do about these kids, but I knew so much of it started because they came from broken or unstable homes. Perpetual poverty was a problem too. Parents working several jobs to keep a roof over their heads left these teens unsupervised and getting into mischief. Even the ones from the suburbs doing this for kicks, I had to wonder why their parents weren't stepping in. My only answer was they were too busy paying bills to pay attention. And if they were paying attention, they didn't effectively discipline them, but allowed them to do what they wanted. It made for very narcissistic kids who thought the world revolved around them.

"Well, thanks for taking care of this for us. We'll see you back at the station."

Angel took Min-Ji into the curtained area and handed Malcom off to him, then joined me.

We left the ER and headed for James' room. James was awake when we walked in and looked alert but also very upset.

"Mr. Osgood?" I said, approaching the hospital bed.

"Yeah." His voice was barely a whisper.

"Sir, I'm Detective Kendrick, and this is Detective Reyes. I am very sorry about your loss."

He nodded, his eyes glassy as he murmured, "Thank you."

"We're working very hard to catch the person who did this to you and your wife. I was hoping you could tell me what you remember."

He swallowed and reached for the Styrofoam cup of water on the swivel table. "I tried to talk her out it."

"You tried to talk who out of what, Mr. Osgood?"

"Mariah. I tried to tell her what she was doing was wrong. That it was going to bring trouble, and we didn't need the money. She liked the thrill of it. Getting away with something. She always liked to push the envelope."

"So your wife knew she was selling stolen goods?"

He nodded slowly. "My wife was a lot of things, but she wasn't a bad person. She didn't think she was doing any real harm. Just getting one over on powerful corporations. She didn't see..." He trailed off. "Mariah grew up poor. She went to school, worked hard, got good grades, even got her degree in design, but when we got married, she dedicated herself to charity work. She said she wanted to help others who grew up in her situation. Then she got this idea to start her own online store. That was about three years ago. At first, she was legitimate. She bought inventory and sold it at a slight mark-up, but she wasn't making much money. I'm not sure when she started using stolen inventory."

"How did she get the stolen inventory?"

"A woman would bring it to the house. I didn't know about it until I met the woman at our house and asked Mariah about it. That's when I found out, and I asked her to stop. We argued about it, and she said—" He started to get upset, his chest heaving in grief.

"It's okay, Mr. Osgood, if you don't want to tell us about the argument right now." I kept my voice calm.

He shook his head. "It's okay; it's just...she said she was going to quit. She said she had already put in a few orders, so she would have to take them, but after that, she'd stop."

"Sir, I know this is hard, but can you tell us what happened the day you were shot?" Angel asked.

"Mariah and I were going to a charity event. I was supposed to come home and change, and then we were going to go together. When I got there, there was a car I didn't recognize in the driveway. I...I thought..." His voice broke, and he started sobbing. "I thought she was cheating on me."

His voice had been so low, so soft, I had to pause for a moment to realize what he'd said because it wasn't what I'd expected. "Wait, you thought she was cheating on you even though she knew you were coming home to meet her to go to a charity event?" The idea of an affair had been a scenario I'd floated at the scene, but I hadn't expected it to be accurate.

He nodded, looking miserable. "She's done it before. Had done it before. She likes...liked pushing boundaries."

"Okay, so you thought it was a man and she was cheating. What did you do?"

"I carry a gun, a .357 Magnum. I had it in the car, so I went in with it. I wouldn't have killed the guy, I just wanted to scare him, but what I walked in on..." His face crumpled, and he started sobbing again.

Angel and I exchanged a glance and gave him another moment to get himself back under control. It took a couple of minutes, but once he'd caught his breath again, Angel asked, "James, what did you see when you went inside?"

"I went up the stairs, calling for Mariah I think, I can't remember exactly, but...but when I got to the landing by the kitchen, I saw her. She was lying on the floor, there was blood, so much blood...and then...then a woman came from upstairs. She had her hands full of clothes." He shook his head and had a confused look for a moment. "I'm not sure what happened after that. I remember a bang and clothes flying at me, or maybe it was the other way around, the clothes flying at me and then a bang?"

"Do you remember firing your gun?" I asked.

"Did I?" Once again, he looked confused. "Did I hit her?"

"No, sir. We don't believe so. The bullet was lodged in the wall," Angel explained.

"Oh." His face fell. "She got away?"

"Yes, sir. Do you know who she is?" I asked.

"Did I not say? It was Lacy. At least that's what Mariah called her when she introduced her to me."

I held up the camera still we got from the hospital security cameras. "Sir, is this Lacy?"

He studied the eight-by-ten glossy image. "Yes, that's Lacy."

"Do you happen to know her last name?" Angel asked.

"No, I don't think I was ever told her last name." He continued to stare at the image. "Wait...was this taken here at the hospital?" He looked up, fear on his face. "Why was she here?"

"She has been here, and we've got an officer posted right outside your room now, so she won't be able to get to you."

His frightened gaze met mine. "She was going to try to kill me, wasn't she?" he asked, his voice low and scared.

"I won't sugarcoat it, she was, but we stopped her. She managed to get away, but we made sure you were okay and that you will still be safe while you're here," I explained, keeping my voice assuring and calm.

"Thank you."

"We'll let you rest, and once we find her, we'll let you know so you don't have to worry."

He nodded, but when the door opened and a nurse came in, he jumped as though he was ready to dive out of the bed and crawl under it.

"Oh, I'm sorry, I just came in to check Mr. Osgood's vitals. I can come back—" the nurse said, her eyes wide.

"It's okay; we were just getting ready to leave," I said, giving her a smile. I turned back to Mr. Osgood. "If you need anything or feel unsafe, just call out; the officer is right outside your door."

"Okay, thank you," he replied nervously.

Angel and I left the room. "Well, we have a first name to go with the image now," I said.

"Maybe we can get a hit on her. I wonder..." Angel started, and then stopped walking.

"What?"

"We should show this picture to Rice and Jackson."

"That's a great idea. Let's go."

36

KILLER IDENTITY CONFIRMED
MARCY

Saturday Afternoon

As soon as we reached the precinct, we headed straight to Robbery and Homicide. A lot of the kids patrol had managed to grab coming out of Splendor, no thanks to Hummel and Vance, were cuffed and seated with different R and H detectives, giving statements. Jill Rice was seated with a girl who looked to be about thirteen, and I just shook my head.

"You see Jackson?" Angel asked.

"He's not at his desk. Rice is though."

We headed over to her and waited for her to finish up with the girl, who looked scared to death.

Jill glanced over and saw us waiting for her and held up a finger.

I nodded.

She told the girl she was calling her parents, then picked

up the phone and dialed. The conversation went pretty much how I expected with the irate parents screaming at Jill over the phone.

Jill waved to one of the patrol officers. "She can go to holding. Her parents are on their way."

"Yes, ma'am." She gently gripped the girl's arm and helped her up. "Come with me."

As soon as they walked away, Jill stood. "I understand we have you two to thank for this chaos," she said wryly.

"Hey, this is on these little thieves, not us." I waved my hand in a circle encompassing the room.

She smiled. "So what's up? Have you caught your home invasion perp?"

"Not yet, but we have a first name and an image of her. Wanted to know if you recognize her."

"Let me take a look." She held her hand out for the photo. Taking it, she said, "What's the first name you've got?"

"Lacy."

Jill nodded slowly. "I know her face, and the name is ringing a bell...one second." She sat back down at her desk and started typing on her computer. She pulled up a record and then turned her screen toward us. "Lacy Miller. Twenty-six. Picked her up multiple times for shoplifting over the last ten years. Last time was about two years ago; she did six months for theft, let out on good behavior."

"Doesn't seem to have done her any good considering she escalated from shoplifting to murder," Angel replied.

"Yeah. If I remember right, the girl had a real temper and attitude, so how she managed good behavior, I don't know. Probably one of those overcrowding issues, and they just released her because at that point she wasn't violent," Jill said as she printed off the pertinent information for us.

"You could be right. Anyway, thanks for this information. We need to get a warrant and pick her up," I said, taking the papers she offered.

"Good luck."

With the information in hand, we returned to HSS and went to speak to Lieutenant Chenevert, but found he was with Captain Robinson in a meeting.

"They should be nearly finished up," Jason said as we stood in front of his desk. "I'll let the captain know you're out here waiting." He picked up the phone and spoke to the captain, then looked back at us. "He said to go on in."

Knocking on the captain's door, Angel stuck his head in. "Sir?"

"Come in, Reyes," Robinson called. "Are you making any headway with this case? Did the perp show at the store today?"

"No, sir, however, James Osgood was able to identify the suspect. At least he gave us a first name. We just checked in with R and H and got a full name and address. Lacy Miller. She's got several priors for shoplifting and did six months in jail. We need a warrant for her arrest."

"Great work, you two. I'll get that in for you," Robinson replied. "We were just discussing a complaint that came in from Splendor's store manager."

I dragged a hand through my hair and sighed. "It was complete chaos, sir. It seemed like more than seventy kids in black hoodies with those neck gaiter things covering their faces swarmed the place. Hummel and Vance were outside. Angel and I were inside. One of the kids had a gun and shot—"

"We've seen the surveillance videos; there was nothing else you could have done," Robinson said.

"I should have better supported you, had R and H there as well," Chenevert interjected.

"By the time the tip came in, it didn't give us a lot of time to coordinate things, so we went with what we had," I said. "Patrol did a good job of catching a lot of them coming out of the shop, and R and H is handling the processing." I wanted to complain about Hummel and Vance, but I didn't want to look petty.

"Well, just know that we'll be addressing it at a press conference this evening," Robinson said. "And I'll get that warrant in, but it could be Monday before we can get a judge to sign off on it."

I nodded. "Well, this is her address." I handed him the information that Jill had printed off for us. "I'd like to prevent her from going after anyone else before that warrant goes through, so I was thinking we could send a unit to stake out her apartment."

"I'll talk to Myers," Chenevert replied, "and we'll have someone there within the hour."

"Thank you, sirs."

"I'll let you know as soon as the judge signs off on it. Why don't the two of you take the rest of the afternoon and tomorrow off unless we get the call the warrant is active," Robinson suggested.

Angel and I headed back out to the detective pool, and he said, "You're sticking around town, right? Not heading to Santa Monica? I know Frank was shot, but he seemed to be doing okay, and if the judge—"

I held up my hand and stopped him. "I'm staying in LA until we close this. And yeah, Frank is okay."

We walked outside to the parking lot. "I'm glad. I'm sure

getting that call was scary. You should have called me, Marce. I'd have gone with you."

I nodded. "I know, but I just wanted to get there, you know?" I paused on the sidewalk. "He's thinking about quitting," I said softly.

"Quitting the force? Because he was shot?"

I shrugged. "I don't think he will, but I also think it's more than him being shot. I think it's everything. His brother, getting shot, the fact that criminals are just being put back on the streets after we catch them...he's tired."

"Can't say I blame him, but I would never have thought he'd quit."

"It's not a done deal. He's just feeling the stress. I told him we'd take a proper vacation after this case. He's looking up cruises." I smiled.

"Maybe all he needs is a break. A cruise will be fun. You looking at the Caribbean?"

I laughed. "No, Alaska."

"Oh wow, that's different. Cold."

"Yeah, probably will be, but it's what he wants to do."

"When are you thinking?"

"Honestly? Probably as soon as possible."

"Good to know. You know I've got that trip to Mexico with Callie in October, so by the time you get back, I'll probably be leaving."

"Well, we aren't going to be gone for a month and a half, Angel. A week or two at most." I laughed again. "Listen, I'm gonna head home. I'll talk to you tomorrow."

"Sure, see ya later."

Getting in my car, I called Frank. "Hey, I'm heading home. How are you feeling?"

"Worn out. Old," he said with a chuckle. "How's the case?"

"We've got a name. Hopefully, we'll be wrapping this up soon. Just waiting on a warrant to go through."

"Perfect. I've got another hour, but then I'll head over. Want me to bring anything for dinner?"

"Frank, you shouldn't be driving with your shoulder," I started.

"It's fine. Stafford was kind of pissed I showed up today, but I wanted to be here when they brought in the suspect on the triple homicide. We got him. I'm working on my part of the report, which is why I'm still here."

"So you're going to pack a bag and stay here?" I questioned.

"That's my plan unless you don't want me?"

"Of course I want you. Every day I want you, don't ever doubt that."

"Good, because I want you too. I'll see you tonight."

"Frank?"

"Yeah?"

"I love you."

"Love you too, TT. See you soon."

MONDAY MORNING AT 8 A.M., as I was sitting at my desk, Lieutenant Chenevert came racing down the hall. "We've got it!" He waved some paperwork above his head.

"Finally!" I said, standing up.

Now it was just a matter of time before we ran Lacy to ground, and I couldn't wait. The sooner we caught her, the sooner I could take some time off with Frank.

37

A PLAN IN PLACE
MARCY

Monday Morning

In case Lacy had gone to her parents' house to hide, we decided to check there first. If that didn't work, then MacHenry was our next visit. He might have something from the website. I drove to the Millers' house in Inglewood. We knocked on the door and surprised the older couple who resided there.

"Mr. and Mrs. Miller?" I asked, hoping they hadn't moved from the listed address.

"Yes, who are you?" the gentleman answered.

I held up my badge. "I'm Detective Kendrick; this is my partner, Detective Reyes. We're looking for your daughter, Lacy Miller?"

He shook his head. "I'm sorry, Detectives, but we haven't seen Lacy in about five years."

"Might we come in and speak with you about her anyway?"

He opened the door wider. "Of course, come in." He directed us to a small living room and gestured to the sofa. "Please sit."

"Thank you," I said, sitting next to Angel.

"What has that girl done now?" Mrs. Miller asked in exasperation.

"I'm not at liberty to say, but we really need to find her."

She shook her head. "You tried her apartment?"

"Yes, ma'am. We've had someone watching for her. She's not been there all weekend," Angel said. "What can you tell us about Lacy? Why haven't you seen her in five years?"

"Look, Lacy has always been difficult," Mr. Miller explained. "Always in trouble, stealing, lying, fighting. She's got anger issues. We tried to get her help, but she wouldn't cooperate. She dropped out of school her sophomore year of high school, ran away from home so many times. We did what we could for her until she turned eighteen, but after that...well..."

"She's a smart girl, our Lacy, but not in a good way. She's manipulative, and when we told her we wouldn't play her games anymore, she left and didn't look back," Mrs. Miller added.

"She struggled keeping a regular job because she continuously got angry about things that were not in her control. If things weren't going her way, she'd take what she wanted and then get fired," Mr. Miller continued.

"Do you think she's dangerous?" Angel asked.

"She does have a temper, and if she were backed into a corner...yes, she's capable of hurting someone in the heat of the moment," Mr. Miller replied.

"Has she?" Mrs. Miller asked quietly.

Seeing as they hadn't seen her in five years and they didn't seem to be lying about that, I said, "It's possible that she did, but we need to find her and talk to her to be sure."

"If you hear from her, would you let us know?" Angel asked, offering them our card.

"Yes, of course."

We left and got back into the car. Angel had driven today, so I was in the passenger seat. "Well, that was a bust."

"At least we ruled their place out. Let's go see if MacHenry has anything. I've got an idea, but I don't know if it's plausible, so we may need to check with Rice and Jackson again."

"Oh yeah? What are you thinking?" I questioned.

"Let's talk to MacHenry, and then I'll tell you."

"Cryptic. Okay."

An hour later we were standing in the Tech department. I was looking at the website on the screen as MacHenry pointed out the latest addition to the website that Stephen had discovered. "What does she think she is? Discount Walmart?"

"She has expanded into just about everything, hasn't she?" He shrugged. "You gotta admire her entrepreneurship. This was a great find by your brother, by the way."

"It was, but really? She's stealing from others to make a profit for herself. She's nothing more than a murderer and a glorified fence," I replied.

"Still. Take a look at this." He pointed at a high-end 4K home theater projector. "This projector is only sold in one place here in LA. Chapman's."

I stared at the screen. "Does that say fifteen thousand dollars?" I gasped. "Is she delusional?"

"To be fair, that projector sells for almost twenty-five thousand."

My jaw dropped. "No way."

MacHenry nodded. "Absolutely. There's several other things on here that are pretty pricey too, but that projector tipped me off that it and probably the rest of these electronics came from Chapman's. I know they've been hit a couple of times now."

"Mac, you just saved us a trip up to R and H," Angel said with a grin.

"What did I do?"

"I've got an idea, and I was going to ask Jackson or Rice if certain stores were getting repeatedly hit by the same crew like Carlos suggested when we talked to him about his own trouble with these shoplifting crews. I think you just answered that for me."

I looked at Angel and asked, "So do you think they'll hit Chapman's again?"

"Why wouldn't they?"

"So what do you want to do? Stake them out and hope Lacy shows up?"

"Not exactly." He grinned. "Mac, do you think you can make tracking devices that can be inserted into some of these electronics?"

MacHenry pushed his glasses up and nodded. "A challenge I live for."

"Whoa, wait a minute," I said.

"What's wrong?" Angel asked, frowning.

"First, we need to clear this with the lieutenant and the captain because it sounds expensive. Second, we need to talk to the owner of Chapman's and see if they're even willing to allow us to do this."

Both of them deflated like party balloons losing their helium.

"I'm not saying we can't do it, but we need to get approval first."

"Yeah, okay," Angel agreed eventually.

"Tell you what, I can start working on a design, and once you have approval, I'll start making them," Mac suggested.

"That's fine, but no actual materials until we get approval." I stared at him until he nodded. "Good. Now let's go talk to the bosses."

38

TRACKING THE GREEN DOTS
MARCY

Monday Afternoon

"Do y'all think this plan will work?" Chenevert asked, looking skeptical.

"I do, sir," Angel said adamantly. "She's already sold out of a couple of the stereos, TVs, and computers that she was advertising. If I were an unknowing consumer, I'd be buying from her because her prices are well below market value. She's going to want to keep that profit coming in, which means she's going to hit the store again. If we can get trackers in some of the products she takes, we can follow them back to wherever she is."

Chenevert rubbed his jaw. "Okay, talk to the store owner. See if he'd be willing to work with us in whatever capacity we need while I run this by the captain. I don't want to authorize this expense without his approval. I'll let you know what he says, and then, assuming the store owner agrees, you can have the Tech team make what you need."

"Thank you, sir." There was way too much excitement in Angel's voice. He was like a little kid making Christmas plans.

"I'll give the store owner a call," I said before we left Chenevert's office.

Angel said, "I'm gonna go check in with MacHenry, see if he's got a plan."

Rolling my eyes, I said, "Fine. But don't build anything until we have approval."

"Yeah, okay."

At my desk, I looked up Chapman's store number and then called.

"Chapman's Electronics, this is Amanda; how may I help you today?"

"Good afternoon, this is Detective Marcy Kendrick with the LAPD. I was hoping to speak with your store owner?"

"Oh, yes, of course," the young woman replied. "I'm going to put you on hold; it'll be just a minute."

"Thank you." I waited, listening to the classical music that played over the line. It was actually relaxing, and I didn't mind it, unlike some of the other hold music I'd had to listen to over the years.

"Detective? This is Alex Chapman; what is this about?"

"Good afternoon, Mr. Chapman, I was calling because in the course of an investigation I'm conducting, your store has come up."

I went on to explain how he was connected, and he admitted that his shop had been hit twice now, losing him nearly five hundred thousand dollars in merchandise.

Hearing that, I was pretty confident that he'd agree to what I was asking.

"If you have a way to stop these mobs, I am more than willing to help in whatever way I can, Detective."

"That's great, sir. So we would like to install tracking devices into some particular items. I promise it won't compromise the actual electronics, but it will allow us to follow them to whoever is behind all of this."

He was quiet for a minute and then said, "Very well, Detective. When would you like to do this?"

"What time do you close today, sir?"

"At eight."

"Would it be possible for us to install everything after you close?"

"Yes, I can arrange that. But what about my paying customers? What if one of them buys one of the units you've tracked?"

"We'll come up with a way for your associates to know which ones have the trackers. I need to go and make sure we'll be ready to do this tonight."

"I'll see you this evening, Detective."

After hanging up with him, I hurried to the Tech department. "We've got the shop owner's agreement; did Chenevert get approval?"

"Yep. We were just waiting for you to get the shop owner's approval," Angel said with a grin.

"Can we have these ready to go in"—I looked at my watch—"four and a half hours?" That would give us an hour before Chapman's closed to get there.

MacHenry looked over at his commander, who said, "We can probably get about ten made in that time with the whole team working on it."

. . .

ANGEL, MacHenry and I pulled up to Chapman's Electronics at 7:53 p.m. The devices the Tech team had come up with were about the size of my pinkie nail.

When we entered the shop, I held up my badge and asked for Chapman.

"Detectives, let me get this place closed, and then we can help you find the items to put those trackers in," he said.

It only took us an hour to get all the trackers installed. "So, we've resealed all the boxes, and we've put little green dots on the boxes with the tracked products in them." I pointed out the tiny dot next to the sticker with the UPC code. "We've put them in the same place on all of the boxes, so you don't have to search too hard for it."

"I'll show my staff and make sure they know to look for those dots before selling anything." He frowned. "What happens if they don't show before I run out of products and need to sell these?"

"You saw how easily we installed them; if you need to sell one, find an excuse to open the box and remove the tracker before you do."

"Do you want me to put it into a different electronic if that happens?"

"With nine others, I think we'll be okay, just hold onto it for us, and we'll collect it if that occurs."

"Very well. How are you going to track it? Do you need to wait in a van in the parking lot or what?"

MacHenry shook his head. "No, it will relay off of cell towers, and I can track them with this." He held up a small handheld computer. "It's a bit like that Life360 app."

We stayed for a few more minutes and then left for the night.

THE NEXT TWO days we waited on pins and needles for Lacy to send her crew to the store to grab more merchandise. The waiting had been stressful, and the only thing that broke up those days of sitting at my desk waiting to find out if she'd gone for it was having lunch with Katrina and Lindsey. They only knew each other because of me, but had become friends as well, so it had been a nice day of catching up for the three of us.

By Thursday, I was afraid that we'd made a mistake, that she'd decided to hit another shop instead. I was close to pulling the plug on the plan when MacHenry came jogging toward my desk, a big grin on his lips.

"They're on the move," he said, waving his little hand-held machine.

"It worked?" I asked, almost surprised.

"Did you doubt it would?" MacHenry looked crestfallen.

"I never doubted your trackers would work, I doubted she'd hit Chapman's again," I said as my phone rang. I picked it up and said, "Kendrick."

"Detective? It's Alex Chapman. They were just here, about forty of them. They took damn near everything that wasn't behind glass."

"Thanks for calling, Mr. Chapman. I can tell you that we have confirmation that the trackers are working. We'll do our best to get your product back to you soon, and officers are en route to pick up the surveillance footage and dust for prints."

"I appreciate that, Detective. Good luck."

I hung up and looked between Angel and MacHenry, who were watching the trackers on the handheld. "Do we have a destination yet?" I asked as I texted Lindsey to head to Chapman's with her team.

"Well, they're in multiple moving vehicles at the moment. They all seem to be heading in the same direction though," MacHenry replied.

"I just filled Lindsey in, so I'm going to let Chenevert know. Get a plan in place to head out once they reach their destination." I strode down the hall to his office. "Sir? The crew hit Chapman's. MacHenry is following the trackers now."

"As soon as y'all've got an address, I'll get the search warrant filled in, and I've already got Judge Harris ready to sign off on it no matter what time it is," Chenevert replied. "I'll give Myers a heads-up as well and have patrol on standby."

"Thank you, sir."

With so many moving parts in this plan, I was once again glad to have not only a competent lieutenant, but one who was a team player as well.

I thought back to the conversation I'd had with him when I attempted to turn in my weapon after shooting the Washington kid. He'd looked at me like I'd grown two heads for being worried about it. He'd made me sit down while he called IA, sent the surveillance tapes to them immediately, and then informed them since it was obviously a clean shoot, I was keeping my weapon and going back to work.

I'd been shocked, to say the least. I'd expected to have to use my backup for at least a week, but I hadn't even been without my service weapon for a half an hour. For me that was unheard of. Of course, Chenevert had said the only reason he was able to do that was because the tapes were pretty clear, but then he'd added that he'd always have my back with the Brass as long as it was a justified shot. He wasn't a back the blue no matter who, but he'd always back a good cop. I didn't know if he knew how much that meant to me, but I was grateful to have him as our new lieutenant, and because he had my back, I'd have his.

I headed back to Angel and MacHenry, who were standing in front of our desks, watching the handheld machine like they were watching the best baseball game on TV. "Do we have an address yet?"

"Not yet, they've converged on one spot though, and I used Google Earth to check it out, but it's an abandoned lot. I think they're transferring the electronics into one vehicle."

"That makes sense. I mean, if I were her, I wouldn't want the crew to know where it ends up," I suggested. "She probably has some kids she trusts who help her move the product out though, so she's most likely not alone wherever this stuff ends up."

"You could be right. Let's give it some time, see if it moves."

"Sounds good. I'm going out to the Lobsta truck; either of you want anything?" I asked.

"I'll take a crab roll and chips," MacHenry said.

"Get me the Lobsta roll and a whoopie pie," Angel added, pulling out his wallet.

I waved him off. "I got it."

Twenty minutes later I rejoined them with the food. "Any movement?"

"Yeah, they're on the road again. Just waiting to see where they end up," MacHenry replied.

The three of us ate as we watched the little beeps move

on the handheld machine. I was cleaning up when Angel said, "I think they stopped."

"Let me Google Earth it again," MacHenry said, tapping on the screen. A moment later, he said, "Bingo. We've got it. It's a storage warehouse in East LA. One of those rental places with climate control."

"Got an address?" I said, poised to write it down.

MacHenry rattled it off, and I took it straight to Chenevert so he could get us the warrant.

39

STANDOFF AT A STORAGE WAREHOUSE

MARCY

Thursday Afternoon

This time, not only did Chenevert send us out with patrol for backup, but he'd also arranged with Robbery and Homicide to send several of their detectives to help with the scene. We didn't know what we'd be walking into, and technically, the shoplifting part of this case was theirs. They were better equipped to deal with the stolen merchandise and the stores it belonged to.

I was the lead, and everyone was going to take their cues from me. We'd viewed the warehouse, which wasn't huge and was one of several on the property, to determine the points of entry. It was surprising how much detail we could get from Google Earth.

In the briefing room, we'd met and coordinated with Jackson and Rice from Robbery and Homicide as well as Carter and Sands from our department and several patrol officers. I had decided that Jackson and Rice would go in the front, followed by Simon Carter and Oliver Sands, who would hang back in case anyone tried to escape, while Angel and I went in the back. I'd ordered everyone to wear a vest, just in case. Patrol was split between all three teams. It might have been heavy handed, but considering how violent this woman had gotten, I didn't want to take any chances.

"Keep your eyes and ears open," I said before we all headed out. "Listen for my signal; we're going in quiet. No sirens. I don't want to give them a heads-up that we're there."

"Yes, ma'am," was chorused through the room.

We rolled out, and as I drove, I said, "I'm glad it's Carter and Sands with us and not Hummel and Vance."

Angel snickered. "Yeah, they'll be lucky not to be busted down to traffic duty after that mess at Splendor. Street cameras showed them down the block, out of place when the store was hit. I heard Chenevert dragging them for it."

I glanced at him, my jaw dropping. "And you didn't tell me sooner?"

"Got distracted. It's not like I'm friends with them or keep track of them."

We reached the property and slowly crept our vehicles into place around the right warehouse. Angel and I got out and joined the four patrol officers who were on our team near the back door. We waited a couple of minutes to give everyone a chance to get into position.

"Move in," I said into my radio.

Angel and I moved toward the back door, and we heard Jackson shout, "LAPD! Freeze!"

Within seconds there was a volley of gunfire and screaming.

"Shit, get the door open," I shouted at Officer Garcia.

He popped the lock on the door and yanked it open as Angel and I stormed in. Inside, multiple teens with guns were shooting at Jackson and Rice as well as the patrol officers with them, while others were running for cover or trying to escape.

I scanned the chaotic scene for Lacy Miller. I didn't see her anywhere, and I was worried that we'd somehow missed her when Braun shouted. I spun around and saw her running out the door. "Shit!" I took off after her.

Lacy swung her arm back and fired off a couple of rounds without looking as she flew through the door, and I had to throw myself to the side to avoid being hit. It didn't stop me from chasing after her, though. I worried about those bullets and where they went. The large warehouse was in complete chaos, and more shots were being fired from both the LAPD and Lacy's crew.

I glanced back to see Braun and Garcia were following me. They looked okay, and I could hear them panting just behind me. I hoped Angel wasn't far behind either.

"Lacy Miller, you are under arrest!" I shouted, seeing her rounding one of the other buildings.

She skidded to a stop, spun, and started to raise her weapon, a Glock from what it looked like to me, but she was still a short distance ahead of me, and I couldn't be sure yet. "Fuck!" she shouted, sounding panicked as she looked for an escape.

Raising my own weapon, I screamed, "Drop it!" as I continued to rush forward, my gun trained on her torso.

Her eyes widened, and a second later she must have realized how close she was to dying because she dropped the gun and held up her hands. "Fucking bitch!" she yelled. "Why do you have to ruin everythin'?"

I finally reached her and kicked her gun away, then grabbed her hand, spinning her around. "Lacy Miller, you are under arrest," I said, putting the cuffs on her hands. "You have the right to remain silent—"

"Fuck you, bitch," she spat at me.

I could hear shots still being fired, but I had to believe that we were making headway. I kept my eyes on her, and once Lacy was in cuffs, I passed her on to Garcia and Braun. "Finish reading her rights to her," I directed.

Angel was about a foot away, his gun still out but pointed at the ground, and I knew he'd had me covered.

We turned and went back toward the warehouse, re-entering through the back door. I noticed several of the teens were now disarmed and on their knees, their hands cuffed behind their backs. Several officers stood guard as their partners cuffed the teens, keeping them safe from the teens still on the loose. Moving deeper into the room, Angel and I started toward a couple of armed teens who had their backs to us and were aiming at the officers in front of them. The two of them popped off a few shots; they seemed to be aiming low because they hit the boxes on the ground between our officers. It looked as though they were trying not to hit anyone with their shots, but that could change at any second.

I signaled Jackson what we were doing. He acknowledged me with a slight nod, but held his position, his gun trained on the teens as well, watching their hands and how they were aiming their weapons in a downward trajectory. I knew he'd be ready if they decided to really aim at them.

My heart was racing as we crept up behind the two. "Drop it," I said, pushing my weapon into the back of one of the teens while Angel did the same to the other.

Seconds later Officer Carmichael was putting cuffs on one while his partner, Lloyd, was cuffing the other. They carted them backwards as they read them their rights, taking them out the back of the warehouse toward their patrol cars.

I scanned the room and breathed a sigh of relief as the last of the shooters were rounded up. "Scene clear," I said into my radio. "Send in the medics."

"Yes, ma'am," I heard in response.

"Anyone injured?" I shouted, my voice echoing around the room as Angel and I moved to the center of the warehouse.

Jill and Keith joined us, and then Carter and Sands entered the room and headed for us too.

Jill holstered her weapon and said, "Bruised, I'm sure; took one to the chest." She poked at the hole in her vest.

"Damn, that has to hurt," Angel said, looking at her with concern.

"Go get seen," I directed, knowing that Chenevert had a couple of ambulance crews on standby for us as well. "The EMTs should be here now."

She nodded and shared a pointed look with Keith, then headed for the door.

"You good?" I asked, looking at him. Then I noticed blood on his sleeve. "Are you kidding me right now? Go."

He gave me a cocky grin and said, "It's nothing. A scratch. Besides, look at this place. It's going to take us hours to get all this wrapped up."

"Go. I'll get Chenevert to send another team."

"But—"

I just gave him a look, and he finally gave in.

Angel snickered, but not loud enough for Jackson to hear him, thankfully.

I looked over to Carter and Sands. "What about you two?"

"We caught the ones fleeing; none of them had weapons on them," Carter replied.

"Good to know."

"What now?" Sands asked.

"Now I call Chenevert, and we get CSI here along with another R and H team. Once they arrive, we start getting names and start sending them to the station."

For the next hour we all began to question the various teens. Jill returned after being seen by a medic; she had been right and was merely bruised. Keith, on the other hand, wasn't just scratched, much to his displeasure. He'd had to be taken to the hospital because he'd needed a small-caliber bullet removed and stitches to close his wound.

Finishing with the last teenager, a girl named Sarah who was only fourteen years old, I pulled out my phone to text Frank.

> Hey, wrapping up the scene and heading back to the precinct to interview our suspect. It might be a late night.

Frank was hanging out at my place, and this morning he'd mentioned fixing us steaks for tonight, but I didn't want him to start anything when I didn't know when I'd get home.

> Everyone safe?

He sent back a minute later.

> We're all good. Love you.

He immediately texted me back, and I smiled.

> Love you too, babe. Glad everyone's good
> and you caught your suspect. Alaska, here
> we come.

> Can't wait.

I replied and then pocketed my phone and got in the car.

"Ready to go speak to our suspect?" I said, turning the car on.

Angel looked up from his phone and nodded. "Yep. Just letting Callie know I'm okay."

Leaving the scene, I started counting down the minutes until I could be on that cruise with Frank.

40

OPPRESSED

MARCY

Thursday Evening

By the time we reached the precinct, it was nearly seven p.m. I was anxious to speak to Lacy and close this case, but the captain asked us to wait. Lacy had spent the last couple of hours being belligerent and fighting anyone who came near her, so they'd put her in a holding cell.

"She can cool her heels until morning. We can hold her for a couple of days before we charge her, so we have time. Besides, I want to have every ounce of evidence against her before we go at her."

I sighed. "Yes, sir."

"Cheer up, Kendrick. You've caught her. The hard work is done." Robinson smiled. "Good work, by the way. Both of you."

"Thank you, sir." Angel nodded.

"I'm just glad nobody else was murdered before we caught her," I said.

"Go home and get some rest, Kendrick. You too, Reyes."

"Sir, before I leave, can I talk to you for a moment?"

"Sure, what's up, Kendrick?"

"Well, sir, now that this case is basically wrapped up, I wanted to let you know that I'm going to be putting in for some vacation time. Frank wants to take a cruise."

Robinson nodded. "How's he doing?"

"Physically, he's doing okay. I think he really needs to take a break, so this time off will be good for him."

"Getting away from here is probably wise. Let me know when, and I'll make sure you get that time off."

"Thank you, sir." I was glad to have gotten approval for the time off. Even though I loved my job, I probably needed a vacation as much as Frank did. Knowing it was going to happen soon had me feeling less burdened than usual.

I headed home and surprised Frank, who was happy to see me. Together we grilled out and then sat and watched the ballgame together before falling into bed and making love until way too late. I fell asleep with my head on the good side of his chest and his good arm wrapped around me.

FRIDAY MORNING I dressed and had coffee with Frank before going back to the station for our interview with Lacy. I was nervous because I knew that Chenevert and Robinson would be watching, though I shouldn't have been. It wasn't anything I hadn't done a million times before. It would just be the second one I'd done with Chenevert watching, and I didn't want to disappoint him. The first one hadn't really counted in my mind because he'd been out searching for a VCR for a lot of that interview.

"You okay?" Angel asked, looking at me as we waited for word that she was being brought over.

I wiped my sweaty palms on my pants. "Yeah, I'm good." And then I met his gaze and bit my bottom lip. "Okay, I'm a little nervous about the lieutenant watching this interview." I rolled my eyes, knowing I was being ridiculous.

"Why? You're great at these. He's going to be impressed."

I wrinkled my nose and felt my cheeks flush. "You think?"

"I know. Stop worrying." He chuckled as he rolled his chair over next to me and leaned in to whisper, "Keep it up and Hummel will accuse you of having a crush on the new lieutenant."

I felt my eye twitch at the thought that I was giving Hummel any ammunition to use against me. "Right." I gave him a sharp nod.

Angel's phone rang, and he rolled back over to answer it. "Okay, thanks," he said after a few moments and then stood up as he dropped the phone back in the cradle. "We're up."

I picked up the file folders I had on the case, and we walked to the interview room. Opening the door, I noticed Lacy in an orange jumpsuit, her hands and ankles cuffed, a chain threaded through them and attached to the table like she was dangerous. Despite her slumped posture, I knew she actually was dangerous and deserved having those cuffs on her.

Next to her sat a pale man with thinning gray hair in a blue suit that didn't look as though it was made for him; a brown briefcase sat in front of him on the table. I didn't recognize her lawyer. Not that I knew every lawyer in LA, because of course I didn't, but we did tend to see many of them repeatedly.

"Good morning, I'm Detective Kendrick, this is Detective Reyes, and you are?" I asked the man.

"David Howell. Public Defender." He raised a hand for me to shake.

Angel and I sat down across the table from them. I nodded at Angel.

He reached over and pushed a button. "Friday, September 6, 9:42 a.m., interview with Lacy Miller. In the room with Lacy Miller is myself, Detective Angel Reyes—"

"Detective Marcy Kendrick," I said and then nodded at Mr. Howell.

"And David Howell, lawyer for Ms. Miller."

"Thank you," I acknowledged. "Ms. Miller, do you know why you've been arrested?"

"Some shit about murderin' those bitches. It wasn't my fault. This whole thing is rigged. You're just a couple a racist cops, pinnin' shit on me."

I narrowed my eyes at her. "Ms. Miller, we have an eyewitness. One you tried to murder, twice."

She sucked her teeth. "Bullshit. That's what this is. You only came after me because that's what you all do. Always oppressin' me and my people. Never lettin' nobody but your own get ahead. I was just doin' what I had to, to get by. You ain't got nothin' on me."

"Ms. Miller," I pulled a photo of the Glock from the folder, "when I arrested you yesterday, you had this weapon on you, didn't you? For the recording, I'm showing Ms. Miller a photo of the weapon that she had been holding at the scene when we arrested her."

She shrugged. "Don't know, it's just a photo. That's not

proof of nothin'," she muttered, then looked at her lawyer. "What are you even here for? You ain't stoppin' them from sayin' shit."

"Ms. Miller, I'm here to make sure your rights aren't violated. So far, they haven't been."

She rolled her eyes. "Useless," she muttered again.

I could see she was close to breaking, to giving me a confession. I hadn't expected it to happen so early in the interview, but I could see in her eyes that she wanted to brag. Lacy wanted to tell me because despite her claims of being oppressed, she was proud of what she'd done. I just needed to push her a little bit further.

"Ms. Miller, your prints are on this weapon. Not only that, they are also on the bullets in the weapon, and the striations from the gun match those on the bullets recovered from the bodies of Helena Richards, Mariah Osgood, and Bella Jones. Do you have anything to say about that?"

"All three of 'em got what they deserved! Fuckin' bitches payin' us nothin' when we did all the fuckin' work. We were the ones takin' all the risk while they lived their princess lives and ordered me around like I was some kinda servant. I was sick of it. They didn't deserve any of that shit. They didn't work for it. I did. I had to work for everythin'. I deserve to live that privileged life, not them," she ranted.

The switch had been flipped, and she was now doing exactly what I expected she'd do when I saw that look in her eyes a minute ago. I was cheering inside, but I kept that feeling buttoned up as I watched her lawyer. He'd been trying to get her attention and shut her up, unsuccessfully, thankfully, but he could still succeed.

Eventually Mr. Howell shouted, "Ms. Miller, please be

quiet!" and slammed his hands down on the table, making it rattle.

She jerked in her chair and stared daggers at him. "You don't fuckin' tell me what to do! Nobody fuckin' tells me what to do!"

This whole thing was going to be much easier than I'd imagined. Her temper and disgust of us had her saying things she would be better off not saying. It was also causing her not to listen to the lawyer who had been appointed to her. I didn't want to get too giddy though and have her shut down before we were finished. Just because I'd pushed the right buttons didn't mean she wouldn't walk it back. I needed her to keep sharing and not listening to counsel.

"Ms. Miller, what do you mean by you were taking all the risk? Can you explain that to me? I just want to understand what kind of risk you had to take."

Her glare was hateful, but she didn't hold back. "We were the ones gatherin' their stupid orders. Millions of dollars' worth of product, and they was givin' us a few hundred. Who the fuck did they think they were? Fuckin' cunts stayed safe in their fuckin' houses when some of my crew can't even find beds for the night. And that lyin' bitch ass Bella runnin' off to Reno every weekend, fuckin' stole from us, didn't even bother to pay us for the last two jobs!"

"I know Bella was the third one; did they all stop paying you? Is that why you went after them?" I asked.

Angel stayed quiet at my side, just listening. We hadn't planned this out, but she was giving us everything, and neither of us were about to stop her.

"No, what do you think, we're a bunch of fuckin' whiny bitches? I couldn't let them disrespect us like that. Nobody disrespects my crew. I didn't even plan to shoot Helena like that. She grabbed the gun. And I wasn't 'bout to leave without gettin' what I came for."

"What about Mariah Osgood? Did she disrespect you and your crew?"

"Fuckin' bitch is the reason Walrus got shot. It was her shit they were jackin' when that motherfucker shot him. More I thought 'bout it, the more I figured she deserved it. She acted all haughty, like we were beneath her. Her and that nobody she was fuckin' married to. Always ignorin' me when I was around, actin' like his shit didn't stink same as everyone's."

"So did she also try to grab the gun from you? Is that what happened?"

"No, she didn't even see it comin'. Blasted her in the kitchen." Lacy laughed. "Shoulda seen her face." She laughed again like it was all a big joke.

I smiled, pretending I found it amusing as well, when all I wanted to do was get out of there and away from the clearly insane woman seated across from me.

"Ms. Miller, I am advising you to stop talking," Mr. Howell reiterated, looking desperate.

I couldn't blame him. His best bet would be to get her to plead guilty and hope she didn't end up with the death penalty. California had a moratorium on the death penalty currently, but that didn't mean it wouldn't be enforced again when or if the new governor got into office.

"Oh, shut up. I'll say whatever I want!" she screamed at him.

"And what about Mr. Osgood? You shot him as well. How did that happen?"

"Fucker came home early. He walked in yellin' for Mariah. He was wavin' that fuckin' gun around, threatenin' me, and I shot him before he could shoot me. 'Sides, he saw me, knew I'd killed his fuckin' wife."

"I see. And did you think you'd killed him?"

"Well, yeah, I shot the fucker in the head; he looked dead." She shrugged. "He shoulda just died."

"Were you aware Mrs. Osgood was pregnant when you shot her?" I asked, wondering if that would even make a dent in her story.

"Who the fuck cares?" She shrugged as if I'd just told her the circus was coming to town.

I went on with my questions. "Did anyone on your crew know you had killed them?" I wanted to see if there was anyone we could charge as an accessory or an accessory after the fact.

"Duh, they knew when I had them start helpin' with fillin' orders."

"What about before you did it? Did you tell anyone what you were planning?"

"Just Moxie, she's my girl."

"Is there anything else you'd like to share, Ms. Miller?"

"I'd do it all again if I could, maybe make sure the fuck-er'd died though."

"So you don't regret killing them to fuel your ambition?"

"No. Why would I?" She smirked once again.

I could see that there was no humanity in her; she was mentally deranged. We'd probably have to have a psych eval done on her before she could stand trial, but I absolutely believed that she knew exactly what she was doing and just didn't care. To her Helena, Mariah and Bella were just bugs beneath her sneaker. Something to be squished and discarded.

"Interview with Lacy Miller ending at 10:21 a.m.," I said

and nodded at Angel. "Lacy Miller, I am formally arresting you for the first-degree murders of Helena Richards, Mariah Osgood, the unborn Osgood child, and Bella Jones, as well as the attempted murder of James Osgood." I raised my hand to signal the officer outside the door to come and get her.

Mr. Howell sighed. "I'll be in touch, Ms. Miller. I'll do what I can for you."

"Fuck off," Lacy said, glaring at him as she was led away.

"She's not of sound mind. I'm ordering a psychiatric evaluation—" he began.

I held my hand up, stopping him. "You do that. I've seen enough serial killers to know when I've sat across from one. She's not crazy, not like you think. She's a narcissistic sociopath, but she is not incapable of standing trial. She knows right from wrong, but chose to commit crimes anyway for her own reasons, as she explained during the interview."

"You're not a psychiatrist; you can't—"

"You're right, I'm not, but again, I've met enough people like her to know what she is, so get your psych eval, and we'll have our own done. I'll see you in court."

41

ESCAPING TO ALASKA
MARCY

Three weeks later
Friday

I put on my black skirt, lavender blouse, and black blazer, then slid my feet into low black heels. I was headed to court again for the third day of Lacy Miller's trial. She'd decided to plead not guilty despite her lawyer telling her it wasn't a good idea. She'd gone through two psychological evaluations, and both psychiatrists had come to the same conclusion. She was a narcissistic sociopath. She had no remorse for what she'd done, no regard for the law or any social mores and was extremely violent and aggressive.

"Do you think they'll put you on the stand?" Frank asked.

"If they're going to, they'd better do it today." I smiled. I wasn't sure that they would, but the prosecution would be wrapping up their case today, and I had been told I needed to be there just in case.

"You sure you're okay with not sticking around town to hear the verdict?" he asked, coming up behind me and wrapping his arms around my middle.

"If it doesn't wrap today, I'm fine with it. She's going to be found guilty, I have no doubt. And I'm not missing this cruise with you." I turned in his arms and kissed him. "Tomorrow morning we fly out of LAX and land in Anchorage, and I'm not missing a second of it."

"Two whole weeks of nothing but you and me and glaciers, wildlife, and exploration. I can't wait."

I kissed him again. "I've got to go. You're checking our itinerary, making sure we've got everything packed that we need, right?"

"Stop worrying. I promise we'll have everything ready to go before we go to bed tonight."

I nodded and started for the door. "Oh, and you're going to touch base with Stephen, right? Make sure he's going to keep an eye on my place?"

"Yes, go." He laughed and shooed me out the door.

I headed for the car and drove off with a wave. I was picking Angel up, and we were going to the courthouse together. It didn't take me long to get to his place and honk for him. He jogged out to my car and got in.

"Morning," he said as he buckled his seatbelt. "One more day, right?"

I nodded. "I can't believe it's tomorrow, but I'm so looking forward to it. I don't think I've ever taken two straight weeks off of work. I'm not sure I'm going to know how to handle it." I laughed.

"Well, you're going to be missed, I can tell you that. Chenevert is probably gonna put me with Hummel and Vance." He made a face of disgust.

My laughter grew. "Well, they need all the help they can get."

"Just you wait; when I'm down in Mexico with Callie, you'll be with them."

"Oh, heck no. Maybe I won't come back...I'll just take a whole month," I teased.

"I can't believe I'm not going to see you for a whole month; it's going to be weird."

"Yeah, but a good weird. And it's not like you aren't going to get a bazillion texts with pictures of everything we see. I expect the same from you and Callie on your trip."

"True." He smiled. "Oh, did you hear? The DA got a conviction on Carlos Renaldo for aggravated assault with a deadly weapon and battery, as well as for receiving stolen goods. He was sentenced to ten years and has to pay a $150,000 fine."

"What's going to happen to his stores?" I asked, wondering if he actually had anyone to watch over them while he was incarcerated.

Angel shrugged. "No idea. He's married though, so maybe the wife is going to take care of them."

I pulled into the courthouse parking lot and found a spot; then we went in. We took seats right behind the district attorney who was prosecuting the case. Lacy wasn't there yet, but her public defender was. He looked just as disheveled as he had in her interview, but somehow, he seemed more harried and disorganized than he had before.

Lacy was brought in, walking between two guards, her hands cuffed, but she was wearing a nice outfit instead of the orange jumpsuit: a pair of black pants and a red top. She glared at me as she passed me and Angel and then took her seat.

When the judge was announced and we were all told to rise, she remained seated. He was not happy, and I had no doubt he was going to hold that against her. The DA got started; he called James to the stand and got his account of what had happened at his house. Lacy's attorney objected a couple of times, but the judge overruled it.

Then the DA called Samantha Greenley. She walked in, and Lacy lost her composure, her anger blasting through the courtroom as she screamed at her, "How fuckin' dare you, Moxie? How could you go against me, you fuckin' bitch? You're dead!"

Judge McNiel banged his gavel on the desk multiple times, calling for order, then said, "Mr. Howell, if you cannot control your client, then she will be removed from the courtroom, and we will have this trial without her here." His voice was harsh and stern.

"I'm sorry, Your Honor," he said and then turned to Lacy, whispering to her.

Lacy threw herself petulantly back into her seat and glared at the witness stand, where Ms. Greenley was now sitting. She was sworn in, putting her hand on the Bible, and agreeing to tell the truth, the whole truth and nothing but the truth.

Lacy slid her finger across her neck, and Judge McNiel banged his gavel again.

"Mr. Howell, please explain to your client that her actions are leading me to add witness intimidation and threatening a witness charges to the list of charges she is on trial for."

Again he whispered to her, and she sat there sullen and glaring at him.

For the next hour, the DA questioned Samantha, who I

learned later had taken a plea deal and agreed to testify for the prosecution in exchange for a lighter sentence. She told the court how Lacy had originally intended to rob Helena Richards. That she had planned the home invasion with her, but hadn't been part of the scene. She wasn't aware that Lacy had killed Helena until after it had happened, so she didn't know what exactly happened, only what Lacy had recounted.

For the second attack, Samantha explained how Lacy had decided that since she'd got away with Helena's murder easily, she should take out Mariah as well. The DA asked Samantha if, at any time, Lacy had mentioned vengeance for the shooting of a boy named Daniel Jacobs, whom they all called Walrus. Samantha said no and that Lacy hadn't even known his name. She didn't like that he'd been shot, but it didn't really bother her.

It seemed that everything Mr. Howell attempted to set up as a justification for what Lacy did, the DA showed it to be false. In the end, he hadn't needed to call me or Angel. He rested the case, and then Mr. Howell got up and, at Lacy's insistence, put her on the stand. It was her downfall.

She spewed her nonsense and tried to paint herself as a victim, but it all sounded weak and hollow. I could see by the jury's faces they weren't buying it. Eventually, Howell gave his closing arguments, and the judge dismissed the jury to go deliberate.

Angel and I headed out of the courtroom, expecting them to take at least a few hours to return a verdict, but we were wrong. We were eating a couple of hot dogs and drinking sodas when we got word that they were back.

"That was fast," I said, pitching my canned drink and the rest of my hot dog in the garbage bin.

"Probably good for us. If they were going to find her innocent after that, I think there would have been a longer discussion."

We returned to our places, the judge was announced, and we sat down.

"Mr. Foreperson, I understand you have a verdict?"

"Yes, Your Honor."

"Very good. Ms. Miller, please stand," Judge McNiel said.

Mr. Howell stood and gripped Lacy's elbow, making her stand too. She yanked her arm away, but stayed standing.

"Mr. Foreperson, on the four counts of first-degree murders of Helena Richards, Mariah Osgood, the Osgood's unborn baby, and Bella Jones, how do you find?"

"We find the defendant, Lacy Miller, guilty of four counts of first-degree murder, Your Honor."

"And on the count of attempted murder of Mr. James Osgood, how do you find?"

"We find the defendant, Lacy Miller, guilty of attempted murder, Your Honor."

"I'll kill you! I'll kill you all!" Lacy screamed.

"Bailiff, restrain Ms. Miller. I will not have her making a mockery of my courtroom," Judge McNiel said, banging his gavel.

The bailiff rushed over and attempted to contain her as she thrashed, whacking him, her lawyer, and anyone who got close to her. It took three court officers to get a hold of her and then drag her out of the courtroom.

Once it was calmer, Judge McNiel said, "Mr. Foreperson, jury, I thank you for your time. You are dismissed. Mr. Howell, I will set Ms. Miller's sentencing for Monday morning at nine a.m. If your client cannot contain herself, then she will not be allowed in my courtroom. Do I make myself clear?"

"Yes, Your Honor."

Judge McNiel banged his gavel again, then said, "Court is dismissed."

"So what now?" Angel asked, checking his watch.

"I have to go to the precinct, but after that, I can drop you off at home." I'd glanced at the time on my phone and knew I had plenty of time to make the meeting I had with Police Chief Warren. Court had been getting out around three every day, so I'd scheduled this meeting for three thirty. It was only two forty-five now.

"Sounds good."

At the precinct, I made my way up to the police chief's office. I was early, but I was hoping he'd see me earlier. I checked in with his secretary and then sat on the leather bench to wait.

At three twenty, he called me back. "Detective Kendrick, come in."

"Thank you, sir." I stood up and walked into his room. "I appreciate you taking the time to speak with me."

"Of course, of course. Have to make our media darling happy." He was jovial about it, and it was all I could do not to roll my eyes.

"That is what I wanted to discuss with you, sir. I know Lieutenant Chenevert has spoken to you, but I wanted to speak with you about why I am asking to end my part in the media circus."

He sat down and nodded. "Chenevert was adamant that he couldn't spare you while the case was going on, and I understand you're going on leave for a couple of weeks, but we can schedule the next round of interviews for when you get back."

"Sir, with all due respect, I'd like to stop doing interviews. They have become less about El Gato and more about me personally, and they've brought up things from my past, my mother's death, the deaths of people close to me, that I simply don't want bandied about the press."

He frowned. "Well, you are a very intriguing woman, Detective. Is it any wonder they're interested in you?"

"I understand that, sir, however, these aren't things I want shared with the public, and I shouldn't have to."

"Right, right. It's not really helping the LAPD to look good when you walk out of interviews angry..." He trailed off. "I suppose it's time to hire a new public relations person to start taking care of these things..."

"I think that's a fantastic idea, sir," I agreed.

"You sure you won't change your mind when you get back?" he asked as he stood up.

I smiled and stood up too, walking toward the door. "No, sir, I'm very sure I won't."

"Alright then, Kendrick. Have a safe trip, and we'll see you when you get back." He opened his door for me and held out his hand for me to shake.

I gripped his hand and shook it, then said, "Thank you, sir," and left his office.

I met Angel in the HSS detective pool, and after saying goodbye to everyone, we left. I dropped him off at his house and then went home.

"You're home sooner than I expected," Frank greeted me with a grin.

"My vacation has officially started." I wrapped my arms

around him and then kissed him. "I've been looking forward to this for weeks."

"You and me both, TT, you and me both."

THANK YOU FOR READING

Did you enjoy reading *Pay Back*? Please consider leaving a review on Amazon. Your review will help other readers to discover the novel.

ABOUT THE AUTHOR

Theo Baxter has followed in the footsteps of his brother, best-selling suspense author Cole Baxter. He enjoys the twists and turns that readers encounter in his stories.

ALSO BY THEO BAXTER

Psychological Thrillers

The Widow's Secret

The Stepfather

Vanished

It's Your Turn Now

The Scorned Wife

Not My Mother

The Lake House

The Honey Trap

If Only You Knew

The Dream Home

The Detective Marcy Kendrick Thriller Series

Skin Deep - Book #1

Blood Line - Book #2

Dark Duty - Book #3

Kill Count - Book #4

Pay Back - Book #5

Made in the USA
Columbia, SC
06 October 2024

46f6037b-ab9d-43c2-86ac-b35567b39e9dR03